Take To The Sky

By

Gregory Jonathan Scott

ISBN: 0991467442
ISBN-13: 978-0-9914674-4-0

DEDICATION

Thank you to my longtime love Scott Burkett, who is my true inspiration. You have always supported me with everything I've done, including my journey into the great big world of writing. You *are* my real angel.

Thank you to my friend, Toni Hanks, who has added so much inspiration during the entire time I've spent writing of this book.

Thank you to Jen Gerschick and Andrea Mason. You two are my northern motivation who might have crossed paths with an angel.

Take to the Sky – The first book of its series

Cover Design by Greg J Meier - Cover art is for Illustrative purposes only and any person(s) depicted on the cover is strictly a model.

Edited by Tina Marie Adamski

First Edition October, 2014

Also available in downloadable electronic version

Published by Gregory Jonathan Scott LLC

http://gregoryjonathanscott.com

https://plus.google.com/u/0/+GregoryJonathanScott/posts

https://www.facebook.com/gregoryjonathanscottauthor

https://twitter.com/GregoryJonScott

WARNING: This Book contains material that may be offensive to some, which includes graphic language and adult situations.

Trademark Acknowledgements:

The author acknowledges the trademarked status and trademark owners of the following trademarks mentioned in this work of fiction:

Aeropostale: Aeropostale

Agusta A109 LUH: AgustaWestland - A Finmeccanica Company

Air Supply: Air Supply

Disney's "Angels in the Outfield": Caravan Pictures and Walt Disney Pictures

MiG-29: Mikoyan-and-Gurevich Design Bureau

Snapchat: Snapchat, Inc.

Superman: DC Comics, A Warner Bros. Entertainment Company

ACKNOWLEDGMENTS

To Tina Marie Adamski, I am thankful for your dedicated guidance, unparalleled input, and your patience in co-piloting this project. With your help, this beautiful story came to life.

To my dreams and experiences that turned into the words on these pages.

Chapter 1

"Must hurry." Kellan ran deeper into the dark, pushing through long ragged tree limbs and tall tangled grass. His bare feet found every rock, pointy stick and twisted root along the way, but he kept on running. A moonbeam shone through the lone cloud in the night sky, hitting him just right, and the feathers that flowed down his back reflected blue light as though they were iridescent.

He glanced back once, noticing that the laboratory he was running from looked more creepy-dark than he ever remembered seeing it before. Thick twisted vines covered the building and clung to the peaked roof that had aged badly over the years. Even with several windows gleaming bits of light here and there, the place looked eerie. Knowing he'd been stuck there for as long as he had was pulling on his emotions. The effect of that knowledge being that his will to continue moving grew stronger than ever.

"Keep going. Must hurry." Breathing heavily, Kellan dashed away from the dark monstrosity, keeping his body close to the ground as a way to avert anyone seeing him leave. Nobody had ever escaped that place. Never. The complex was beyond penitentiary secure, tighter than a prison. No one was able to get in and certainly nobody could get out. Not even the geniuses that dreamt up the creations hidden within those scary walls were allowed to come and go at will.

Kellan went on running, low to the ground. With his well-planned adieu came mind-bending exhilaration, the thrill of being free, accompanied by a spiraling dread of what was yet to come. But without allowing himself further distraction, his focus on his triumphant getaway stayed strong. He was determined to fly. Take to the sky.

~~~~ O ~~~~

In the middle of a wooded lot that could only be seen from the ground if someone followed the carefully hidden drive that lead up to it stood a massive turn-of-the-century building made mostly of stone, with a few patches of brick stashed here and there. Many years ago the place was home to many 'crazy' people. A cuckoo's nest was what it was known as by most people, but honestly it was widely recognized for being an "Asylum for the Mentally Insane." This being a better title for it in those days and one that helped people understand what it really was. As a medical center, it looked more haunting than inviting. The place was at one time filled with lost souls that had no idea who they were, and most seemed to remain crazy only because of the drugs that were administered to them by the staff.

Just before the words "Insane Asylum" were etched above the entry door, the hospital was closed down because some half-witted fool set the place on fire. That particular fool wasn't someone forced to stay there by injection, but a doctor who was considered brilliant. One who went rage-wild one evening due to an overdose of a drug he was administering to himself when nobody was looking. Stupid fool couldn't keep his sticky fingers off the happy drug. He had to go mess everything all up.

A few years after the fire took out most of the building, those parts which had been refurbished still smelled a bit cooked, like burnt timber and rotten cherries. This was mainly blamed on the building never being completely taken down to the ground and replaced with a new one. Much of it was left half-baked, which actually made a good cover for what it was ultimately
~~~~

turned into. The place was dingy outside from all angles, probably inside too, and it towered creepily in front of the moon in a way that made it manage to always look like a postcard perfect image of Halloween. A glimpse of it at nighttime with the purplish black sky behind it brought on a rather bone shaking experience, and anybody in their right mind would be crazy to take to the grounds or step foot inside the building for a closer look. Call people smart in that respect, or crazy; whatever, but everybody steered away from that wicked place for good reason.

Quite a while back, though long after the original one, the building was forced to close down due to a second fire that roared through its halls, caused exactly the same way the first one was. It was funny how that worked in a place meant for drug therapy. The crazy person wasn't always the ill-fated individual *behind* lock and key, but sometimes the one *holding* them.

The government eventually took the place over and changed the hospital from an asylum to a secret laboratory that was operated and funded by the state. Some crazy shit came out of there and it wasn't because somebody with a mental illness went in. It would seem that a government-funded lab such as that would be better off hidden in the hills of Montana or Idaho, not in a summer getaway destination like Traverse City Michigan. It was secretly referred to as 'The TC Lab of Modern Science.'

What were they thinking?

Scientists and clinicians in their white lab coats walked the halls, and from what was understood by the nearby townspeople, most didn't even leave the place. They spent most of their time there like they were serving a permanent residency. None were even seen leaving on holiday to be with their families, if they had any. It was said that they lived and breathed for the next experiment.

Who were really the 'crazy' ones?

~~~~ O ~~~~

With the night air getting cooler, Kellan crept across the dark, wooded grounds until he came to the high fence that surrounded the laboratory's property. The wire-covered wall stood about twenty feet tall, and every few feet in either direction, seeming to go on forever, were posted signs that stated
~~~~

"Electrified and Dangerous", presumably meant to keep people in as well as out. The placards seemed to serve their purpose well since Kellan never saw anybody try to scale the walls during the twenty-eight years that he'd been held captive in that awful place.

With the moon still high in the sky and aimed right at Kellan like it was a spotlight following his every footstep, he stopped just short of reaching the fence, looked to the top and saw the grotesque coils of barbed wire that spiraled horrifyingly along its peak. Even for him it looked impossible to escape over the top of. For anyone else, getting to the outside world wasn't happening at all.

Attached to Kellan's left ankle was a fine jewelry piece the lab clinicians put on him and made sure he wore at all times. It was pretty and sophisticated, almost like an old-fashioned penal wrist cuff, but appeared less shackle-like than the typical house arrest anklet. He was in such a hurry to get out of the building that its presence slipped his mind. More irritating than the band being strapped to him was the red light on it that blinked every few seconds. If he didn't look at the thing, he forgot it was there.

Out of sight, out of mind.

The anklet kept tabs on him, and was designed to notify the lab's security if he strayed too far away from his block. Kellan knew the mechanism needed to be taken off straightaway before the techies noticed his disappearance. Kellan was strong, and the fine metal lost its battle against his strength as it broke free with one quick tug. He threw it back toward the lab, hopeful that the action would stop any Seekers who became aware that he had left.

Kellan took another look behind him, checking the grounds for anyone who might see him before he jumped fence. Once assured there was no one there to witness it, he backed up several steps and took off running at full speed toward the fence in front of him. The fifteen-foot high fence criss-crossed with heart stopping electricity. His feet pounded the ground, arms churned at his sides. Nothing would inhibit him from fleeing the horrendous place he'd been locked up in for so long. Nothing.

In one swoop, his pearly white wings unfurled from his shoulder blades, snapped out wide to either side of him before rising high above his head. With a hard downward beat of those wings, Kellan lifted himself off the ground and into the sky.

~~~~ O ~~~~

Kellan was possibly one of a kind; a magnificent creature genetically engineered in the same laboratory he was running from. Gene splicing had been a factor in his creation, which involved genetic material from two separate species that would not normally gestate if joined naturally. Kellan was a product of combined avian and human genetic material, which gave life to his incredibly unique abilities. He surprisingly grew into one of the more superior creations in the lab, and was being trained to carry out missions planned by the American military.

Kellan knew his escape would not go unnoticed for long, and may possibly have been identified already.

Beating his wings, Kellan flew. With each stroke, he flew higher. Kellan floated on the wind. Like most birds, his bones were webbed internally, allowing them to be filled with air pulled from his lungs. The added air in his bones gave him the extra lift he needed to carry his solid form through the sky. He was heavy, his body hard with muscle. His breastbone was larger than the average human being's was, with a deep Y-shaped collarbone which extended down his chest to help support his large wings. His pectoral crest was oversized and thickly muscled, broadening his shoulders to provide the reinforcement needed to bear the weight of his double limbs. Kellan's heart was large, and it pumped about forty beats per minute, slower than normal humans. Sometimes less when he was idle, but it sped up when he needed it to. He had a healthy heart, like an athlete's. It needed to be healthy and strong to do the job required of it.

Kellan flew freely and let the wind rake through the disheveled wisps of his light blond hair. He split the sky with his twelve-foot wingspan as he soared. His wings carried his one-hundred-eighty pound frame higher in magnificent flight. It was amazing, a phenomenon, and completely astonishing that a human could fly.

While living at the TC Lab of Modern Science, Kellan was given as much time to fly outdoors as he wanted, the only restriction was that he fly solely on nights when the moon was at its darkest. It was the best time to hide away what wasn't supposed to be seen by anybody on the outside of the fence. Tranquilizer guns were always at the ready, pointed straight at
~~~~

him, ready to pierce his skin if he tried to really take flight or do anything unexpected, like fly the coop.

Kellan was an advanced design, one that had astonished his creators. He needed special attention at almost every turn. Not that he would cause trouble or intentionally hurt anyone, since his soul was so gentle, but because he was unique and special, a birdman that could fly.

Before attaining success with Kellan, that superior being; there were many gene reassignments performed that amounted to closure and disposal, experiments that went wrong. As a result of trial and error, Kellan was the first of his kind who was strong enough to survive the rigorous cell division, to create such a human life, and only the government knew of his existence. The secret of his reality was kept hushed for twenty-eight years.

Incredible!

Kellan went on flying with outstretched wings, keeping his flight pattern sporadic, finally enjoying life for the very first time. He flew as far away from the people he thought of as villains, the ones that taught him to fight, and would next teach him to kill. He wasn't having it, he couldn't. It wasn't in him to take another life. The thought of it was horrifying to him. So instead of doing what they wanted, he ran away.

Kellan dipped his shoulder, rolled quickly to the left, hard and strong, and then rose higher above the trees. It was dark out in front of him, but his avian vision allowed him to see as clearly as if it were mid-day.

Just like that, he was gone. Deep into the night.

Chapter 2

Kellan flew fast, he always had, it seemed like only a few minutes passed from the time he flew the coop until the time he reached the North Bay where the straights connected the two Michigan peninsulas. He was far enough away from TC and it seemed to be a good place to hide out for a while, so he planned to fly down and find cover somewhere among the trees.

Down below where he soared was the two-spire suspension bridge he'd only heard about and seen in pictures on the internet. In real life, the thing was a magnificent piece of architecture that crossed the waterway with a span that looked over five miles long. To Kellan, the bridge appeared to stretch for about a million miles between the two masses of land, and the lights that traced the drooping suspension cables helped him see from one end to the other without a problem. From the stretch of lights alone, he could tell it was huge, and when he flew closer to it, the structure was simply massive. Kellan felt miniscule in comparison to it, and its enormity outright gave him the creeps.

The sensation of crisp fall air felt good against his face and he could sense it was getting colder by the minute. The brisk night sky, combined with feeling freer than he'd ever felt before, was exhilarating. The air that stroked his bare skin felt fresher than any he'd experienced at TC.

It only took three good wing beats to quickly push him up the side of the tower that suspended the south end of the bridge above water. He straightened out, bringing his arms to his sides, as he swooped skyward, hugging the massive support until he reached the top, where he perched and let the cooler breeze from the north come at him and comb his light blond hair. His wings fluttered; filled with air, and a few loose feathers pulled free in the wind and spun down toward the water.

Being up high helped Kellan stay clear of any TC officials who may be looking for him. The vantage point also made it easier for him to keep a sharp eye on everything around him for miles, even in the dark. It was high where he sat, but to him it was nothing extreme, it felt natural. He was part avian, was used to it, enjoyed it, and it was certainly part of his nature to take on high places without fear.

Kellan sat a while at a place that felt like the top of the world before he decided to stand up and freefall toward earth like a reckless hawk diving toward its prey. He closed his eyes, leveled his arms out to his sides and let himself drop backward over the edge of the mile high tower. He plunged downward, spinning and turning with the wind. It was like he was part of it, and his racing heart thumped from the exhilaration of not knowing where the bottom was. Seconds into the back flip dive and just in the nick of time, he snapped his wings wide open, pushed them back toward his feet, rolled to the right and skimmed above Lake Michigan while dragging a finger over the surface, making a small wake that trailed behind him. He was hawk-like, and did everything a bird would do except screech and claw for fish.

Dawn hadn't yet broken and he predicted it must be closing in on three in the morning. With that thought, Kellan realized he'd been awake since five a.m. the day before. He cursed himself and figured it would be a good idea to find a quiet place to get some rest. He needed it, but the unsettling thought came to mind that while resting he would be leaving himself vulnerable. Exposing himself to risk of being netted by the TC officials and dragged back to where he just escaped from. He realized a peaceful night's sleep was not on his agenda, but his superior genetics ensured a few hours rest was all he needed to be at peak performance and ready to take the sky at full speed.

While Kellan searched for a place to nap in the wooded brush along the lake, he spotted a house standing alone at the edge of the bay. It was a charming two story home, and from what he knew of residential architecture, it was more or less a new century craftsman with the typical dormer windows protruding from the rooftop that looked like a set of eyes with a pair of bushy brows. The door, which was painted red, resembled a pair of lips. Taking it all in, the house seemed to be a face that appeared surprised to see him.

Even hovering more than two hundred or so yards from the home, he could clearly see the house from this distance as though he were right next to it, looking in a window. He was actually able to see the digital clock display on the microwave oven above the stove. His vision was razor sharp, impeccable like most birds, which gave him the power to see everything as if all objects were only a few inches in front of him, even in the dark.

The house was dark inside and out, which led Kellan to believe that everybody on the inside was either sleeping or no one was in the house at all. He wasn't sure enough about that, and he wasn't going to risk peeking in any of the windows to find out. That was too dangerous for him.

His birdlike features would be freakish to anybody that saw him in the world outside the walls of TC, so it was in his best interest to stay far enough away from the doors and windows of the cute summer cottage on the lake.

Kellan was a strong man inside and out, however he felt oddly vulnerable; at risk, and had no desire to be alone. The feeling came on suddenly, but he certainly didn't want to be at the lab either.

He brought himself down out of the sky and stood quietly for a minute on the beach, looking around. Left, right, above, in front, and then behind. He was being cautious, as he should be.

Turning away from the house, Kellan walked toward the wooded lot to take a seat under a large maple tree. He spotted it on the way in and picked it out as his resting place due to its apparent safety. It was monstrous like the bridge, which made it seem fitting to be standing there so near the bridge. There were actually many of these trees, mostly smaller than this one, which presumably made up a beautiful forest that shaded the ground when the summer's hot sun beat down.

Kellan made himself a spot to lie down with several fallen leaves he scooped into a pile. It wasn't the most comfortable against his bare skin, but it was the best he could do with the resources he had. As soon as he laid head to ground, he fell into dreamland fast. He was mentally exhausted more than he was physically beat, and truly needed rest in order to go on.

Kellan must have dozed heavily for several hours judging by the way the sky had seemingly changed so quickly and reappeared so brightly when he saw it next. He woke what seemed to be just a few minutes later, to find the sun shining in his eyes and a shadowy figure standing over him.

Terror instantly came over Kellan, totally exposing him, wings and all. He wanted to run or fly away. He panted hard, in shock and gripped by total horror. He had no idea how he should react to this new set of eyes on him. He didn't know how the ogler would react to him. All he knew for sure was that he needed to run away again.

Kellan sprang to his feet and snapped his wings out sharply to his sides. Bringing them back in, he turned and ran for the open beach. It was bright, and a risk, but he took it anyway. He had to. He needed to fly.

"Wait. Don't run," the shadow-caster said, his hand leveled out in front of him to set the birdman at ease. He stared intently, astonished at what he was seeing, while shushing the perky dog standing next to him, his head cocked to one side.

Chapter 3

Neil was the shadow-caster who lived in the Craftsman home that Kellan saw earlier. During Neil's morning walk with his half-pint dog, Dylan, he kept an eye on the dark clouds that scuttled across the sky the entire time. Unless he missed it, there was no mention of a storm on the morning news, but it looked like it was coming in from the east. It was forecast to be a brisk sunny morning, not a gloomy one that dropped bird people from the sky.

What was happening and who was this man with wings?

Seeking an immediate distraction for Dylan, Neil threw a stick he found on the ground at his feet. Kicking up dirt, his Sheltie chased the airborne stick. Most of the time, Dylan was bright-minded, but when a toy or a stick was in play, the dog went crazy for it.

Forgetting about the amazing angel, Dylan took off after the flipping stick as expected, and with an abrupt forward skid that tossed sand out in front of him, he quickly stopped, looked back at

Neil as if telepathically saying, *'Are you coming or what?'*

Surprisingly the birdman didn't run or fly away, but instead stopped just before taking to the sky.

Neil called Dylan, telling him to sit by his side, and like a good dog, he did exactly that.

During the dog's playful romp, Kellan slowly brought his wings down from above his head, pulled them to his sides where he tucked them tightly against his back. He turned and looked at Neil, pressed a pointy finger to his lips as a gesture of asking him to not speak of what he was seeing. He bowed his head toward the ground, giving the impression of being ashamed of the way he looked.

Neil nodded his head. "Oh-My-God, it's beautiful," he hummed.

Together with the dog, Neil cautiously took one step at a time toward Kellan. His heart pounded faster and his head spun with wonderment. "How and where?"

As if he had a pistol pointed at him, Neil raised his hands to a surrendering position, showing Kellan he meant him no harm. He crept even slower than before, keeping an eye on Dylan while the handsome pooch trotted proudly beside him. Neil looked up at the stormy sky, wondering if the birdman came from it. Could that be? Neil couldn't quite fathom the possibility of this being an angel because his spiritual attention was not in its right place at that moment. His hands moved down to his sides slowly, still watching Kellan intently. "Where did you come from?" He whispered to keep from frightening the winged man away.

Dylan made a noise that sounded like a cry, followed by a glance at Neil as if to be thinking, *'What the heck is it?'*

Kellan lifted his gaze from the ground, shifting his piercing cerulean eyes to look directly into Neil's. They were wolf-like, almost ice white. Kellan's wispy blond hair and pearly feathers flickered together in the wind. He looked strong and stood tall in front of Neil and the Sheltie. The little bit of light peeking through the cloud-filled sky made him shimmer like an angel. A holy angel. He was magnificent and borderline dazzling.

For reasons unknown to Neil, Kellan was shirtless and wore no shoes. He stood only in a faded pair of denim jeans that were about two sizes too large. To keep them in place, he had them cinched around his waist by a heavy rope with frayed ends. The ensemble gave Neil the idea that wherever he came from, he had left in a hurry.

Kellan appeared to be feather-light, except for his smooth bulky chest, which looked thickly muscled to Neil, and he figured it had to be that way in order to support the weight of his wings and arms. Kellan's skin tone was pale white, almost lavender, presumably from being locked away from the sun for so many years.

Even though Neil and his dog seemed to pose no threat, Kellan still had his senses focused on escaping. He was not taking chances. Not now.

Chapter 4

It was still early Thursday morning and the thump-thump of a helicopter in the sky circled the bay beneath the clouds. It was government issue from what Kellan could see, and he knew it was on a mission to find him and take him back to the science lab.

By now they would certainly know he was missing.

"Not good," Kellan bit the words off, turned away from Neil, and ran back to the wooded parcel instead of flying.

Caught up by Kellan's fancy footwork, Dylan went crazy and started barking. His blank stare back at Neil made it appear he was asking, *'Where's mister bird person going?'*

"Hush!" Neil screeched at Dylan. He pointed to his feet at the same time he watched Kellan duck out of sight.

Kellan walked backward until he disappeared into the trees along the lake, all the while keeping watch on the beach where the chopper moved in closer, its nose bobbing along the ground like it was sniffing for food.

The beating props of the chopper sounded like thunder and

were getting louder as the whirly-bird inched closer to the ground where Neil and the perky dog were standing. Neil stood still and then knelt down to grab Dylan by the collar, his hair snapped by the force of the wind, sand blowing in both their eyes.

Kellan stayed low and still until the chopper lifted and finally moved away. The machine in the sky only had to hover around for a few seconds to know that Neil wasn't part avian. The missing wings made it obvious to them that he wasn't the birdman they were looking for.

Neil allowed a few minutes to pass before making any effort to go look for Kellan. It was important that the coast was clear and to wait long enough to be sure the chopper wasn't planning a surprise return. He stood up, let Dylan loose and walked slowly toward the brush where Kellan had gone. "Be a good boy and go find the angel."

Dylan first looked at Neil, then yapped and took off running toward the trees at the same spot Kellan had disappeared. Dylan's hind end wiggled every time he hopped forward like a jackrabbit. Ears flopping, tail wagging.

Quietly, Kellan perched himself on a tree branch rather than standing on the ground. He instinctively knew that was the way birds did it and he was safer that way.

Out of nowhere and seeming nervous, a tiny iridescent hummingbird zipped from around the backside of Kellan's head, flitted up, down, left, and right in a matter of seconds to observe Kellan from all angles. It stayed inquisitive the entire time, hovered close by until it knew exactly what Kellan was and how the big birdman fit into the same world as it did. The tiny bird and its invisible wings whizzed in closer, stared Kellan straight in the eyes before it flipped backward as quickly as he had moved in.

The hummingbird was unfamiliar to Kellan; he'd never seen a real one before and wasn't sure if it was a bird or a bug. Birds he knew about, but buggy birds? That was another thing. That sounded like something the scientists at TC would create.

Was the little guy considered an insect or a bird? Kellan had no answer for that. But being just as cross bred as he thought the hummingbird was, he could easily relate to the bird-bug's exclusivity. He realized they weren't that much different from each other. Both intriguing, and a marvel most would like to get a closer look at.

The humming bird showed no real signs of fear around Kellan until he took a poke at its beak with his fingertip. He probably shouldn't have, but he was too curious not to do it.

Distraught, the hummingbird sputtered and flew away, moving so fast that watching it with the naked eye wasn't possible. It left no sign that it had actually been there.

At the same moment the tiny bird zipped away, Dylan rushed over and looked up at Kellan perched on a branch about ten feet off the ground.

A few steps behind the spunky Sheltie, Neil walked slowly, avoiding any sudden movements so he wouldn't frighten the birdman away. He took a deep breath, inhaled fresh air, and stayed calm.

Neil remained tentative at first about getting too close to Kellan because the beautiful man seemed to have mysteriously just dropped out of heaven. The idea of Kellan being heaven sent was the only explanation Neil could come up with.

Had Neil died? Was his angel of glory here to take him to a more magnificent place above the clouds?

Neil wasn't sure what the winged creature would do if he made any sudden movements. Truth was that Neil's nursing instincts kicked in and told him to help the birdman instead of running away from him.

There were a few sporadic movements from Dylan each time the angel shifted its wings or moved a limb. A groan and a growl escaped the dog, along with stomping of restless paws.

The last thing Neil wanted was for Dylan to freak the angel out and scare him away after he'd tried so hard not to. "Hold still, Dylan. Now sit." He tugged on Dylan's collar to make him understand.

Dylan turned back and looked at Neil, finally settling down a little. He was normally an extremely well behaved dog, but how could Neil blame the pet for wanting to get a better look at what he'd never seen before? Neil was having a hard time keeping himself contained, so he understood how a dog was not able to keep his anxiety in check. In truth, a man with wings *was* a creature to get excited over. It was somewhat of a wonder.

Neil stood and looked at the angel for the longest time, and the angel stared back at him. He was more beautiful than anything Neil had ever seen, which made it difficult to pull his eyes away. The power of his beauty was as absurd as it was undeniable. He looked like a ghostly sculpture that once stood in a chapel and suddenly came to life. His hair and eyes were brilliant, deserving of being called angelic. The angel had a few bruises, but from what Neil could tell, there were none to be concerned about.

Many questions came to Neil's mind. The two most important seemed to be, where did he come from and how did he get here?

About five minutes later, Neil stopped staring and Dylan finally took his place on the ground beside him. Figuring the angel man was able to speak English, Neil took a chance and asked in a whisper, "Do you have a name?"

"Kellan," was all he said, followed by a short nod. With concern on his face, he shifted in a way that appeared to ready him for takeoff. He spread his wings slightly and his muscles tensed.

"I'm Neil." He pointed to himself. "It's okay, I won't hurt you."

Kellan shifted a little and looked at the dog.

"It's okay, he won't hurt you either." Neil patted Dylan's head and stroked it a few times. "This is Dylan."

Dylan's tongue came out and relaxed across his lower jaw that made him look like he was smiling. He was cute as hell.

Kellan didn't say anything more after his own name, so Neil got the impression that the angel didn't speak too many words, or might not know much English at all. Neil wasn't sure about anything at that moment, he was star struck and feeling a little nuts. An angel perched in a tree in front of him just didn't compute as real.

Neil wondered if he should help Kellan down from the tree, but that seemed a bit silly. Besides, the birdman might think he was trying to hurt him, so with that thought, he decided to keep a fair distance. For the time being anyhow.

There was a short pause before Neil asked Kellan if he needed shelter for the night or if he was hungry. He wasn't sure he'd get an answer, but he asked him anyway.

It was a start.

Kellan only shook his head, still keeping his words behind his tongue.

Turning toward his house, Neil pointed and said, "I'm just up the way if you need a place to rest, or need any clothes." It seemed strange to say, but a welcoming invitation may be just what the doctor ordered. The birdman seemed frightened, but maybe his actions were because he was in protective mode.

Kellan rotated his head from one side to the other as if he was looking around for a predator getting ready to pounce on him. "I'm fine," he spoke, still perched in a way that made him look tense and ready to fly away at any second.

"Omigawd," Neil hummed. He felt a slight smile on his face when he heard the angel's deep voice speak a few more words.

The small bits of communication seemed like tokens of trust, and that trust was something they would need to help them both cope with what they were about to face. It was some sort of miracle or paranormal event that had caused this birdman's unexpected appearance, Neil knew that much. Either way, he was close to being sure the whole thing was going to get ugly, if all of what was taking place, including the helicopter searching for the angel, was real. He couldn't look away or dismiss the whole scenario from his mind. It was too late for that. He had been pulled in. He was involved.

Neil didn't want to lose site of the magnificent creature he had stumbled upon, but he believed stepping back was the best thing to do, to give the angel some private space. He sought to build trust with the angel and the best way to do it was to walk away and let him make up his own mind to follow. The last thing Neil wanted to do was smother the poor winged soul.

When Neil finally stepped out from under the trees and back onto the beach, towing Dylan with him, he wondered if he was ever going to see Kellan again. He found himself glancing back a few times as he walked away, seeking Kellan out, hoping he hadn't left. "What am I doing?" he mumbled. "This is crazy. Go back."

Dylan ran ahead toward the house as if everything was back to normal and there was never an angel sitting in the tree down the beach. It's amazing how a dog's mind shifts from one moment to the next, forgetting about what's behind them and only thinking of what's ahead.

"This is crazy, go back," Neil repeated.

Chapter 5

There weren't too many other buildings or homes nearby, just the woods all around the cabin and the lake in front of it. It was a tranquil and secluded place, and that's what made it the perfect hiding place for Kellan. It was not widely known that Neil's house was sitting alone on so many acres of land along the beach or that it stood so close to the foot of the Mackinac Bridge. The large trees surrounding it did a fine job hiding it.

The view out the front window and from the front porch was magnificent, what most would consider breathtaking. The massive bridge in the near distance looked close enough to touch, even though it was about two miles away from doorstep to suspension span.

That morning, Neil left the door to his house wide open as a way to let the birdman know he was welcome inside if he wanted. It was most important to Neil that Kellan was safe. Secondary to his safety came his really wanting to know more about the mysterious angel that appeared so close to his home. Neil continued to look impatiently over his shoulder every few minutes, but every time he did, no angel stood in the doorway.

Several hours had passed with no sign of Kellan on Neil's doorstep asking to be invited in. It wasn't surprising by any means, but it was most certainly building anxiety within Neil. His heart skipped a beat every time he heard a noise that sounded like footsteps at the front door. He wanted the angel to visit, wanted him to come in.

Throughout the day, Dylan watched Neil pace the floor and take to the window with a pair of binoculars what seemed about six hundred times. Neil was eager to know what the birdman was up to and hoped he didn't fly off without saying goodbye. The window peeping couldn't go on too much longer because it was getting late and the sky outside was growing darker. Unless the binoculars Neil possessed had night vision, there wasn't any chance he was going to see anything more than a foot or two in front of him with them. To continue spying was senseless.

"Okay, one last look and I'll shut the place down." As usual, Neil talked to himself or to Dylan if he was listening. This was a product of his typically being alone with just the dog for company. He grabbed the binoculars one last time and pointed them at the place he last saw Kellan sitting. Good news, he was still in the tree, looking around and poking at the hummingbird that decided to become his friend earlier in the day. "That's good, at least he's still there," he carried on to himself before lowering the lenses and putting them away. His brown eyes burned.

Kellan hanging out where Neil left him implied that Kellan either trusted him enough not to fly away or he at least felt safe in that tree.

Fly away? That sounded strange.

Neil proceeded with closing the place down, shutting windows, latching doors, and turning off the lights.

With every turn Neil made, Dylan followed him as he normally did during the evening's lock-up ritual, making sure the evening finished with a not-to-be missed snack. After the last lamp went dark, Dylan trotted to the kitchen, stood by the cookie jar and stared at Neil until he came about and handed him the final snack of the day. The treats were always part of the ritual and were not to be left out. Dylan always saw to that and would be a herding pest until Neil gave in to tradition.

That night played out a bit differently than it normally did and the perplexed look on Dylan's face came across as comical while he stood waiting at the foot of the living room stairs and looked back at Neil. His little mind was rumbling what it always did when things didn't go the way they were supposed to, *'What the heck are you doing, Neil? This a-way.'*

Neil smirked as he read Dylan's mind. "Tonight we sleep down here, Hunny bunny." Neil pulled bed sheets and blankets from a nearby closet and carried them to one end of the sprawling sectional in the living room. "I have to keep an eye on that angel, so we stay down here tonight."

Before Neil started making the sofa into a comfy bed, he flipped on the flat screen with a tap to the remote control he lifted from the end table. He scrolled through the broadcast menu until he found a channel that coincidentally was playing the Disney film, "Angels in the Outfield."

How appropriate was that?

It seemed to be the perfect film choice to be playing on the widescreen. With any window peeking luck, perhaps it would coerce Kellan into thinking it was okay to come in and visit a while. Angels inside and angels outside. It was perfect.

As a result of snapping the bed sheet over the sectional, the idea sparked in Dylan's head that playtime was about to start. He ran in place for a second on the slippery wooden floor before taking a flying leap into the back of the sofa, getting tangled in the sheet as it slowly floated downward on top of him. A few excited yelps came out of him as he rolled around and took in the cool fabric wrapped around his little body.

"What are you doing? Get off – Move," Neil snapped broken words.

One last yip and then Dylan stopped horsing around, cocked his head to the left and stared at Neil. *'What?'* could be seen in the expression on his cute little face.

"I said move. Now move it." Neil spat again, more playfully.

Dylan stood up on the sectional and walked across the cushions to the other end where he clumsily dropped down. Then out came the tongue, which gave up that famous smile and a look that bore, *'What's wrong with you, I didn't do anything.'*

During the entire time Neil was making the bed, he continually glanced out the windows and watched the door, wondering if Kellan was finding his way toward the house. Seeing no sign of the angelic creature told him to turn in and focus on the flat screen that showed angels really do exist.

Dylan cornered the sectional and plopped down at Neil's side where he waited for a hand to naturally reach out and pet his fur, down the back and up around the ears, again and again for the best part of twenty minutes. *'I love you, Neil,'* and *'Oh this is the life'* were certainly painted across Dylan's face as he lay still, enjoying the fantastic head-to-rear massage.

About thirty minutes into the movie, both Neil and Dylan had dozed off.

Neil was in and out of slumber a few times, mostly because he kept checking the front door so he wouldn't miss an angel walking through it.

Dylan turned restless and soon got down from the hot sofa to sprawl out on a floor that was much cooler on his tummy.

~~~~ O ~~~~

It was time. Time for Kellan to make a move. Staying in one place for too long wasn't a good idea, and if he didn't know any better, the chopper that circled the place earlier that morning had a hit on him and was waiting for the right time to strike. He couldn't take the chance of that happening. He wasn't going back to that place he considered a jail cell. It was like a prison with no future.

Hours ago and sometime close to when the sun was setting, the hummingbird Kellan got to know during the day flew off to find a place it could take shelter for the night, something Kellan should consider doing himself.

The night air was getting cooler and the dark waves on the lake made it seem eerier than it should be. Kellan wasn't afraid of the dark, but nighttime wasn't really his favorite time, and he preferred that the night sky be left to the bats and other flying scavengers that had no desire or business flying around in the daylight. He normally shied away from darkness, but sadly, he had to use the night to keep himself hidden, and it worked to his
~~~~

advantage while the government hunters looked for him. If he couldn't see the hunters, then he figured the hunters couldn't see him. Wasn't that how it worked? He hoped it was.

Kellan shivered for different reasons, not always because he was cold, in fact that rarely took place. But this time he shivered because the temperature dropped, plummeted quickly, and being shirtless and barefoot wasn't helping the matter. His bare chest which caught the cooling breeze seemed to make his chilling circumstance worse. He shivered, couldn't stop shaking, and every few seconds his teeth chattered, hit together until they ached. He actually felt like crying, but he didn't. It wasn't just because he was cold, but because he felt alone and somewhat terrified by not knowing how he was going to survive. He was a big boy now, actually a man, and crying wasn't going to fix anything about the situation he had shaped.

He had his entire escape planned out for quite some time, maybe months, but he still wondered if he did the right thing by running away from the only place he ever knew as home. The laboratory where he was created housed the only people he knew and maybe loved. He thought the decision to take off was the right one, but something inside him now told him differently.

He needed to quickly fix his anxiety before he blew himself to bits from the inside out. Flying always eased his troubled mind, so up he went.

There was liftoff.

Kellan was airborne again.

Chapter 6

It was midnight, and Neil's on again, off again slumber was shattered by a loud crash directly overhead, like it came from the roof or the sky above it.

What the hell?

Dylan's rest was interrupted by the thunderous bang as well. Instead of rousing his lazed spirit to serve and protect the way a real hero should, he ran next to Neil and whimpered like a true chicken shit.

Another loud crash came from outside. This time Neil sat up, startled, and threw the blanket to the floor, covering most of Dylan. Neil wasn't fully awake when the second boom hit, so the crack he heard didn't register right away as being a thunderstorm. He blinked a few times, trying to focus.

The widescreen was blank from receiving no satellite signal and the only light in the room was flickering from the fireplace coals.

"Holy shit, that was loud." Tired, Neil shuffled to the door to swing it shut.

Dylan trotted behind him.

It was raining hard outside and the sporadic flashes of light jumping from cloud to cloud lit up the sky like there were fireworks going off. Tension built with every crack and with each bolt of light came a boom that shook the house.

Before Neil had a chance to close and lock the door, Dylan squeezed through the open crack, charged outside and started barking at whatever he saw move with the wind.

"Dylan," Neil hollered. "Get back in here."

Hearing the authoritative command, Dylan stopped at the edge of the covered porch, but went on barking at whatever was moving outside on the beach. He whimpered a few times before changing his tone to a low growl.

Eerily standing on the beach several yards from the bottom of the steps in the pouring rain was Kellan. Waves from the lake rolled and crashed behind him and every time lightning flashed his full form lit up like a flare of white light. He looked saturated to the bone and he stood ghostly with his arms crossed over his massive bare chest. Shivering.

Neil lowered his voice to what was almost a whisper. "Dylan, hush. Get in here." Neil stared out at Kellan as the water drops on him flashed in the lightning while walking out the door next to Dylan. "Kellan?" He still marveled over how beautiful the angel was, and still had a hard time believing such a being actually existed. Neil's chest went tight and his vision spiraled, blinking away flashes of light that reflected off the angel standing outside.

With no place to go, not even up, Kellan stood in the downpour with his head bowed toward the ground to keep drops from running in his eyes. Icy rain splashed across his shoulders and ran down his back, somersaulting through his feathered wings. He was thoroughly soaked and a deluge of droplets ran down his chest in rivulets of silver sparks, tracing every gutter of his muscled form.

Kellan walked toward the house, slowly at first, and then a little quicker when he noticed Neil opening the door a few inches wider, proposing it as an invitation to enter.

Was it okay? Was Neil okay?

Kellan's wings flittered when gusts of wind circled and rushed up against him, and it pushed him toward the house as if telling him it was alright to go. He didn't hesitate when he noticed Neil seemed gentle. He sensed it. It was a bird thing.

When Kellan reached the rising steps on foot, his wings snapped at his sides and shook off water. When they came back down, they lifted him up the steps until he reached the top where he descended softly, the tips of his toes first.

Neil stood in the doorway and watched Kellan drift above the stairs. "Oh My God," was all he said, while he marveled wide eyed at the miracle that floated in front of him.

Kellan pulled his wings inward, tucking them neatly in place behind his back. He stood quietly for a minute, contemplating Neil and his reactions as he lowered himself to the porch decking one toe at a time.

Neil swallowed, pushing his heart back down his throat where it belonged. "It's okay, you can come in." He moved inside the house, one slow backward step at time, one hand still holding the door open so Kellan could enter.

Kellan shook rainwater from his hair, followed by a few observant glances around the covered porch. "I'll be fine out here, if that's okay with you?"

Neil held up both hands placating Kellan. "Yes, yes. Of course it's fine. Would you like me to bring you a blanket, or a light sheet, or something to cover you for the night? It can get pretty cold out here this time of year. The wind off the lake can be chilly."

"A blanket would be fine. I'd like that," Kellan said.

Neil was content that a conversation was being exchanged between the two of them. "Okay then, I'll go get what you need. You can wait here 'til I get back." He stepped backward through the door, keeping an eye on Kellan, more afraid he would miss something than anything else.

"I don't frighten you do I?" Kellan asked when he saw what could be fear in Neil's expression. He'd been told countless times by the doctors at the lab that he was a frightening and hideous freak of nature, that if anybody other than the lab clinicians saw him, they would call him a monster, and would have no qualms about shooting him dead to save themselves. Because of what they said, Kellan always thought of himself as an ugly disfigured creature, and figured Neil could actually be one of those people who would kill him on the spot because he were afraid of his hideous form.

"Frighten me? Not at all. Gawd no!" Neil brought his hands down to his sides and stepped away. "I'll be right back. Please don't go anywhere."

Kellan loosened up and let himself smile after Neil went inside. How could he not? He noticed Neil was trying so hard at making sure he was welcomed and comfortable, that it struck Kellan as being cute.

After Neil left to fetch covering, Kellan tiptoed around the front porch to catch glimpses of his surroundings, register everything in his head to make a mental map of the place in case there was a reason for a quick escape. He wasn't the type to meddle in anybody's business, always kept quiet and to himself, but he was out of his normal element and certainly needed to be aware of every part of his environment. He learned to be observant at the science lab, and was now taking that training with him on the outside. Kellan was not the freak of nature he'd been told all his life, but he was a rare and wondrous breed, and anybody that saw him would consider him as nothing less. And because of that, he needed to be on guard.

There was good reason to call Kellan beautiful. For the love of God's green earth, he was a blessed angel. His hair was a pure blond shade that anyone would expect to be seen on an angel, it made him look scared, holy in a way. And his body was block solid and muscular, the way a well-bred warrior's would be. He was like a mystic jewel with wings. Kellan was not to be seen by anyone, he needed to be kept a secret. Until Neil, no one knew he existed, except for the TC doctors and a few select government agents. That's it.

Neil quickly returned to the front porch with a large patchwork quilt that was meant to keep Kellan warm while he slept. If he wanted it, the blanket would suit him perfectly by holding back the chill that was already creeping in across the massive body of water. If not the quilt, then the sheet Neil also brought out with him.

Keeping his footsteps soft, Neil stepped closer to Kellan,

holding out the folded bedding.

Even though Kellan intuited Neil to be gentle like himself, he still backed away before taking the covering from Neil. Kellan always remained defensive the way he'd been taught, naturally on guard. Mostly due to the way he'd been treated by some of the doctors at the Laboratory in the woods.

Without warning, a crack of thunder came down from the sky and scared Neil into retreating, and along with him, Kellan jumped closer to the door. Neither of them had the desire to hang around outside after the ear shattering noise that just broke through the patter of the rain on the rooftop.

Frightened as well, Dylan shot inside, ran across the room to the fireplace, and looked back toward the door right when the angel started walking through it.

Kellan strolled inside the house, side stepped Neil, and let the wet weather follow behind him as it wanted to. He tried real hard not to think about all the troubles he may be facing ahead, like who's watching, where they're hiding, when they're going to appear to possibly hurt him and the ones he was with. He also tried not to think about Neil who might run a blade through his heart, or point a pistol at his skull, but he had to take the risk. It was for the best and better than being locked up in that science lab where he felt like a captive animal at a city zoo.

As Kellan stepped into the living room, he appeared massive compared to Neil. They stood about the same height with similar body types, except that the added wings on Kellan's back made him appear twice Neil's size and double his weight. Neil looked scrawny next to the larger and more impressively built Kellan.

So many questions were coming to Neil that he wanted to ask Kellan— Where did he come from? Did he have a family? Was he an experiment gone wrong? Why show up on his doorstep? Did he trust him? These were only a few he would like answered.

While Neil observed Kellan and thought about how he was going to ask his many questions, Dylan rushed up to the angel and carried on with the typical ritual that dogs normally do when meeting new people. He sniffed every part of Kellan's body that he could, gathered and memorized his scent to help him recognize Kellan in the future. Dylan was a little short to reach Kellan's crotch, but it was noticeable that he really wanted to start there. Dylan was as intrigued with the unusual creature in his house as Neil was and the only way he knew how to get to know him was to run his wet nose over most of Kellan's body.

Kellan didn't seem to mind being worked over by Neil's dog and his nose. He was used to animals and lived with many; however with the unknown Dylan, he remained on guard the whole time he was being sniffed, and kept an eagle's eye on the door that Neil left open, just in case. While holding his own wits with the dog, Kellan could tell by Neil's mannerisms that he didn't seem like the kind of a man who would hold him hostage or hurt him. If there was any reason Neil planned to hold Kellan captive, he probably would have already closed and locked the door and used the dog to block the exit.

Not being too sure how Kellan was going to sit down with a set of large feathered wings attached to his back, Neil asked if he would like to have a seat anyway.

"No thank you, I'm fine. I can stand." Kellan wasn't a sitter, he perched like most birds did, leaning forward on a branch or in a way that his wings dangled neatly behind him. He moved closer to the fire and shook his wings the same way he did after taking a bath, sharp twitches to remove as much of the water as possible. Tiny water droplets hit the floor and dried really fast from the heat of the fire.

Neil whispered so that only he himself could hear, "Omigawd." He couldn't contain himself or pull his eyes away. He initially noticed Kellan's wings. Who wouldn't? To Neil, Kellan's wings were almost more attractive than the rest of him. Not really, but they were so impressively gorgeous and new to him that his eyes were drawn to them like he was looking at a pretty face or a beautiful work of art. Neil wasn't quite sure if it was because he'd never seen wings on a man before or the fact that they were truly magnificent and beautiful. They were large, pearly-blond in color, and looked like flowing silk. They shimmered each time the light of the flickering flames from the fireplace bounced off of them. Kellan's chest was what Neil noticed next. He appreciated a man's well-developed chest, and Kellan's was large and muscular, just the way he liked a man's chest to be. The angel's stomach was perfectly trim with light traces of blond hair that ran up the deep gutter in the center, and each ripple across his abdomen was visibly defined when it caught the flickering firelight. From behind Kellan, the glowing light magically silhouetted him, which cast an impressive full body halo all around him. He was heavenly and idol-like, almost more glorious than Neil could handle.

Kellan glanced around the room they were standing in while he let the rest of the mist on his damp wings dry. The place was pretty quiet and cozy, the way a living room should be. He saw many dark colors all around, or maybe they just seemed dark because the room was dimly lit by the fire alone, there was no other source of light in the room to aid in brightening the place up. There seemed to be a lot of older items scattered here and there, as if most of them were left by a grandparent, or the house actually belonged to an older person, and Neil was just occupying it for the time being or perhaps taking care of the place while the actual owners were away. All the bits and pieces around the house didn't seem to really fit with his modern day appearance.

Like Kellan, Neil was twenty-eight as well, born the same year but only a few months apart. Neil was the younger of the two, surprising the world during the first week in January, where Kellan made his winged appearance at the end of March.

Neil looked like a contemporary man, one who would be measured as tall, dark and handsome, well almost tall, if just clearing six foot was considered tall these days. Neil was either graced with great genes or he was one of those gym bunnies that worked out every day. It was clear by how his beastly form stood out beneath his Aeropostale pull over that he was solidly built.

Dylan was still running his nose over Kellan, mostly sticking to areas below his knees. At the laboratory Kellan sometimes thought that the animals were his only true friends, and with his perception of that, he was used to being licked and loved in ways only pets knew how. With that in mind, Kellan gave no thought to pushing Dylan away.

Turning his back on Kellan, Neil excused himself, "I'll be right back, but don't go anywhere. Please." He left the door to the outside open as a pleasant way of making sure Kellan felt at ease and less confined in a strange place. "Can I bring you anything? Would you like some tea?" He asked as he walked away.

"No thanks, I'm good." Kellan kept an eye on Neil as he walked from the living room and into the kitchen. The distance between the two rooms wasn't very far and the open floor plan allowed Kellan to see every move Neil made. While he watched Neil, Kellan knelt down and gave Dylan a massage up and down his back, from head to tail, finishing with a gruff wrangle behind each ear.

Dylan liked that. He exuded excitement by backing himself tighter up against Kellan, bumping his wiggling rear end against his knees while he flapped his energetic tongue.

When Neil returned to the living room with his cup of herbal tea, he could tell that Dylan and Kellan were bonding in a way that could actually turn into a longtime friendship. Aside from both seeming to be more animal than human, Neil was able to pick out how connected the two of them were quickly becoming. Dylan was certainly lovable, and Kellan seemed to be too.

Kellan rose from the floor after letting Dylan go, gracefully turned, and just like that, he liked looking at Neil's strong face, chiseled cheekbones and cowboy-square chin. He liked the softness he saw in Neil's dark shiny eyes. They told Kellan he was honestly gentle.

Kellan never looked at anybody the way he looked at Neil, that deeply, that profoundly. Not even his secret crush, Seth at the lab, who never knew Kellan liked him romantically or even thought of Kellan in the same way.

Quite opposite of Kellan's appearance, Neil had dark chocolate hair that dangled fine wisps in front of his deep brown eyes. His sun tanned skin tone against Kellan's almost translucent white flesh made the contrast between the two of them like night and day.

Neil's tranquil gaze held Kellan's attention for a few silent moments before eventually being snapped out of it. It could have been the thunder rolling in the distance or the crackle of the fire that dragged him out of the trance Neil had put him in. Whatever it was, there was an intense connection made just then.

The weather outside was starting to simmer down from what they both could tell. The rain diminished to a few staggered drops and the thunder rolled further and further away. There was something soothing about the end of a storm that made everything seem like it was going to be alright. Both Kellan and Neil seemed to feel the same about that.

It was half past midnight and Neil still had lingering questions on his mind that he wanted answered. But before he had a chance to ask any of them, Dylan trotted over and hopped on the sofa next to him.

Impatiently, Dylan inched closer to Neil, intently staring at him, waiting for much needed attention. When no response came from Neil, his little body moved closer until he was practically in his lap. His paw lifted and came back down with a thump against Neil's leg. When his existence went unnoticed by Neil, a whimper escaped Dylan and he paw slammed Neil's leg again. Prolonged unawareness by Neil made Dylan move in even closer and he climbed even further into Neil's lap where he rocked and made himself known. Dylan needed that cookie and he needed it quickly.

"Alright, for the love of Harry," Neil grumbled, pushing himself up from the sectional.

At the second Dylan felt Neil budge he jumped off the sofa and ran for the cabinet in the kitchen he knew so well as the cookie door. When he got there, he barked, accompanied by uncontrolled pony hops in front of the wooden door.

Kellan admired the interaction between Dylan and Neil. He could see that Neil was the type of person who looked out for others, not only himself.

Neil returned to the living room and left Dylan to munch on the cookie in the kitchen alone.

The fire showed signs of dying out and needed another log or two to keep it alive, but before Neil stoked the flames, he checked to see if the added heat was okay with Kellan.

"Of course." Kellan stepped aside, bumped into the table next to him, almost knocking the lamp over with a swish of his wing. He spun around to grab hold of it before it toppled to the floor and broke, and when he did, the tip of his feathers swiped Neil's cheek.

Instead of protecting himself, Neil immediately held up an arm to block Kellan's wing from reaching the fiery flames. That could have been bad in so many ways.

Clearly the place was not meant for an angel. Big wings and flight practices were better suited for the out of doors.

Exited by all the commotion taking place, Dylan barked and hopped around as if it were playtime.

"Hush," Neil told Dylan.

Dylan stopped and sat down on the first command like the good dog he really was.

"I should be more careful." Kellan sat down sideways on the end of the sofa sectional, letting his big wings fall back over the edge where they touched the floor.

"It's okay. Worse things have happened in here. I have a dog that was once a rambunctious puppy." Neil let go of the fire stoker and turned to sit on the opposite end of the sofa where he'd left his tea.

Just as anxious to be part of the team, Dylan jump on the sofa between them, dropped down like his legs gave way, looked at Kellan first and then over at Neil, tongue hanging out and smiling, content and loving every bit of the friendly visitor.

Enjoying the silence for a few minutes, Neil reached for his tea and sipped instead of asking any of the questions he had stored away in his head to ask Kellan.

Kellan was first to break the silence. "Do you live here alone?" He was curious, wanted to know if the place was Neil's, if he shared it with anybody, or if it belonged to somebody else like his parents or even his grandparents. By the dated décor and placement of knickknacks, he figured it was grandma's place.

"I do. Well, Dylan and I do." Neil patted Dylan on the head, giving him the simple affection he loved so much.

Dylan exploded at Neil's touch. The briefest attention always got him riled up.

Kellan chuckled when Dylan stirred. "It's quiet here. Very nice."

Neil spoke briefly, "Yep, we like it here too."

Kellan looked over top of Dylan at Neil, staring at him. He found Neil to be an attractive man, at least to him he was. Neil's dark eyes seemed to hypnotize him and Kellan liked his strong jaw line that was shadowed with a full day's growth of facial hair. It gave Neil a rugged appearance, the kind that Kellan found appealing. Kellan grabbed a sneaky glance at Neil's chest and could tell by his snug fitting shirt that Neil was in good physical form. He needed to be if he was going to keep up with a fast flying angel and a rambunctious dog all at the same time. Kellan forgot all about Seth from the lab after being spellbound by Neil's solid good looks.

Neil looked over the fine rim of his teacup, catching eye contact with Kellan. He held his gaze without looking away, giving answer to Kellan's curiosity whether he liked him back. "I'm sorry, I didn't mean to stare, but"—Neil shook his head—"I'm sure you get that a lot."

Kellan smiled at Neil. "It's okay, I don't mind if you stare." His smile changed to a compelling grin. "I'm fine with it coming from you." His feathers fluttered and then relaxed. "I don't actually get a lot of lookers. The only people who have ever seen me are the doctors and staff at the lab and now you and your little dog."

Neil's curiosity perked up after he heard Kellan mention doctors and a lab. As a member of the medical field himself, the nurse in him wanted to know where Kellan came from and how he got there more than ever. Neil's mind went spiraling in several directions because he'd always wondered if secret eccentric research was going on somewhere in a hidden lab buried a few miles underground that was run by the government. Being that Kellan appeared out of nowhere somewhat solidified his beliefs on the subject of the existence of underground laboratories where fucked up shit went on. What else could it be? It explained the chopper that pinpointed his location earlier that day. Military helicopters don't just appear in the sky in Traverse City for no reason. They had to have been looking for someone who got away, in this case, a runaway angel. And the winged creature that showed himself on Neil's doorstep contributed to the idea that they were looking for *this* angel that escaped the confines of their laboratory. The whole possibility of the existence of these mysterious labs kind of reminded Neil of Dr. Frankenstein's monster. Only this one was so much more handsome than the movie version of the creature and was somebody he would definitely like to keep.

"What's on your mind?" Kellan asked, looking hard into Neil's eyes.

Neil blinked a few times to regain his focus on reality before he answered. "This is so fucked up. I mean… I'm sorry. I didn't mean that." His hand went to his forehead where he banged the side of a fist against it a few times as if trying to knock some sense into his clouded brain cells.

Kellan laughed. "I know it's a bit of a shock to see all this." His hand grazed his naked chest.

Neil went on, "I mean… You being here in my house." —He swiped a hand out in front of him—"Wait… NO... Not you being fucked up. Oh Gawd, that didn't come out right either." He gripped his teacup with both hands again. "I mean… Who would have thought in a million years that I would be sitting in my living room, catching glimpses of crackling flames in my fireplace, while drinking green tea with my dog and a beautiful man with wings?"

Kellan laughed again at Neil's neuroticism and really liked that he called him beautiful.

"This shit doesn't happen" —Neil focused on the tea inside his cup—"not to me." He looked like he was about to lose his mind.

Dylan laid his head on Neil's lap and looked up at him with eyes of trepidation. The look on his face was saying, *'What the heck is going on? I'm here for you if you need me.'*

Neil stroked Dylan's head, taking from him what he was offering: Love. His fuzzy head was warm to the touch and the soft fur helped bring Neil's anxiety back down from where it took off to with his realizations. Perhaps the shock of everything just settled in all at once and he wasn't as level headed about the whole thing as he thought he was. He took a deep breath and miraculously settled down almost instantly.

Dylan sensed it and calmed down too.

Kellan lifted an eyebrow and with it went one of his wings, like they were somehow connected. "You were saying?"

Neil sat rigidly at the very end of the sectional, feeling oddly ashamed for mentioning that Kellan was the main reason that everything around him was currently all fucked up. There was a long silence before he said anything, being careful not to make the same mistake twice. "How long have you been here?" He asked a simple question.

"Your place - here?" Kellan pointed at the floor. "Or do you mean at the Lab?"

Oh crap, another question.

"If you don't mind, let's start with the lab. I'm figuring you weren't one of the doctors?" Neil leaned in to hear better, and the funny thing was, so did Dylan.

"Until now, I've been living at the Laboratory over in Traverse City. You know of it?" Kellan wasn't sure if Neil had any idea the place existed, or if anybody did for that matter, so hearing Neil's answer intrigued him.

Neil had no clue there was such a place in Traverse City. "Is the lab inside one of the hospitals on the bay?" His brow came down tight in the middle, almost making him appear angry.

"No, it stands alone. That place has too many weird things going on inside of it to share a building with an organization that has any other purpose. From what I've seen, they couldn't risk anybody poking a head in on one of their experiments and then blabbing about it to the outside world. That place is top secret." Kellan gave Neil an angled glare, reading his expression to make sure he really didn't know about the Laboratory.

If Neil didn't know there was a building hidden there in the woods, then there was the possibility that others didn't either. How could a great big place like that remain a secret for twenty-eight years, Kellan's entire life? The monstrosity stood three plus stories tall in the middle of a rural tourist town. There had to be somebody who knew about it. What did everybody think the place was?

"Where is it? I know of all the hospitals in that area, but can't place a free standing laboratory in the city." Neil's eyebrows pulled tightly together again. His forehead wrinkled in the middle.

"You may know of it as the old Mental Institution up off thirty-seven," Kellan said, pointing in every direction because he really didn't know which way he was facing.

"What? That old place? I thought it burnt down long ago, and was too damaged to be of any use." Neil moved over to the fireplace and poked the logs.

"There was a large fire, but the place was refurbished a few times and its most recent use is as a Laboratory," Kellan said.

"Odd. Seems I would have heard something if it was being used as a medical facility of some kind," Neil replied and then sat back down on the sofa next to Dylan.

Kellan's manner seemed so natural as he sat stroking the feathers on his right wing. His eyes stayed fixed on Neil as he spoke. "That place isn't a hospital anymore. It's an experimental Lab where people like me and other strange creations are made. The place is so huge, and I don't know about so much of what goes on in there."

Neil's face went blank for a minute. "Wait, what did you just say?"

"The place is an experimental Lab?" Kellan repeated.

"Well that too, but you said you were *made* there?" Neil stopped and swallowed. The mere idea of a person being made like a recipe whose ingredients were written on a card had him every bit as interested in the process as the technician who put all the ingredients in the mixing bowl and then turned it on.

"That doesn't freak you out, does it?" Kellan said.

"I can't see how anything could freak me out after seeing you."

"What?" Kellan sighed.

Neil grinned. "You're a man with wings here in my living room. I'd say at this point I've seen just about everything."

"No you haven't," Kellan replied. "But I *have* seen it all." He stood up and walked over to the fireplace where he folded his arms across his chest and opened his wings to stretch them out and let in a little air to dry the places that still felt damp.

Neil couldn't tell if Kellan was cold or if he just had a moment of insecurity. "Since I was a kid, I always heard that place was haunted."

"That's exactly what *they* want you to think. They want to keep you and everybody else out. Part of the building actually may be haunted. Many people did die in the fires there and they might still be there walking the halls." Kellan didn't want to discount the fact.

"Who are *They*?" Neil asked.

"The State. The government. They own and run the place, and what goes on inside those walls supposedly stays inside the walls. Well, I'm now the one exception." Kellan hadn't abided by that rule at all. He told Neil almost everything about himself and what he went through at the Lab. He told him that each day was sort of like living in a prison cell. He felt he could trust Neil, but if he couldn't, he didn't care who Neil told at this point. Well, deep down he did, but his resolve was wearing too thin from keeping his secrets to himself. Twenty-eight years of holding it in was way too long. He needed to tell somebody, let someone else know how he had lived and understand what he felt. Kellan gave Neil more than what he probably should have, but he needed somebody he could trust, and telling him everything without holding back might bring Neil closer. And he wanted that, he wanted to feel close to someone. Kellan was in dire need of a friend, and hopefully Neil was that person.

Neil sat quietly and listened, letting Kellan take his time while telling his story. There was a lot of information being given to him all at once, which he probably missed half of. But the one part of Kellan's story that stayed with Neil, and what he found to be most interesting, was when Kellan spoke of a lab technician by the name of Seth. That bit of information let Neil know that Kellan was more infatuated with the same sex than with the opposite. It seemed to Neil that Seth was Kellan's first crush, maybe his only. Neil smiled at that and did his best not to let it turn into a wide grin across his gorgeous face.

"How long ago did you leave the lab? Was it just this morning?" Neil asked.

"Actually, late last night is when I flew the coop." Kellan laughed at his attempt at being witty, but that moment seemed to be a good time to lighten the mood. They both needed a laugh.

"And you got to Mackinac that quickly?" Neil raised a brow. "That was fast, it's over a hundred miles. Did you fly the entire way?"

"With wings, do you think I walked?" Kellan laughed again, this time actually trying to be funny.

Neil laughed back, and with a swish of a hand, offered Kellan some tea from his cup. He pushed the cup toward Kellan, expecting him not to take it, but he did.

Kellan sipped from the cup, tasting Neil's herbal essence mouth that was on the rim. It was like a first kiss, sweet and subtle. "Mmmm. Good. Ya know what? I'll have some of this delicious tea." He brought his wings in like an accordion, tucking them against his back on either side of his spine, and handed the teacup back to Neil.

"Sure. I'll get you a spot." Taking the cup, Neil set it down on the table next to the lamp that had almost taken a nose dive to the floor earlier. He then stood for a few seconds, captivated while staring down at Kellan's beauty, like he was looking at a gold bar for the very first time. He wasn't sure he would ever get over how magnificent Kellan was. How impressive he was with the solid muscles in his massive chest and shoulders, developed to support those mystical wings. Neil wondered if Kellan had other parts of his body that functioned the same way a non-hybrid man's did. To satisfy his inquisitiveness for the time being, he glanced down at the front of Kellan's jeans and could see there was definitely something stowed away behind his bulging zipper. He wondered if Kellan was bred that way or if it was just good luck in the choice of genes the scientists used. Neil wanted to find out, but first it was teatime. "I'll bring in the kettle. You and Dylan hang out here."

"I can get it," Kellan insisted, and stood up to take the cup back.

"Don't be silly. You're my guest." Neil lifted a hand and made the snap decision to serve his handsome visitor as if they were in a fine teahouse.

When Kellan agreed to let Neil take on the role of a maître d', he dropped his hands and pushed them into his back pockets. Every muscle in his upper body went tight. Each ripple in his abdomen flexed as he exhaled. He was rock solid and it caught Neil's attention again.

Neil lost focus, stopped and stuttered while he took in Kellan's purely human masculine beauty. "Um—do you take sugar or—um—any milk in your tea?" He liked Kellan's shirtless pose and was having a hard time remembering why he got up to go to the kitchen in the first place.

"I was never allowed much, if any, sugar at TC, so please, no sugar or milk for me. I'll take what you have, as is. Are you sure you don't want me to get it myself?" Kellan's chest flexed when he breathed, and his smile went crooked when he noticed Neil's interest in his half-dressed body. He discretely flexed for him again, holding his impressive position.

"Stay, I've got it," Neil harped, like he would have if he was talking to Dylan. Not harshly, but with cheerful firmness. "Damn, he's fine," he whispered to himself as he left the room.

Kellan stepped back when he heard Neil's assertive response that sounded commanding yet sexy. Kellan's smile still held true because he knew that Neil was only taking strides to make his situation better. And even knowing Neil for the short time he had, he could tell that he was a giver who looked out for other people more than he did himself. It seemed to be in Neil's nature. Kellan liked that about him and that thought made his sideways grin go full.

Returning to the warm living room with a kettle of hot tea in one hand and an extra cup and saucer for Kellan in the other, Neil saw that Kellan was still standing in front of the fireplace looking into the flames like he was trying to stay warm. "Here's your tea. It might help warm you up a bit. Are you cold?"

Kellan turned around to face Neil. "No, I'm good, I just like fireplaces. We didn't have anything this cozy at TC. I'm just enjoying what I've never had. I'm actually getting kind of hot, but I'll be fine."

"Maybe I should get us some coolers instead, but you look good with your shirt off and I don't mind keeping you that way," Neil blurted out. "Oh Gawd, I'm sorry. Did I just think out loud? I didn't mean to. I take that back."

Kellan's chuckle quickly turned into laughter. "No, please, don't take anything back. I like that you like me this way."

"You do?" Neil's voice lowered as he shyly spoke.

"Yes I do," Kellan answered. "At the Lab, there wasn't anybody that liked me for me. They just wanted me for what I could do for them. Nobody really, *really* liked me."

"That's crazy talk, you're gorgeous. What's not to like? And I don't just mean winged beautiful, I mean you are an outstandingly gorgeous man with a handsome face as a bonus."

"That's nice to hear. I've always been told I was a freak, unsightly, Quasimodo ugly." Kellan looked to the floor, like a boy that was just scolded by a pointy finger in the face.

"Kellan, that's crazy talk. You're far from being a freak, and anybody that looks at you can see you're not unsightly. Other than being different from the typical human, you're a thing of beauty and I honestly mean that. Ohmigawd, you have to know this?" Neil was shocked by what he was hearing and leaned in closer to Kellan, making sure he was fully aware that nothing compared to the beauty that he projected.

There was a hiss of pain from Kellan upon hearing Neil's words of affirmation, but it dissolved quickly as Neil carried on.

Like a heartsick man in love, Neil looked deeply into Kellan's eyes as he spoke. "There is nothing wrong with you. You have to believe that." He scooted closer to Kellan, handed him the hot teacup and reached for his other hand and held it in his own.

Kellan gave back a grim smile when he looked up at Neil from beneath his shadowed brow. It was easy to see that he still held more than a hint of what appeared to be pain or maybe worry. It wasn't clear, but from what Kellan had recently encountered, it was probably pent up anxiety caused by running away from the only home he had ever known. It was evident that what he had been told about himself, what he left behind was still very much a part of him.

Neil went silent, eyes locked on the inspiring angel as he inched inexorably closer to him. Kellan's movements were hypnotizing and Neil couldn't remember ever feeling the way he did just then.

Neil's heart sped up the closer they got, and Kellan's cherubic lips looked enticing, begging for Neil to press his against them. It was sensual. That magical moment had arrived naturally, as if it was meant to be.

"You must have been sent from Heaven," Neil whispered, and his warm breath caressed Kellan's mouth as he moved in closer.

Chapter 7

Breaking through the depths of sheer silence and heard over the crackle of the fire, Dylan barked and ran to the door, continuously looking back at Neil and then at the door between huffs and snorts.

The mood suddenly shifted from romantic to grim, but Kellan was not giving up that easily.

"What the shit?" Neil groaned and pulled back from Kellan.

Dylan kept on barking as bright lights circled the beach and then zeroed in on the house, piercing the darkness beyond every window. A bright light shone in the back of the house and one in the front.

It was *The* chopper, most likely the military bird that came by early in the morning, back again and it brought a companion.

"Shit!" Neil snarled again. "We need to get out of here, or at least we need to find a way for you to flee."

Kellan had never uttered a curse word in his life before but this seemed like a good time to start. "Shit, where the fuck am I supposed to go?" His wings automatically sprang from his back like two flags opening up on a windy day. He was standing, on guard all over again, the same way he was last night.

Neil made one of his famous snap decisions and pushed Kellan toward the kitchen. "Get in the pantry. Hurry. I need to stay here so they aren't suspicious of an empty house that has a barking dog and an active flame burning in the fireplace."

Kellan hesitated a minute. "The pantry? They will surely find me in there. Is there room?"

"No they won't, I promise. Now go." Neil pushed him again, harder this time against his back, between his wings. It was the first time he really touched them. They were silky, just like he'd imagined they'd be.

Dylan was still barking at the front door, which added havoc to all the commotion going on in the kitchen.

During the rush to hide Kellan, Neil swung open the pantry door that Kellan expected to be a small closet but wasn't. Beyond the narrow door were a set of shelves that secretly hid another small room. Nobody but Neil knew it was there: until the moment Kellan was pushed through it. Neil grabbed hold of a hidden lever and pushed the shelving unit lining the back wall open. Reaching back, he grabbed Kellan's hand and awkwardly pulled him through the doorway. Inside the room in the middle of the floor was another trapdoor that would take them below the ground into a storm shelter. It would be safe and hopefully the chopper crew wouldn't know to look there.

"Go quickly. I'll meet up with you soon," Neil said and handed Kellan a flashlight. "Here, take this with you."

Kellan shook his wings and tucked them tightly against his back to make it easier for him to fit down the narrow stairway. It smelled damp and musty, but at the time he didn't care, he needed to hide. As he stepped down, he gripped Neil's hand in a way that made it clear he didn't want to let go. Slowly he loosened his grip and slid his fingers from Neil's, looked up and watched the door above his head drop down into place. When it slammed shut, it was like being in a prison cell all over again.

Giving in to the helicopters' noise, Dylan finally cooled down and stopped barking. He knew he couldn't win over the loud thumping sound of the chopper blades.

How did they know and what made them come here again?

Neil quickly closed up the pantry, grabbed a book and a blanket and went to the front door as if nothing was any different in his house from any other day. He looked out at the lights shining down on his house and tried to block out the noise of the still turning chopper blades by covering his ears.

The area on the beach in front of the house was limited in size and not designed with an aircraft landing pad in mind. Foolishly however, one chopper touched down successfully while the other one stayed high in the sky. It seemed rather idiotic to land on the beach with sand and water beneath the gale force winds being created by its blades, but all the rain that fell earlier helped to at least keep most of the sand on the ground.

Neil stepped through the doorway and onto the porch with Dylan at his side, squinting to keep any flying debris from getting in his eyes. Instead of being pelted by junk and stuff, he and Dylan backed up toward the house and waited for whoever was in the chopper to come knocking on the door. They stood in the open doorway, hopeful of discouraging the strangers from trying to get in.

Just as Neil suspected, the strangers came knocking. Two men from the army green helicopter climbed the steps and met him in the door's archway. They were dressed in black suits, white shirts and black ties that made them look like FBI agents, and Neil was sure they were armed, he just couldn't see the guns, tasers, or knives. The dark sunglasses they had on in the middle of the night were a dead giveaway that they were up to no good. The lenses had to either have been designed for night vision or made with x-ray capabilities so they were able to see through walls and shit. There had to be a good reason for wearing sunglasses at night and Neil was pretty sure it wasn't to look cool.

At the doorstep the two men in black tried to be polite, but failed miserably. They were dry and orderly, clearly interaction with the human race was not their first talent. They crowded the front door and studied what they were able to see inside over Neil's shoulders. After asking several questions that didn't make much sense, they harshly pushed their way in to look for the missing person they mentioned.

Really? Missing person?

Pushing back at the two big black clad men, Neil blocked the doorway with his hand jammed against the doorframe. "You can't just shove your way into my house. This is not a public toilet."

Dylan growled like the guard dog he was supposed to be.

The men took a couple steps back when they saw the dog's teeth glisten and what looked to be a plan to attack their throats and tear them to shreds.

They explained to Neil that they were looking for a man who had escaped from a hospital for the criminally insane, mentioned that they spotted him in the area and he may possibly be hiding in one of the homes on the lake. They told Neil it was in his favor if they were allowed to search the property in order to protect him and keep him safe. The men were lying and Neil knew it.

"I'd know if anybody unwanted was in my house, so there's no reason for either of you to enter," Neil lied too. He'd cross himself, saving Mary and the angel in his house if he didn't still have his hand propped in the doorway to block the hoodlums from getting in.

"Its official business and we're checking every house on the strip, so I'd recommend that you let us in to check things out." One of the oversized men pressed, looking above Neil's left shoulder, already checking for other people inside the house in a way that suggested he was in law enforcement.

"This is nuts," Neil bravely grumbled.

Dylan licked his chops.

"Are you going to let us in or do we have to call in additional force?" The other man threatened with a stupid grin on his face and a forehead that wrinkled above his shades.

Neil couldn't let that happen. He wanted them gone for Kellan's sake. He wanted them gone for his own sake. "Show me some identification that proves you are who you say you are."

They each flashed a badge beneath their coats that indicated they were military police, and because they flew in on an Agusta A109 LUH military style fighter copter, they must be official. Neil honestly had a good idea they were who they said they were because of whom he was hiding in the shelter underneath the house.

Even though Neil lied to the black suited men by telling them that nobody was in the house but himself and the dog, they still insisted that he let them in to take a look around.

Neil clearly knew why they were in the house, and the way he was trained in nursing school was not to give out good or bad news to the patient, it's up to the doctor in charge do all the talking. With that in mind, he kept his mouth shut most of the time while they searched. He only spoke when it was necessary to do so or if he wanted to cause a distraction.

The two brawny men in black followed each other around the house in a single file, one in the footsteps of the other. If the man in front abruptly stopped, he would get one hell of a cock up his ass. Both appeared to be packing huge dicks.

Neil did the same by following the suits around the house single file; however he made sure to keep several steps behind. When one of them opened the pantry door and traced the inside with an evil eye and a gloved finger, Neil panicked internally and Dylan whimpered.

"Shit," Neil silently screamed in his own head that resounded back as *"fuck me."*

The uninvited black clothed invaders continued searching the house while Neil tried to keep them away from the pantry as best he could. He hung out in the kitchen for a while but then decided it would be less conspicuous if he sat down in front of the fireplace to read his book, *Heartbreak Beat,* make believe everything in his house was business as usual and let them carry on with their hunt so they would hurry up and leave.

When the men first arrived, Neil's manner seemed natural and casual, but as time dragged on and they were still roaming through the house, his mood changed, and became snarky. "Are you here to save me or what?" He was bothered enough by their intrusion that he didn't care how he sounded. He just wanted them out of his house.

The two men didn't respond, and from what Neil could tell, they just looked at him through dark lenses and scowled. Both of them at the exact same time, like they were tethered at the brain.

Twenty long minutes later, they finally left empty-handed.

Thank God.

Chapter 8

As soon as the men in black walked out the door, Neil shot from the sofa with Dylan by his side, running to the window to watch the choppers lift into the sky and fly away. One after the other, the two aircraft headed north toward the bridge and then made a U-turn south, spot lights sweeping the bay. Unless there were more choppers hidden out back in the trees, Neil was pretty sure all the shady guys were gone. He waited a few more minutes before heading to the pantry door to be with Kellan, his new friend who just happened to be an angel who, not coincidentally, was wanted by the men in black.

Neil wasn't an unscrupulous person, but he was proud of himself for having been able to deceive the bad guys into believing he was alone in the house. His wicked side came out pretty easily, but that didn't matter, he had a winged man in his house that seemed holier than thou who would most likely be able to banish his malevolent deed with a blink of an eye.

Neil had an intense need to get back to Kellan so the guy

knew everything was all right on the top side. Before he did, he moved to put out the fire in the living room. First he pushed the coals and sizzling logs to the back of the fireplace and then reduced the oxygen flow to it by closing the glass doors.

As if any loud noise would bring back the men in black, Neil whispered, "Dylan—come." He tapped his thigh a couple times to lead him to the kitchen.

One last sneaky look around before Neil opened up the pantry door and stepped in. "Come," he whispered to Dylan again and then shut the door behind them.

Before Neil opened the trap door to the storm shelter, he knocked on the floor with his heel and quietly announced it was him who was about to enter. He heard a light knock back which let him know it was okay to open the door.

Neil tugged on the door hidden in the floor and propped it back against the wall so he could enter. "It's okay, they're gone."

At his feet looking up he saw Kellan's wide eyes, pupils blown from being in total darkness. Neil pasted on a smile for Kellan, even though he was still a bit shaken by what just occurred. He had to, for Kellan's sake.

"Can I come out now?" Kellan asked.

"It may not be a good idea. I'm not sure if they'll be coming back," Neil answered.

"Are you coming down then?" Kellan sounded concerned and then poked his head up through the open floor.

"We both are. Me and Dylan." Neil needed to lock the cabinet door first, just to feel safe.

Kellan held the flashlight on Neil so he could see what he was doing. The lock clicked into place and then both he and Dylan turned to take the steps down through the floor.

Neil grunted when he lifted Dylan and then grunted louder when he took each step to the shelter below with the thirty-six pound dog in his arms.

Dylan hated those stairs because he slipped down them once before and from that day forward he insisted on being carried. Dogs will be dogs.

"There's a light switch next to the doorway to your left. Can you hit it?" Neil grumbled on his way down while he spoke to Kellan.

The light beam from the flashlight swept across the room until it landed on the switch next to the archway. "Ah. Found it."

The overhead light traveled fast and the room lit up in a hurry.

Kellan had no idea the area was set up so nicely. As far as he'd known, anything underground was considered a dungeon. He'd spent his fair share of time in more than a few of them. It was supposed to be dark, dank and dingy. This place wasn't. It was actually cozy, set up like a small studio apartment for a single person, with everything needed to live in the place for about a week or two. Plenty of food. Lots of water: piped in as well as stored. A cooler if needed, but most of the items on the shelves were nonperishable edibles so a place to keep them cold wasn't really required. The ceiling was a bit low, but the floor space looked to be about twelve feet square. At the opposite side from where they came in was another door, which opened to a tunnel that would take them outdoors in case the entrance to the house became blocked. A single lamp with a softer light stood on a small table next to the only bed in the room. One bed. One Pillow. Close quarters. Great deal.

"This is it. We can spend the night down here so that we're clear of those hoodlums' snare if they decide to come back. What do you think of the place?" Neil asked, putting Dylan down on the bed where he liked it.

"It works." Kellan was still looking around the room, intrigued a place like this existed beneath the earth's surface. "Those guys were looking for me, weren't they? What did they look like?"

"They were two big black guys, the football player type – meaty with cinder block feet." Neil brought his clawed hands in front of him as if holding an imaginary football, giving Kellan a grizzly look. "They kind of scared me, but I knew what they were looking for and as long as I let them believe I had nothing to hide, I figured I was going to be alright. Shook me up a bit, but as you can see I survived."

"I wonder if I know who they are," Kellan pondered.

"You probably do. If not, I'm pretty sure they know who you are," Neil said.

Dylan stood up on the bed and stared intently while

whimpering.

"What's he want?" Kellan asked, pointing at the dog.

"A cookie," Neil said.

"Does he have any down here?" Kellan looked over at the shelves full of food but didn't see anything for the dog.

"He does. Over there." Neil flipped his hand toward the top shelf above the water basin near the door that led outside.

"You think he'll let me give him one without out taking off a finger?" Kellan asked.

"Anybody that gives him a cookie, he'll be sure to spare the finger in case a second one follows." Neil told the truth. "What do you eat?" he asked.

"What do you mean, what do I eat?" Kellan smirked and then began chuckling at the question. He handed Dylan a cookie.

Neil shrugged his shoulders. "I don't know? Bird seed? I haven't a clue. I need to know these things. You're an experiment, remember? What the hell?"

"Do you *have* bird seed?" Kellan inquired. "I'm kind of hungry."

"What? Really?" Neil pulled his arms to his chest and crossed them, concerned Kellan would starve if no bird food was stocked.

"I'm having you on. You can relax." Kellan started laughing at Neil. "I eat the same thing you do. I'm pretty much like you: a human, except I have wings. It's the only difference. Every other part of me is the same."

"Good to hear." Neil's mind wandered and he grinned. "Well, that answers a few other questions about you I had."

"Really?" Kellan's face went curious. "Like what?"

Neil suddenly turned shy and abandoned his thoughts. "It's nothing. I have my answer."

Kellan had a good idea what Neil was thinking and it gave him hope.

It was getting late, almost morning already and the sleep requirement for a human was between six and eight hours within a twenty-four hour period in order to properly function. As for Kellan, he could survive on much less, but more was better.

Kellan looked over at the bed Dylan was still standing on. "You can have the bed. I'll sleep over here on the floor. I'm used to a hard surface."

"What? Don't' be silly. The bed is a queen, large enough for all of us. We can share it," Neil commented.

"Don't forget I have these great big wings. I take up quite a bit of space. I might crowd you." Kellan grinned.

Neil liked the idea of that. "We'll manage," he said. "Now, help me with the sheets so we can get some rest. The sun will be up soon."

Kellan snapped the sheet open above the bed and let it slowly float down over Dylan. "You get in front, I'll take the back."

Neil loved the idea of that.

Dylan snorted.

Chapter 9

Neither Kellan nor Neil could really tell, but they both seemed to think morning had arrived and passed. It was darker than dark in the small room underground and nobody was able to see a hand in front of their face. Well, Kellan could, but he was built like that. It was pitch black. The windowless room kept it that way. There was no sunshine poking at them through yonder windowpane, so how were any of them supposed to know if it was time to rise and shine?

As it turned out, morning had arrived and passed them by, and they were still lying in the same order as when they fell asleep earlier that morning, tightly wrapped in a clingy bundle. Kellan pressed up behind Neil with his arm wrapped over his side, kind of hugging him, and his face was buried in the back of his head.

Dylan still at their feet, not ready to get up just yet either, so it seemed.

There was a decent sized surprise that actually brought Neil to full wakefulness and that fanciful surprise came from Kellan as he rested against his backside. It was evident Kellan was happy to wake up with him, so Neil smiled and pushed back against the angel behind him.

Life seemed good.

Kellan had never been in such an intimate position with another man before. His first thought when he woke up was to pull back and mind his manners, but he didn't. Everything about it felt good to him and his natural reaction was to push hard against the man in front of him and bring great release to himself, but he didn't do that either. Even though he was feeling a little skittish about the whole bonding thing he was experiencing, he enjoyed being close to Neil and could sense the affection he had been missing in his life for so long. He didn't want to let it go. He liked it. He wasn't going anywhere. Not yet anyway.

Neil on the other hand was quite familiar with the whole man-to-man connection in more ways than one. He'd been in this position a few times before, with and without clothes on. Over, under, on top and on the bottom. Every which way. He'd had his share of midnight romps in the past, a short-term boyfriend or two, or three, okay, make that four, but this time was a bit out of the ordinary. He wouldn't call it a romp, but spending the night with an angel had never entered his mind and wasn't in any of his plans until he was in heaven sprouting his own set of feathers. Well, there was this one time at summer camp where he met a guy who wore a pair of angel wings while they fucked each other in the back of a tipsy camper, but that didn't count. That wasn't real, this was. Neil stayed put and decided to wait for Kellan to make the first attempt at pulling out of the tangled knot they were in. He wasn't moving before he had to, no way, no how.

Neil really didn't sleep most of the night because he couldn't stop the thoughts and images crashing around in his head. An angel slept next to him all night long and the hardened evidence pressed up against his spine excited Neil and at the same time tore him down. He could feel the warmth that Kellan was passing on to him solely by his touch, but at the time, Neil couldn't bring himself to act on his need to explore. He wanted to feel more of Kellan. Kiss him, hold on to him, passionately make love to him, but he wasn't too sure how everything worked with a real angel. As Kellan said earlier, everything was the same except for his wings, but to remain respectful, Neil laid still and imagined how it could be. If there was a moment that Neil wanted time to stand still, it was that moment.

Was this some kind of punishment for love?

One puff against Neil's ear and then Kellan rose.

Neil swore it was a kiss.

"We shouldn't stay here too long," Kellan said. "Is there a clock down here?"

First looking at his illuminated smart phone screen, Neil yelped, "Holy crap it's four in the afternoon. Is it possible we slept that long?" He jumped out of bed, or literally rolled off the edge.

"I don't think we fell asleep until about five or so in the morning, so yeah, I'd say we slept that long," Kellan replied, scooting to the edge of the bed to stretch his wings.

Neil was flabbergasted, he never wasted the day away by sleeping through it. He must have really been exhausted. Maybe it was a good thing. Those men that showed up late last night, bordering on early morning, may still be out looking for Kellan, which made hiding out all day that much more an appealing idea.

"I'll go have a look up stairs. You hang tight a minute by Dylan's side. I'll be back to get you when I know the coast is clear." Neil aimed a finger at Dylan and then moved it over and pointed at Kellan.

Before opening the pantry door, Neil pressed an ear to it and listened. No noise was good noise. He pushed. The outdoor light coming in the windows almost set his eyes on fire. It was shocking to his retina and they spiraled until able to focus. "Shit, that's bright." His arm went up like a vampire blocking the purity of the sun's rays. "It's fine. You can come up. But leave this door open in case you need to get out quick."

Dylan was okay with running up the steps, it was going down them that he had the issue with.

"I'm going to make something to eat. You like breakfast?" Neil asked.

"I do. Even though it's almost five in the evening, I could go for that. Whatever you have." Kellan went to the window and looked out just to make sure they were alone. No creepers were invited to their breakfast dinner.

It took them about thirty minutes for the meal to be prepared and devoured. It was a good breakfast style dinner. Probably the best Kellan ever had in his life. He was used to his meals being served on a tray, much the way they were prepared in prison and it usually consisted of the four food groups with no added flavor. He was fed all the right portions with no salt, sugars or byproducts. Some days it was protein overload and tasted like sweetened bananas. The laboratory made sure the food he ate would not inhibit his ability to grow into the warrior they wanted him to be. An effort in which they succeeded, because Kellan was as strong as an ox, but looked as gentle as a dove.

After dinner, Kellan, Neil and Dylan went out to the front porch to sit and enjoy the last bit of the sun before it had a chance to set. It was tapping at the horizon fast, which cast the perfect shadows to keep Kellan hidden. Too much light and the man would glow. The thing that bothered Kellan most was that he couldn't enjoy the sun at the lake any more than he could when he was held at TC. He was destined to being a creature of the night and it was all due to his winged secret.

Dylan dropped down next them and it sounded like a pile of bones being tossed across a wooden floor. Boom-did-a-boom, and then a clunk. A huff followed and then his head went low before he rolled over on his side to relax, ready to rest again. He loved the outdoor life and unlike most dogs, the hotter the better and more so if there was direct sunlight on his back.

Breaking the silence, Kellan asked, "Do you have a job, Neil?"

Looking over at Kellan with one eye squinting to block the last ray the sun was giving off, Neil answered, "Not at the present time. I've taken on this estate from my grandparents and until I can figure out what to do with it or where I'm going, I've decided to just take some time off so I can make sense of my life. Don't get me wrong, I love being a nurse, but the hours can be brutal."

Perfect, a nurse, just what Kellan needed. He didn't care to be reminded of his time at the Laboratory; it was still a raw wound in his mind, an ache that would never disappear. He would have liked to happen upon somebody that was not tied in with the medical field. Aside from the nurse issue, Kellan did like Neil. He even liked the way he felt when he held him in bed. He wanted that and needed it in his life. He was a lover, not a fighter.

"Hello, did I lose you?" Neil noticed Kellan disappear into his thoughts.

"No. Sorry. When you said nurse, my head went back to TC." Kellan shook his head and told the truth.

Neil sat up straight. "That's fine, we don't have to talk about it. How about we change the topic or go for a swim?"

Kellan hissed, "Look at me, do I look like I swim? That's one thing they missed when they put me together. No flippers."

"I see. We can just walk the beach then," Neil said.

"Sure. But let's wait for the sun to go down. Gotta keep my secret you know." Kellan shifted on the bench until his wings swung around and touched the floor.

"What's it like to fly without an engine?" Neil leaned in.

"Hey, I have an idea. How about I take you on your first flight?" Kellan leaned toward Neil and tapped him on the nose with a gentle finger. He bit his bottom lip and then pulled away.

Neil sputtered a bit, hoping for a kiss just then. "That would be great. I'll give it a try."

"Leave it to me," Kellan said.

As soon as the clouds crossed in front of the moon, Kellan stood in front of Neil, holding out a hand for him to take it.

"Are you sure about this?" Neil wondered.

"Very. Come on, take my hand and let me give you all I've got," Kellan said.

It was dark now and the sky was theirs.

Kellan stepped in front of Neil and held both his hands. "Now just relax and follow my lead." He leaned into Neil and for the first time, he kissed him lightly on the lips. "That is for good luck," he whispered.

Chills raced up and down Neil's spine. Not from fear or from being cold, but from the sheer tenderness of the angel's kiss. It was just a peck, but for some reason it was the best kiss he'd ever had. He cleared his throat, looked to the ground, and a giddy smile crossed his face.

With his voice still low and soft, Kellan said, "Remember to follow my lead." He loosened his grip a little on Neil's hands and circled to his backside. He pressed his firm body tightly to Neil's back and gripped him firmly around the waist. "Now, I want you to bend at the knees and on the count of three, I need you to jump. I'll take it from there."

Neil's heart was pounding faster than it ever had before. "Oh God—oh God—Oooh GOD," just came out of him.

Kellan laughed quietly and hummed in Neil's ear as if instilling his own calmness over him, "I got you." He kissed Neil, making him quiver.

This time, "Ohmigawd," came out of Neil.

"Ready?" Kellan asked.

"Mm-hmm. I think so," Neil replied.

Bending at the knees, down they went. One—Two—THREE.

"Let's fly!" Kellan whooped.

Chapter 10

When Kellan naturally snapped his wings out at his sides, they sounded like the crack of a flag in the wind.

Neil roared as soon as they took flight, it felt like he lost his breath. He needed to let the noise explode from him because he panicked and the uplift made him feel like he was going to throw up. For a split second he had a nightmarish image of himself tumbling helplessly toward earth and nobody was there to catch him. It was different than all his dreams, this was reality.

It was a little funny to Kellan so he laughed, but held on tight to Neil who dangled like a wet rag beneath him. He said it again, "I've got you." Then hugged him tighter. It was a good feeling when he held Neil. He liked it.

They went higher into the night sky, free like a couple of birds. One helping the other.

Kellan dropped a shoulder and dipped, making a wide open curve to one side until he flipped shoulders and plunged hard the other way, quickly taking Neil to the left and then just as fast to the right. He took him up high and then back down again until they just about met water below them. The tips of Kellan's wings skimmed the surface and splashed droplets everywhere, creating a manmade rainstorm neither one was expecting.

Another bend in Kellan's wing caused them to roll over that put Neil square on top. As quickly as Kellan spun, he corkscrewed just as fast, winding up putting Neil in the same spot he started, back underneath him. Kellan laughed again when he heard Neil grunt.

Despite Neil's anxiety, he found the sky to be exhilarating. Not many birds flew this high and certainly no wingless people. Some falcons and hawks made it to this altitude. In fact, Neil swore that one flew in close and checked them out.

Kellan's wings were powerful and every beat took them further into the sky. As high as they were, the land below resembled a chessboard. Dark square patches everywhere.

When they left the water and flew above the bridge, the cars looked like busy ants traipsing back to the hill with food in their thriving lineup. Kellan would always pick something minuscule out down below, like a car or a bus, whatever, and would bring it into focus like it was only inches away. He could do that. Those crazy maniacs at the lab made sure he could see for miles. It was part of the plan. He bet they were cursing his name right about now. Well so what?

The two of them soared freely through the air like an arrow from a crossbow, being cradled by the wind, doing whatever they wanted and going whichever direction they chose.

They buzzed around the sky for a while before Kellan toyed with an idea to bring his new crush Neil a little closer to him. "Follow my lead, I've got you," he whispered the familiar words. Within a few seconds, he channeled the breeze under his left wing, dipping to the right. Slowly and gracefully he rolled over, and at the same time spider-spun Neil in his arms until they were face to face. With another downward stroke of his wings, Kellan was soaring on his back with Neil on top. He smiled, pulled Neil tightly to his bare chest, closed his eyes, and kissed him. Just like that they transferred affection for the other while flying a mile above the earth. No engine or any strings to hold them up.

Feeling secure, Neil's heart went from racing to a slow

thump. He was calm and knew he could trust Kellan with whatever came their way. The flight was magnificent and it took every ounce of breath he had in him away. He moved his arms and locked them around Kellan's neck as he lay comfortably on top and kissed him back.

It was quiet where they were at. For a moment the two were lost in an airborne dream world.

Without thinking, Kellan dropped a shoulder, gave his wing an angled twist that rolled them over again where it put Neil back on the bottom. They kissed a while longer before Kellan twisted Neil in his arms and had him facing forward again.

Spinning, spiraling and dipping, they zipped in and out of the cables that held the massive bridge in place right before they soared straight upward toward where the sky was even darker.

Infatuation, admiration or just plain trust, whatever the draw, Kellan could easily love the man he was holding in his arms beneath him.

"Let's check one more thing out before I take you back home." Kellan took charge and raced off into the night. He was always fascinated by what he'd heard of Mackinac Island and he finally had the chance to actually see it for real. He understood that there were no automobiles or gas powered engines of any kind there, only bicycles, and horse drawn carriages were allowed to pedal the streets. It was like a place that time forgot and he loved the thought of that. Figured it would be the perfect place for a blossoming friendship and if they were somehow spotted, they would be forgotten too.

Neil hung on tightly to Kellan's arms as they flew far above the bridge toward the secret island off the Mackinac coast.

From a distance, the main island appeared to be shut down and tourists were no longer welcome after dark except for the ones that were already there and had plans to spend the night at the grand hotel or other small dwellings sporadically placed around the island.

"Look, down there." Kellan narrowed his wings and they started to drop fast, heading straight for an empty plot of land near the back shoreline of the island. The part that they were aiming for seemed to be abandoned. It looked like nobody ever went there, which made it a perfect place for the two of them to hide out and be alone. It was a tiny island, maybe an acre in all, with even smaller satellite sandbars all around. Way smaller sandbars, hardly big enough for a bush to grow on.

Neil's vision wasn't as keen as Kellan's, so wherever he looked he saw just different shades of black. The few lights scattered here and there made some areas below appear gray.

"Hang on, were going in." Kellan gripped and hugged Neil tighter.

Even though it was cold outside, the heat from Kellan's bare chest kept Neil warm. He felt cozy, like a lighted fire was keeping him toasty.

The moment the speed at which they descended increased, Neil covered his eyes to help relieve the anxiety he felt from flying so fast. Way fast. Faster than he could have ever imagined, and the closer they got to the ground, it felt even faster, pretty much like the landing of an aircraft right before touchdown.

Before they reached the dirt, Kellan put the airbrakes on by pulling his wings high above his shoulders and then pushing them down hard. Several quick beats passed, and within seconds their fast flight turned into a peaceful hover, with nobody's feet touching the ground. Not yet.

Where they ended up that night was several miles away from Neil's front doorstep, but the speed of Kellan's flight got them there within minutes. Neil's revelation as to how fast they actually flew caused him to realize that if they crashed, they would have certainly been doomed.

"You can open your eyes now, my handsome friend." Kellan set Neil gently on the ground and then touched down himself right before tucking his twelve foot wings back tightly behind his back.

Neil's feet made a very satisfying thud when they met the ground. He stood a minute in a state of shock mixed with exhilaration. He really didn't know how to feel after that fantasy flight. He was woozy and almost felt like he was still flying. He needed to get his land legs.

"You all good?" Kellan asked.

All Neil did was grin and stare, then said, "Unh."

"Okay, then. I guess you are." Kellan massaged Neil's shoulders while gripping them to make sure he didn't crumple to the ground from the thrill ride he just experienced.

They explored the place like a couple of kids, picking up stones and freshwater shells that lined the beach. There was an abandoned houseboat that appeared to have been shipwrecked on the coast of the small island. The way it looked, there were critters and crabs of all kinds making it their home.

They ran up the coast with the wind, kicking their feet in and out of the water the same way the sandpipers were doing until Kellan raced up behind Neil, scooped him up beneath his arms, and flew him to one of the sandbars that had a small tree growing in the middle of it. The entire bar may have been only twenty feet from coast to coast. Kellan's wingspan could almost reach from one side to the other when he opened them fully.

There wasn't much to do there except stand in the middle where the tree was. Neil couldn't make sense of why Kellan picked him up and flew him there, to that particular spot. To be funny maybe? Or perhaps another game of trust? If he wanted off that sandbar, Neil would need to swim to the mainland or ask Kellan to take him.

"Can we get off this sandbar now?" Neil begged. "Between yesterday and today, I think I've had enough of these types of places that lead to predicaments or near death experiences."

"Are you going to swim to shore, or do you want me to carry you?" Kellan jokingly asked Neil.

A large fish circled the small island like a hungry shark, and as fast as it came, it swam away.

Neil dipped his toe in the murky water as a way of testing its temperature, looked at how far away the bigger island was and decided there was no way he was swimming in that dark water. He turned around and stood facing Kellan, looked at him and pleaded, "Would you be kind enough to carry me to shore?" He forced a smile, but it came across more worried than anything else.

Kellan had a good idea Neil was going to ask for help getting off the strip, which is why he was already moving toward him. Kellan's walk quickly turned into a run, a well-trained athletic run, like an Olympic athlete. He stretched his wings above his head, pulled them downward, and flapped them in sync with his steps. The combination swiftly lifted him up off the ground.

When Kellan reached for Neil, he saw his eyes and mouth open wide and his cheeks flush with terror.

No, Neil did not find that funny.

Neil's arms went up to block his face from what seemed like the onset of a major collision. He knew what to expect, but he still roared.

Kellan shouldn't have laughed, but it was funny to him. The newly discovered look on somebody's face when they were about to take flight would never get old. He'd seen it before whenever he took a clinician to the sky. It always felt as new to him as it was to them.

Before crashing into his target the way Neil thought he would, Kellan quickly swooped around behind him and scooped him off the ground. Kellan interlaced his arms under Neil's and locked his hands together across his chest. Kellan took him high, straight up - purposely.

When Kellan banked to the right, Neil's legs swung far out to the opposite side.

Neil uttered, "Ugh," before he placed a cupped hand over one eye and the other over his mouth. He had to, or the sudden feeling of sickness caused by the rapid lift would find a way out.

They dived downward again, toward the dark empty island, pulled up sharply, and then leveled out above the coast. There was a low-pitched whistle that could be heard as the wind crossed over Kellan's wings while they soared. He then banked slowly to his left and then spiraled gently toward the ground, back-flapping for stability with a profound thwapping sound as they landed.

When they touched ground, Neil spun in Kellan's grasp, facing him where they stood.

"Kiss me," Neil said, in a voice almost too quiet to hear.

Seconds before their lips touched, the sound of a chopper came out of nowhere. Just like that, it appeared in the sky.

They immediately pulled back and looked up while the whirly bird moved in closer.

All at once, Kellan pushed his wings back, grabbed Neil by the hand and took off for cover inside the abandoned boat they spotted earlier along the coast.

"Why the boat? Why not the trees?" Neil rambled and tripped forward.

"Because they'll be looking in the trees," Kellan said. "Hurry, get in."

Neil crawled across the ground and entered through the hull of the boat while Kellan pushed him in from behind.

"Move, hun. Move faster." Kellan pushed. "Hurry, they're getting closer."

As soon as Neil was in, he quickly turned and tugged on Kellan's hand, helping him.

It wasn't working. The hole was too small. Kellan's wings were lodged in the entry and it held him captive.

"What's wrong?" Neil screeched.

"My wings, they're stuck. I can't get in," Kellan said.

"What? Hang on, I'll pull you in," Neil said.

"It won't work." Kellan pulled back. "Stay in here, I'll see you soon."

"No. I'll come with you," Neil yelled back, losing his grip.

"It's not safe. Stay here." Kellan pulled himself free and disappeared.

For the first time since Neil met Kellan, he felt a hollow spot in his chest. He was sad and was on the verge of letting his tears flow. He missed Kellan instantly and wasn't ready for him to be pulled from his grasp so quickly. Not like that. Not yet. The darkness outside didn't allow Neil to see more than a few feet outside the hole in the hull, which barred him from leaving where he was. Because of that, he did what Kellan told him to do and stayed hidden inside the grubby boat. Holding still, he laid face down in the musty dirt that covered the ground beneath the boat, certain he would be eaten alive by whatever creepy-crawlies were inside there with him. The thump of the chopper was still out there telling Neil not to move.

Outside somewhere Kellan flew off into the dark, hiding too. He had to divert any attention that may be on Neil away from his hiding spot. Neil didn't need that trouble, this wasn't his fight. He was just a willing passenger.

Kellan flew up into the trees. If for any reason the chopper took after Neil, he was ready for them and would show himself and lead them far away. There he sat; in the tree, waiting. Not even Neil knew he was there.

How did they know where he was?

The thumping of the helicopter rotors hung in the dark sky. Somewhere. Kellan couldn't see it and neither could Neil from his vantage point.

Lying alone in the dank boat wreckage, Neil felt the void in his chest getting bigger. Something was wrong. He'd just met Kellan, but he was missing him as if they were somehow connected. He was aching inside and needed to know Kellan was okay. Anxiety was crushing in on him and his need to get out of the box he was in was growing stronger. They were after his angel again and he couldn't just sit there. Waiting. He then saw a light sweep across the hole in the boat. After inching himself deeper into the space, further away from the intrusive light, he froze.

Kellan was about to strike, flying into view, to lead the chopper away from Neil, but his gut feeling told him to stay where he was. Nothing about the aircraft gave him any clue that it was there for him or Neil. It was too small to be a military chopper and seemed to be there as a tourist, probably looking for a quiet place to land just like he and Neil had. It looked to be more a private helicopter than a military one. He stayed put and watched from the trees.

Still waiting for a clear chance to move, Neil lay quietly. He then heard the thump of the chopper fade, not completely but it sounded as though it was moving away. He wouldn't be able to settle down until he knew Kellan was safe. His ability to move freely was restricted, but he was able to slowly angle himself toward the opening in the hull.

Gradually, everything around Neil went quiet. All the sounds he heard seemed to fade away. Even the rolling waves along the shoreline. When all was silent, suddenly he heard a thump on top of the ruins where he hid and the boat hull rocked.

"Shit!" Just came out of Neil. Then he saw the hand he needed to see. He recognized the hand as Kellan's, and then following that hand down from above came the face, that handsome face that told Neil everything was going to be fine. At least for the time being it was.

"It's alright, you can come out now." Kellan crawled down the edge of the boat like an insect with sticky feet, sat in front of the broken hull on his knees and waited for Neil with one hand extended, wanting him to take it.

To look through the hole in the boat and see Kellan outside on his knees calmed Neil's soul, and Kellan's face was more glorious to see than before he left. It helped take away the uncertainties Neil had about losing him, and to know that Kellan was safe made his heart slow to a normal beat.

Neil crawled out and dusted himself off, bugs and beetles dropping to the ground. He gave Kellan a once over and saw something about him that was different. A new sting of astonishment took his breath away. "Did you... Wait… What? Your wings..." Nothing he said made any sense.

Kellan's wings were changed. "I needed to blend, like a chameleon. Another design flaw those maniacs at the lab made sure I had which will work in my favor instead of theirs."

"It's amazing what they did for you. Really." Neil traced a finger down the edge of Kellan's wing. It still felt like silk even though the colors resembled the bark of a tree, unlike earlier when they shimmered like the finish on a milky pearl.

"Amazing, but a burden," Kellan said. His wings seemed relaxed by Neil's touch. He liked it.

Neil understood the burden of having wings, the need to hide from those that didn't understand, but to have the ability to fly seemed to be worth the trade. He looked to the sky. "They didn't stay here long, thank God. I wasn't sure how much longer I could have stayed inside that moldy boat with the flesh eating bugs."

"I don't think they were looking for you or me. It seemed they were just flying around on a late night tour. Maybe looking for fish?" Kellan assured Neil.

"You're probably right. People do a lot of fishing around here." Neil stood up and started to walk away.

"Hey, wait a minute. Where're you going?" Kellan spun around and took hold of Neil's wrist.

"Home, I guess," Neil answered.

"How you gonna get there?" Kellan stood up. "Don't you need me and my wings?"

"I suppose you're right." Neil grinned.

"Before we fly home, isn't there something we need to finish?" Kellan said.

"What's that?" Neil asked.

Kellan gripped both Neil's wrists tighter and pulled him closer. "You told me to kiss you right before the helicopter came in and interrupted us."

Neil's voice went low, "Oh—Yes, the kiss." His breathing went shallow and just about stopped. He moved in closer and could feel Kellan's thick chest press against his.

Kellan leaned in and took the warm kiss he needed from Neil earlier. There was heat, but most of all, there was passion.

Neil's hands moved to Kellan's chest where he felt the patter of his heart against his palms. The beat was steady and it was fast. Bird-like, from what he always understood. They moved their heads from side to side which eased the way for their tongues to greet and taste the other.

There was a thumping sound similar to that of chopper blades being heard, but this time it was the beat of their hearts pounding together as they kissed.

As their kiss progressed, Neil felt his own erection growing from Kellan's touch, and could easily identify the one bulldozing its way through Kellan's pants and trying to get at his.

Several minutes later, they parted reluctantly. They had to, but didn't want to.

"Shall we fly?" Kellan said.

In Neil's head, he was already off the ground.

Chapter 11

Within a few minutes of leaving the island, they arrived at Neil's home, but before Kellan landed and let him go, he took Neil for one last flight up the coast. A fun one was in store, a ride he would always remember.

With one quick downward wing-beat, Kellan flew a little higher. He held Neil at the waist, nudged him forward until he was head down with his feet up.

Neil hollered as he slipped. "What are you doing? This isn't funny." His eyes shut tight.

Kellan shifted Neil further forward, grabbing each of Neil's ankles in his hand.

Neil hung head-down with his arms swaying stiffly from left to right. He screamed, this time louder.

Kellan laughed, probably shouldn't have, but he did. He took Neil on a crazy flight that left him breathless, taking him around and above the trees, dipped close to the water and then back up again.

Enough was enough. Kellan back flapped against the wind to slow his flight, and gently lowered Neil to the sand, hands first.

The second Neil touched down, and before Kellan let him go, Neil went wild like a chimp in the bush, running sentences together without getting answers first. "Y-You crazy bird. What was that all about? That wasn't funny." He stood up, banged his palms against his legs to rid them of sand and loose shell bits. His hands and jaw stirred in unison.

"Okay, I'm sorry," Kellan said. "I only wanted your first flight to be memorable. Next time I'll go easy on you,"

"Ppphh! Next time?" Neil spat and started to walk away. "I don't think so, there isn't going to be a next time."

"Get over here." Still chuckling in a playful manner, Kellan reached for Neil's wrist and tugged. "Yes there will be, and I promise I'll go easy on you."

Neil jerked and spun into Kellan's arms, hitting his chest hard. It seemed warmer this time and what Neil liked most of all was when Kellan wrapped his feathery wings around him for that added hug. And then there was the kiss. Another beautiful kiss that transported them to a world of their own and just like before, it was perfect.

Hardly a minute had passed when the thrill of the other's touch set off definite arousal inside both their jeans that fought like hell to bust loose and connect in a way that only two men could.

Neil brought his hands to Kellan's bare chest and stroked it. If he wasn't mistaken, his chest wasn't as smooth as it was before, maybe superfine feathers like the downy growth found on a newborn bird. It was shadow black where they were at and the darkness kept Neil from being able to tell for sure, but his exploring hands that roamed Kellan's chest made him grow much harder than he was just seconds ago.

The low moans that came out of Kellan told Neil that whatever was happening between them needed to continue. When he felt Kellan's tongue push between his teeth, he took that as proof that the angel wanted more of him.

Was it a good thing or a bad idea?

The night air was still, too still, almost peculiar enough to be a bad sign. It was like the calm before an approaching storm.

Neil longed for more of Kellan, but wasn't sure it was the best thing for them to do. The idea of getting wrapped up with an angel who just escaped a top-secret government facility might not be a good one. He desperately tried to put his mind elsewhere, anywhere but on the man he was kissing. Anywhere in the universe would do fine, but the thought change wasn't working to save his ass - he was hooked. Neil tried to pull away, but that didn't work either. Kellan was too irresistible coming at him with his mystical appearance and the probability of being marrying material. Having those wings tightly swathed around Neil wasn't helping the situation either. Their clutch pulled him in and held him. Neil went stiff and pulled back more firmly this time.

"What's wrong?" Kellan fought Neil's attempted getaway.

"Maybe we should go inside? It might not be safe out here in the middle of an open stretch of land," Neil said.

"You're probably right." Kellan unfurled his wings from around Neil's back and let him go. "I'll follow you."

Their evening flight to the island and back couldn't have ended in a better way. The kiss and the budding stiffness between their legs validated the feelings they both had. They each desired the other to be more than just a friend to pal around with. It was quickly becoming more than friendly.

They moved their kiss and hard-ons inside the house where it was better suited for them to take things further if the sparks continued.

Dylan gave Kellan and Neil one of his intruder *Ba-rooo-rooo-roo-roo* alert barks as they stepped inside, which then quickly stalled out and turned into an excited wiggling butt when he realized it was them, then morphed into an enthusiastic yip.

"Should I light a fire?" Neil pointed at the hearth. "Dylan, hush!"

"Sure, that would be nice," Kellan said.

"I'll get one started." Neil passed Kellan so closely on the way to the fireplace that their mouths just about touched again. It was purposely done and Kellan knew it.

Kellan shadowed Neil and helped him stuff crumpled newsprint pages under the logs that were already propped in the base of the smoke stack. After handing Neil the fueled fire-starter, he stood behind him and lightly fanned the flames with waving wings.

With Kellan pressed against his back, Neil's concentration went on a downward slide. The erotic image playing in his head caused him to lose focus and his eyelids closed as his head dropped back against Kellan. He wasn't prepared for any kind of intimacy. Not then and good Lord not with an angel. He needed to stay on course, stick to the plan he thought of outside: keep in mind that the two of them hooking up might be a bad idea.

Not now dammit!

Giving in to his desire, Neil spun upward from the floor until he was face to face with Kellan. He was weak when it came to that man with wings, very weak. Not because Kellan was unique, but because Neil sensed some deep emotion for him that he'd never felt before. It was a strong feeling making it seem impossible for him to tear himself away, and it kept pulling him to Kellan with magnetic force.

When Kellan stepped closer to Neil, he did away with any space that was left between them. His hands moved to the top buttons on Neil's shirt where he snapped them loose, slipped his hands under the collar and ran them along the base of his neck and across his shoulders, thumb pads gently tracing his collarbone.

Kellan's touch set off sparks within Neil that enticed him to kiss the man he sensed he was born to kiss. His head tipped to one side and his dark eyes hid behind lowered lids. He shuddered when Kellan's mouth closed over his and Kellan's warm breath ghosted over his skin. Neil drew him in with a gentle embrace while his hands dropped to Kellan's waist where his thumbs neatly laid in the gutters of his obliques.

Neil kissed Kellan with this mouth closed and held it there for a while, not moving or loosening his jaw to take him in. He stayed connected to Kellan, their kiss locking them in place.

Neil unexpectedly pulled away, nipping Kellan's bottom lip as he separated from him, trying to conceal his erection by turning around.

Kellan reached for Neil and brought him back. "No, don't turn away — I like it. Love it actually." He took Neil's hand and pressed it against the front of his own jeans. "You see, you're not alone. You do the same thing to me."

Neil's face lit up with a widening grin that he wasn't able to keep hidden, partly because he was grateful for not being the only one standing with a hard-on climbing his hipbone, and partly for having Kellan's erection throbbing against the palm of his hand. In the same way Kellan did, he liked it, or actually loved it.

Kellan had the same silly grin on his face that Neil did, he couldn't hide his either.

Slowly, Neil dragged his hand away, bringing it to Kellan's chest and felt it rise and fall with every breath he took.

"It's my keel," Kellan said, watching Neil's hand stroke its center.

"You're amazing," Neil said.

Kellan kept watching Neil's hand move across his chest, gliding from one side to the other. "As you can feel, my sternum is thicker than yours, mainly to support the bulk of my muscles that run along my ribcage to my back that are there to hold my wings in place."

Neil fanned his fingers over Kellan's chest, feeling his heartbeat race. "You always feel so warm when I touch you. That will be a great bonus for me on a cold night."

Kellan smiled at Neil. "That's because I'm endothermic. My body produces the heat I need from the inside to keeps me warm all over."

"But I thought I saw you shivering outside in the rain." Neil questioned.

"When I shiver, I'm not actually cold, it's my body producing more heat when it knows I need it."

"My God, what did they do to you?" Neil said.

"It's not what they did *to* me; it's what they did *for* me. They made me into a being that grew more superior and resilient than they expected, and because of how I turned out, they created other hybrids, similar to me but with venomous dispositions, meant to be war heroes that are more easily controlled than me. For the most part these hybrids, or Seekers as I call them, have been used to keep an eye on me and take me down if I ever got away. As you can see, that worked out well didn't it? Unlike me, they made these Seekers with built in switches that can be turned on and off to make them more controllable. The Seekers are the finished product that started with them creating me, however there were many failed trials built and destroyed in between until the engineers got exactly what they wanted. Because I was their first creation with enough usable cells to keep the breed growing, my life was spared. Good for me I guess. Makes me glad I was born this way."

"There are more like you?" Neil said.

"Well not like me, that I know of, but yes there are more. We were never allowed to socialize or come in contact with each other, but that rule didn't get in the way of me seeing a couple of them. The lab flunkies kept us pretty well separated, which I was thankful for because I've heard Seekers can be extremely vicious, because they were built to be killers." Kellan bit his lip.

"Oh." Neil's face went white when he heard the word killer.

"Thankfully I wasn't bred with the instinct to kill, those Seekers were, but I do have the mind to attack. I only attack in a good way." Eager to get off the subject of TC and the Seekers, Kellan waggled his eyebrows to distract Neil. He coerced Neil against his chest, kissed him, and walked against him until he fell backward onto the oversized sectional. He lowered himself down on top of Neil with extreme lust, kissing him hard, invading his mouth with deep penetration that involved his exploring tongue, taking in every part of Neil's mouth like it belonged to him, and was his banquet to survive. The erotic thrill of the connection brought his wings up and his cock to its fullest length, bulldozing against Neil's mounting erection.

Neil pulled Kellan down on him, taking his tongue even deeper than before. His breathing sped up.

With no resistance, Kellan pulled hard on Neil's shirt, ripping it wide open from top to bottom. Buttons popped and scattered around the room, clicking across the hardwood floor and rolling in every direction. Getting a glimpse of Neil's chest between deep heated kisses, Kellan muttered, "My God, you're beautiful." His hand floated up Neil's washboard abdomen until it reached his chest where it stopped to rest. To Kellan it was magical and seemed dreamlike, but it was real, actually happening, and was happening to him.

Abruptly, out of nowhere came the warning alarm that seemed to consistently intrude on their moments of passion. They heard the thump of the copper blades coming from above and to them it sounded like a big one. No, it sounded huge.

They froze and Neil shrieked, "Fuck."

Not again.

Chapter 12

The wind created by the choppers' rotors banged against the window in tempo with Kellan's and Neil's heartbeat, white light-beams pierced every window, bringing daylight inside the house that wasn't meant to be there until morning.

"Shit, we're fucked." Kellan's wings snapped like sheets in the wind and within seconds he had Neil on his feet in front of him.

"No we're not. Get to the storm shelter. Hurry!" Neil pushed Kellan toward the kitchen. "Dylan, Go!" He pointed.

Kellan pulled his wings against his back, and for a split second his feet left the ground. He ran after Dylan toward the pantry door, and behind them, Neil followed with a long handled fire-lighter and stoker in his hand.

Neil slammed and locked every door behind him, the entire time thinking they had no chance of getting away, but refused to let Kellan know his doubts. Staying rational meant getting out safely and alive.

The chopper landed just outside the front door with beating blades that shook the house and came close to cracking glass. Masked men jumped from the whirlybirds and barged up the front stairs, busting down doors with hard kicking feet and ramming shoulders. At the same time the doors dropped, windows shattered when hissing gas canisters crashed through them, blowing gummy glass fragments across the floor along with the smoke they created. Pistol fixed flashlight beams swept through rising fume clouds ready to take out anything that moved.

The whole while the masked men were taking over the house, presumably looking for Kellan, Neil lifted the flaming fire-lighter he brought with him and ran it along the ceiling, trying to follow the footsteps he heard stomp across the floor above. Several footfalls were heard but he still wasn't able to identify how many men were occupying his house. Because it was only a matter of time before the hunters upstairs found them in the shelter, he needed to think fast.

There was another way in and out of the storm shelter and that was the route Neil, Kellan and Dylan were going to take.

"Kellan, take this and grab that coffee canister up there." Neil pointed.

Kellan quickly retrieved the canister and spun back toward Neil, who was already dashing toward another shelf that had a case to carry Dylan in and another satchel with other small items already in it.

"I'll take the can"—Neil reached out—"we're gonna need the money that's in it."

After stuffing the can into the pet carrier, he slid it across the floor to Kellan so he could help Dylan get in it.

Dylan scrambled for the carrier, stood inside and waited for Kellan to close it up. Smart dog.

"This is it. We need to go - Now - Hurry - Head out the back door," Neil ordered.

Kellan grabbed the carrier with Dylan in it and scrambled down the back tunnel as best he could with wings, lighting the way with the measly fire-starter Neil gave him.

"Kellan," Neil said quietly and breathy behind him. "Let me go first."

In a hurry, Kellan stepped aside accidentally banging Dylan into the wall.

Scared, Dylan whimpered.

Neil passed quickly and gripped the doorknob that would lead them outside. "Oh God, I can't believe this is happening," he mumbled.

Hearing Neil, Kellan said, "Maybe you should stay. It might be best if I go alone. It's me they want, not you."

"Are you crazy? I'm in this with you now. I'm not letting them have you like this," Neil ranted, looking up as if waiting for a miracle. "This is it, you ready?"

Without waiting for an answer, Neil busted through the door and took off up the concrete steps two at a time until he was outside in the backyard beneath a canopy of what he'd always thought to be the largest maple trees on the planet. He reached a hand out to Kellan, helping him out of the stairwell. They stood together in the wind while keeping an eye on the chopper in the sky that was still circling the place with a penetrating spotlight. A chill raced through Neil at the same time Kellan's metabolic system went into overdrive which generated enough heat for everybody within a hundred yards.

"My turn. I'll get us out of here." Kellan's wings turned black to match the night, took Neil in his arms, and shot straight into the sky.

To get away from the house as quickly as possible, Kellan took them on a wind-whipping race. After a few minutes and many miles passed Kellan brought them to a coasting speed where they glided closer to the treetops in order to keep hidden.

"Do you think we lost them?" Neil asked.

Kellan back flapped, dropped a shoulder and pulled a wing in tight to one side that took them on a jerky turnabout to the right. "Looks that way, but we're gonna keep going." A repeat performance turned them around and put them back on the same path they were just on.

Beneath him, Kellan held onto Neil with both hands fanned out against his bare chest, feeling the beat of his heart through every finger. It was pounding hard and fast, presumably because of the adrenaline spike brought on by the home invasion they just fled from. It was the first time Kellan actually touched Neil's chest without a shirt in the way and it intrigued him how much deeper Neil's sternum was than his own. The missing keel made his chest muscles feel more prominent to Kellan, made them seem bulkier. He'd never had the pleasure of running a hand over another man's bare chest, and the differences between his and Neil's was what Kellan liked most.

Neil and Dylan dangled below Kellan as if they were luggage. Hanging from one of Neil's crooked arms was the satchel of munchies and money, while Dylan swayed from side to side in the pet case over the other.

It was finally getting more peaceful as they flew, or at least it seemed that way after the near death experience they encountered just a few minutes ago.

"How far do you think we should go?" Neil looked up at Kellan but could only see his chin.

"I'd say we should go a little further, just to be sure. We can hide out in a forest when we find one thick enough to keep us from being seen." Kellan did his best to keep their flight smooth.

Neil noticed there were a few dips added to the flight that felt like turbulence of an aircraft, a couple side-to-side swings to make it less boring, but overall, it was a pleasurable ride. Out of the corner of Neil's eyes he could see Kellan's wings stretched out and flapping over his shoulders, and because he wasn't able to see all of Kellan, the wings actually appeared to be his own. Neil could see the color in them slowly change from black to blond, back to the way they were before taking off from his house on the lake. It was very similar to a recurring dream he always had where he's able to fly, but this time it was the real deal. He was actually flying, in the real sky, with the real earth below him and the best part was that he had a real developing crush pinned to his back.

Gawd, what a feeling. A REAL feeling.

Neil smiled even though he had a good idea that his house was more than likely destroyed by bottle bombs, possibly even blown to bits. At a minimum it would be ransacked by the hunters while looking for clues as to where they were and how they could be found. He had to dismiss the idea of destruction from his mind because he had other concerns to be dealt with. Kellan was one of them, and their safety was another.

With Kellan having the eyesight of a night owl, Neil left the hunt for lodging up to him. Neil had no idea where they were, but figured they were still in Michigan someplace. It didn't really matter where they put foot down because he was with the two life forms he cared most about.

Suddenly, Neil felt a change in pressure and his stomach churned, giving him a clue that they were descending.

Kellan pulled his wings tighter to his sides, aggressively beat them against the wind in a manner that turned their flight into a bobbing hover. When Kellan channeled the airstream in reverse, Neil's feet slowly came down and they landed.

"Where are we?" Neil asked.

"We're on an island at the northern part of lake Michigan just a few miles west of the big bridge. I picked the darkest island out of the three grouped together. The only thing I saw on this one was an old rundown lighthouse and a grassy runway that looked to be overgrown with weeds. The rest of it looked empty and covered with trees, most of them dead. It'll be perfect for us. You see the lights on the bridge over there?" Kellan stepped up next to Neil and took the satchels from him, setting both of the down, the one with Dylan in it first.

Neil shook his hair out and brushed a few strands away from his brow. "Yep, there it is. I can kind of see the bridge. I believe that puts us on Trout Island, and you're right, the only thing here is an old abandoned lighthouse and a small aircraft runway. I actually don't think anybody maintains the place, except to replace that light bulb in the tower, so this will be perfect, nobody will bother us."

"Great." Kellan could feel Dylan getting antsy to be released from the pet carrier, so he quickly opened it up and let him out.

The dog went wild, bringing playtime around Kellan's feet. Dylan grabbed the first stick he found, dropped it in front of Kellan to throw and play catch.

Kellan read the dogs mind. The stick whistled in the wind when he threw it and sailed about ten yards away. After Dylan took off for the stick, Kellan gave Neil a peck on the cheek.

"That's it? That's all I get?" Neil said.

"I'm afraid to give you more. You and I both know what happens when we go at it. It's like a curse," Kellan mentioned what seemed to be a fact.

Dylan ran back with the stick in his chops, dropped it at Neil's feet and stared at him, begging him to throw it again.

Grunting like an old geezer when he bent over, Neil picked up the stick and did just what Dylan wanted him to do. He threw it. "It's just a coincidence."

"Coincidence my tight white ass and big blond wings, it's happened to us three times. Every time I've touched you. It's like they can see everything I'm looking at and are waiting for that moment when I go in for a kiss to fly in." Kellan was sure their interludes were being sabotaged.

"You're being silly," Neil said.

"No I'm not."

"Yes you are."

"Nuh uh," Kellan replied.

"Nuh uh?" Neil smirked. "How old are you?"

"Old enough to get a hard-on when you kiss or touch me."

"Ya got me there." Neil backed down.

"Oh gawd, maybe that's it," Kellan said.

"What's 'it'?"

"My erection," Kellan said.

"What?" Neil snapped.

"Yeah, maybe it sets off some sort of signal when it gets hard, like an antenna." Kellan shoved his hand down the front of his pants and felt around.

Neil laughed at him, thinking he could actually be right. "Let me see. Get over here and I'll check things out."

"Are you nuts?" Kellan squawked. "I just met you. I can't have you probing around in my pants looking for prizes."

"It's no big deal, I'm a nurse. Now come here and drop the drawers." Neil motioned with his hands toward his chest.

"This is ridiculous, I'm not doing it. I never should've said anything." Kellan released half a laugh at this surreal conversation.

"Alright, suit yourself. But I will be searching the skies for choppers when that boner stands stiff."

Grinning, Kellan blushed.

During the bantering about Kellan's electronic erection, neither of them realized Dylan had returned with the stick. It seemed he was done playing, because he ended up lying on the ground chewing the damned thing.

Neil lightly returned Kellan's peck. "Let's go find that lighthouse."

Chapter 13

The lighthouse was clearly run-down and didn't seem to have been maintained in quite some time, and the absence of obvious maintenance made the place ideal temporarily and could very well be their permanent home for a while.

It was secluded from everything and set only a few yards off the coast, making it a house on the lake they could call their own. The weathered lighthouse was pretty much over-run by the elements including possibly even a few animals and more than a few bugs. Its faded clapboard siding desperately needed a fresh coat of paint and by the looks of the rooftop, it also required repair. The dry roof shingles that had curled over the years were a sure sign that it leaked all the way through to the inside when it rained.

They stopped in front of the dilapidated old lighthouse and wondered if it was a good idea to risk entry. The look in Dylan's eyes showed he was thinking the same thing. They crept toward the front door, stepping around overgrown weeds and swatting at flies that should be resting for the night.

Kellan glanced over at Neil with a face drowning in dread, deep down preferring to just hang out in the trees behind the house with the other birds.

When they reached the front door, things took a filthy turn for the worse.

Neil opened and held the rickety door to prevent it from blowing away with the gentle breeze, and when they stepped inside the floor appeared to be alive as critters came to life and scampered away.

"Oh, my stars. Oh my starry, starry-stars." Was all that Kellan said.

"Home-Sweet-Home." Neil somewhat mimicked Kellan's tone.

Dylan barked once, holding back his urge to chase the varmints out of town, knowing it wasn't a good idea to be charging into a place like that without first making sure it would withstand a little dust lifting ruckus.

"Maybe we should sleep outside," Kellan said.

"Nonsense." Neil reached behind his back and tugged Kellan by the belt "We're going in."

Kellan flinched and his wings retracted when he felt Neil's fingers unexpectedly slip down the front of his pants. He liked being manhandled, but was still on edge about going inside the lighthouse.

Dylan yipped a warning, but he followed them in anyway.

"Hand me the fire-starter. It should be in the bag with the money can," Neil said, trying to see in the dark.

They kept themselves huddled together while they walked farther into the house. Thank God the place was small, which made it much easier to see the entire space and keep an eye on everything coming and going.

"Maybe we should split up and look around for anything we can use to make our stay more comfortable," Neil suggested.

"Uh, perhaps." Kellan looked up and watched a spider drop from the ceiling in front of his face. He blew at the stringy web and the arachnid floated across the room and landed on a nearby windowsill. "Eww."

Neil found a dark closet filled with a whole slew of candles, probably kept on hand in case the power went out or perhaps for ambiance purposes. There were plenty of oil lanterns placed throughout the house, several in the main living area, one in the dirty kitchen, and another in the bathroom that none of them even wanted to go near while it was dark.

Kellan located two lanterns and lit the wicks, but kept the flames turned low. While the hunters were flying the skies looking for him, the less light glowing from the windows the better.

Neil stood in the center of the main room, looked at the stone style fireplace, and suddenly went cold. Everything that just took place caught up to him in that split second and he wondered what the hell he did to deserve it.

When Kellan noticed that tension had directly lassoed Neil, he met him from behind, and rubbed his biceps gently to bring him serenity. "It'll be okay. I promise," he whispered in Neil's ear, not too sure his words of assurance held any truth.

Instead of turning around, Neil continued to peer into the imaginary fire in a way that made him seem misplaced.

Kellan couldn't let Neil be left in such a state, it wasn't right. All that took place since they had met was his fault, which meant Neil wouldn't be in the mess he was in if it weren't for Kellan showing up on his doorstep. Everything about it sucked, except for Kellan may have met the man he was destined to fall in love with. He gripped Neil's shoulders and turned him around, moved his hands to the sides of his face, and ran his thumb pads along his square jaw line. He looked him right in the eyes and waited for Neil to come back to him.

As soon as Kellan touched him, Neil pulled himself together. He was normally stronger than that, and could handle just about anything that came his way, even if it was a band of killers who were tracking him.

Still holding Neil's head, Kellan pulled him to his lips and continued with the kiss he initiated at the lake house. It didn't last as long, but was still full of the same passion as before. At the same time Kellan kissed Neil, his wings lifted and lightly fanned the room. A little dust rose and the whirlwind he created spiraled out the door.

Neil perked up. "What do you know? Your erection returns

and not a single chopper has come to visit."

"There you are. I thought I'd lost you." Kellan dropped his hands down to Neil's chest, pushed his shirt aside, and exposed every part of his torso from his hip hugging jeans on up. "Hot damn, you're gorgeous." He glanced at Neil's body from bottom to top.

Not expecting to be considered hot damn gorgeous, Neil laughed quietly, more like a giggle. "Okay. Where are we going to sleep?"

"I'm not really tired, but I suppose we could make a bed right here on the floor in front of the fireplace. There's got to be bedding in this place somewhere," Kellan said.

"I'll go upstairs to see what's there," Neil said.

"You're not going up there alone are you?" Kellan grabbed Neil's hand.

"I'll be fine. It doesn't seem like anybody is here but us."

"Doesn't seem are the key words. You're not going alone," Kellan insisted.

"Alright, pack your wings and follow me." Neil caressed Kellan's chest and felt a prickle against his palm he didn't remember being there earlier. "Oooh, I've gotta ask. Did you just trim the hair on your chest or did I prick my fingers on a few quills?"

The question struck Kellan as funny and he laughed. "It's hair. It was trimmed just a few days before I left the Lab. The clinicians keep my chest smooth so it's easier for those medical monitor tabs to adhere to my skin. It's at the point right now where my chest is itching - drives me crazy. I should let it grow out. What do you think?"

"I could easily get used to that, though you look great the way you are," Neil shyly mentioned.

"Let's go find some bedding before the sun comes up." Kellan pecked Neil's lips and smacked him on the ass.

Neil flinched, and with it came a snort.

Chapter 14

Kellan got a total of three hours rest that night. It was a good thing that's all he needed to feel refreshed and ready to go for another sixteen or so hours. Neil on the other hand needed a few more.

It was probably creeping in on five in the evening and Kellan lay with Neil resting across his arm at his left side. Kellan stayed quiet and still until Neil woke up on his own. They were up until six or seven earlier that same day, so the man had to be drop dead tired. Kellan watched Neil sleep and couldn't take his eyes off his blocky bare chest as it lifted and fell with each breath he took. Kellan laid his hand over it a few times just so he could feel the beat of his heart.

They were night owls now, had to be. The night sky and dark shadows gave them the added protection they needed to keep from being easily seen by the hunters, Seekers and anybody else that might try to do them in.

Dylan noticed Neil stirring, trotted over next to him, stared directly into his face and waited for an eye to open. Dylan didn't care for bedtime much, it was too lonely and he missed essential playtime with Neil.

A feeble groan mixed with a shaky stretch and flickering eyes showed that Neil was coming out of his slumber. "Is it time to get up already?" He groaned again.

"It's time and the clock is about to strike five in the evening." Kellan gently dragged the back of his nails up and down Neil's chest, soaking in as much of the handsome man as he could because it was unknown as to how much time they had together. Their new boy meets boy relationship, be it friends or mates, was rocky and uncertain for sure.

"Wow, it's peaceful here," Neil said. "I can't believe I slept so long."

"You must have needed your rest," Kellan suggested.

"We should go check out my house to see how much damage has been done to it, grab a few things if we can. We might be okay here. This place seems to be a good spot for somebody like you. I mean us." Neil sat up.

"As soon as the sun sets, we can jet," Kellan said.

"Has Dylan pooped yet?" Neil asked.

"He did run out back for a few minutes, did whatever he went outside to do and came back in to sit and stare at you. Not that I can blame him for the staring."

"Dylan's not the only one who likes to stare. What are you looking at?" Neil lowered his brow and crimped his lips.

"You're just so damned good looking." Kellan totally wanted to kiss Neil again, deep throat him with his tongue, maybe even try a few other things, like get naked and have sex with the man – full blown man on man sex with him so his repeat erections could finally get some release. It was a great thought Kellan had, but there was too much at stake to follow through with his sexual fantasy with Neil at the moment. Certainly he wasn't giving up on the idea of plunging his hard-on inside him and pumping him full of cum, it just didn't seem to be a good time for that. Just thinking about linking with Neil got Kellan rock solid and leaking semen.

"Get up. We need to organize this place and then figure out what we're going to do next." Neil grunted, petting Dylan on the way up from the floor.

While waiting for nightfall to greet them, Neil put a few misplaced pieces that were lying around the old lighthouse where he thought they should be. Most of what he moved was nautical crap that might be better off in the garbage. He left a few items out, figuring it went with the theme of where they were at, but shoved most of the junk in one of the bedroom closets so he didn't have to look at it.

The final particles of dust were swept away with a broken broom he found lying on the floor in the kitchen. He went full blast with it, sweeping every floor, nook and cranny, not missing the cobwebs that were the main attraction inside the shack, hanging in every corner like the place was theirs. They clearly had to go, along with the spiders and bugs that lived and died in them.

Kellan followed Neil around like a needy puppy dog, swishing everything with a watered down dust cloth.

The place didn't have many pieces of furniture, which helped make clean up quick and easy. A crooked sofa and a dining table with two chairs were all that was staged in the room. They didn't need much more than that so the minimalism suited them fine.

Kellan stopped for a few seconds and huffed. Not because cleaning wore him out, but because he actually despised it.

Neil noticed Kellan's pause, which gave him an opportunity to lunge into Kellan and force his tongue to the back of his throat all over again.

Grabbing hold of Neil's jaw with both hands, Kellan overpowered his advance by walking into him, compelling Neil to skip backward a few steps. Staying connected, they traded genetic material as their tongues hammered around inside each other's mouths.

Losing his balance and his lusting mind, Neil tripped back against the crooked sofa where he went down with Kellan on top of him. His arms dangled lifelessly at his sides while Kellan kissed him with an appetite that gave the impression of being deprived. Neil's greed was uncontrollable and he gave in to Kellan completely, taking as much as he gave.

Kellan's wet tongue searched deep inside Neil and his

masculine touch had Neil growing harder beneath his jeans.

Teasing Neil, Kellan slowly slipped his tongue from Neil's mouth, pulled Neil tighter against him by the waist, and ground their stiff cocks against each other. One, then the other, Kellan gripped Neil's hands, lifting them above his head where he pinned them. Before a second was able to pass, Kellan's wet lips were back over Neil's, and his hot breath moving into Neil's lungs as if it helped him breathe.

Kellan dragged his mouth across Neil's cheek until his lips reached his ear. Softly he whispered, "I could love you so easily, Neil." He nipped Neil's earlobe with his tender lips.

A wave of heat covered Neil's ear that made him shudder and crumble. When he tried to swallow, his Adams apple jumped and dropped, clogging his ability to speak. Easily love? He could do that too. He was hooked from the very first kiss from his angel.

Kellan leaned in, kissed Neil's throat, moving up over his chin with tiny pecks until he reached his lips, where he stayed.

Taking in Kellan's touch, Neil laid back and breathed him in deeply.

Lowering himself against Neil, Kellan muttered sounds of yearning into his ear. Little by little Kellan toiled his lips along Neil's jaw line until he found the softness of his warm lips again. Neil's tongue slipped into Kellan's mouth where the passion of romance quickly changed to shameless lust.

Passionately veiled by each other's kisses, their bodies entwined and their erections went thick.

Shockingly, Dylan barked.

Both Kellan and Neil twitched and the unexpected noise forced Kellan to pull away.

Neil's legs unlinked from around Kellan's hips and they dropped with a clunk to the floor. "What the fuck?"

Dylan's shrill bark made Kellan's hard-on instantly deflate, and the down-stroke of his wings lifted him off Neil just as quickly. He stood majestically tall and powerful at Neil's feet, his head turning left, toward the door. His broad chest pushed forward, his wings extended wide, and his fists tightly knotted at his sides.

Neil scrambled to his feet just as fast. "Douse the lights." His cock went soft as well.

Coincidence of another chopper invasion, or was there some kind of implant in the angel's dick that set the choppers into action?

They had both developed rock hard erections while kissing, so it made sense that it was the invading helicopters that continuously tried to put a stop to them getting any further than a kiss.

"They found us?" Kellan asked.

"I think so." Neil turned the knob on the lantern that shut down the flame.

It was dark inside the house and as they stood huddled in the middle of the room waiting for another chopper intrusion, they noticed no noise or lights outside.

Neil lifted a finger to his lips, shushing everybody even though there was no evidence of any inside noise.

Dylan ran to the satchel on the floor and barked again, looked at Neil with wide eyes and what appeared to be a grin and waited.

Startled, Neil flinched and squeaked.

Kellan's wings retracted. "Shit."

Dylan whimpered and tugged on the handle of the satchel.

"What the fuck?" Neil said. "Was that what all the barking was about? You wanted a cookie?"

"Thank God, but seriously?" Kellan relaxed and his wings crimped against his back.

Dylan marched in place and waited.

"We should take this as another sign that we're never going to get any further than a kiss," Neil said.

"It's alright. It'll happen when the time is right," Kellan assured him.

Neil shrugged a shoulder and broke into the satchel to get Dylan his dog biscuit.

After everything settled down, Kellan asked Neil if he thought it was a good idea to go check on the lake house to see if everything was still intact.

Neil only had one reason to want to go home. Other than being chased by hunters, there was the undesirable knowledge that his house might be flattened and he no longer had a place to call home. He tried to find a way to avoid going, but he needed to know. “What if the hunters are still there?”

“I can’t guarantee they aren’t, but I don’t know why they’d hang out there all night and through the day if what they’re looking for isn’t there,” Kellan said.

“I suppose you’re right,” Neil said.

It didn’t take long after Neil agreed for Kellan to scoop Neil and Dylan up for another flight of their lives.

Chapter 15

They flew as close to the ground as possible without totally banging the bag Dylan was in against rocks or skimming it across the water. They could see the house as they angled in. Amazingly it was still standing, looking dark and quiet. It was actually left pretty much intact, no major damage from what they could tell, so overall the place looked okay. The inside may be a different story knowing the hunters. They had seemed careless during their last encounter, only interested in getting a hold of Kellan no matter what they trampled or destroyed while doing so. Before Kellan and Neil went in, they hung out back in the trees for a while to be sure nobody was setting up shop on the inside.

"Maybe you should stay out here while I go in first to check things out. You're the one they want, not me," Neil said with his hand pressed against Kellan's chest, holding him back.

"Hell to the no! You're not going in there without me." Kellan pushed against Neil's hand. "I got you into this mess, so there's no way in hell you're going in there alone."

"Yeah but…" Neil started to say.

"Yeah but, nothing," Kellan interrupted. "I'm going in with you. Period!"

Neil could tell there was going to be a battle with Kellan if he persisted in trying to keep him out of the house. Kellan made it clear he wasn't staying outside in the bushes by himself, he was tagging along if Neil liked it or not. There were definite signs of protective instincts bred into that angel, which Neil actually liked, especially when it was directed at him. It put him in a position where he didn't have to be the caregiver, the provider, the nurturing minder all the time. He was always looking after patients at the hospital, so it was nice to be taken care of by somebody other than himself for a change.

"Fine," Neil spat.

Kellan smirked at Neil because he knew that if the hunters or the Seekers were hiding out in the house, he would be the one protecting Neil, not the other way around. Kellan knew how those creatures took after their targets. The beasts won't go down with a simple poke of a hypodermic needle.

After hanging out in the bushes for a while with what seemed to be the same hummingbird Kellan met the day he arrived, they sneaked to the back storm shelter entry that would lead them up into the kitchen pantry.

Kellan watched their backs, the hummingbird still there, while Neil opened the door to the shelter with extreme caution, and as he did, winced as the weathered hinges creaked. For some reason the noise the door made seemed louder than it ever had before.

Dylan took off through the tunnel first, kind of quickly, which was a good sign that nobody was up ahead ready to bring them to the ground the second they rounded the corner.

Neil went in next and then Kellan followed.

Before Kellan had a chance to pull the door closed behind them, bright lights from a white conversion van swept up the lane at the back of the house and burned a dusty beam through the misty air. The lights were aimed right at them, pointing their existence out. On the lake side of the house, the chopper dropped from the sky, rotor blades thumping.

The maniacs were waiting for them to return after all, until then Kellan had never been hunted by the Seekers before, they were coming for him, and they were coming for him as killers.

As quickly as the van pulled up to the house, it spun around with the backside facing the shelter's doorway. Dust and gravel shot like bullets toward Kellan and Neil who were still looking into the bright light outside.

Kellan whirled Neil out of the way at the same moment he snapped his wings open as a protective shield.

Neil glanced up in time to see the rear doors on the van open up and the grizzly beasts Kellan briefly told him about hopped out. They were the Seekers, he was sure of it. The two he saw were injured-ugly with big black wings like those seen on a bat. Their noses were bunched flat against their face and pointed upward much like canine pugs. Even though dark outside, he could see that their flesh tone was shoe-polish black that blended with their leathery wings. They were horrifying to the eye and emanated breath as rancid as trash gone bad. The creatures were clearly more raptor-like than human with strong killer instincts.

They had come for them and the way it looked to Neil, the maniacs were going to win. Those grimy monsters looked stronger than bulls, and to Neil, he felt he brought a knife to a real killers gun fight.

Kellan pulled the door shut to buy time, knowing it wouldn't stop the Seekers, but it would hold them back a minute or two. The three of them took off running in the dark, through the tunnel that took them to the room beneath the house.

"Fuck, fuck, fuck," Neil nervously ranted while stumbling up the stairs to the pantry.

Kellan grabbed Dylan and jumped the steps behind Neil.

As they took off through the house, Kellan's wings were knocking everything he passed by to the floor. All grandma's shit bit the dust.

The Seekers came in the house the same way Neil and Kellan did and the chopper was still beating blades out front along the coast. Their escape was limited to one way out, the side entry leading to the garage. It was their only chance.

Kellan and Neil sprinted through the kitchen toward the exit and instead of turning the doorknob, Kellan turned his back on it and busted through, totally pulling the hinges from the frame. As the door crashed to the pavement and on his way out, Kellan reached for Neil's hand and pulled him through the open doorway with him.

The tug shocked Neil and his knees banged against the floor as he was dragged outside.

As soon as they were out the door, Kellan beat wings against wind. Up they went, Dylan in one arm and Neil swinging beneath them like the tail of a kite. He circled the house and flew straight out toward the lake.

"I need to drop some weight," Kellan said. "I'll put Dylan down on that sandbar over there."

"What? No!" Neil yelled back.

"I have to. I can't fight these bats with both of you in my arms. They're programmed to chase after me, not Dylan. He'll be okay," Kellan said, heading toward the sandbar.

"What about me?" Neil asked.

"Right now, I'm taking you with me." Kellan dived for the strip of sand, back flapped to curb his speed and then let Dylan go. He quickly shifted Neil into both arms and held his shoulders against his chest, legs dangling.

Dylan grumbled.

Quickly, Kellan threw his wings up and then down hard which brought a sudden drop before shooting straight up into the sky at a quick climb. Another beat did it again and this time the sensation made Neil's stomach churn and forced an acidic lump into his throat where it stuck.

Kellan looked back to see how far ahead of the Seekers they were, and when he followed through with a bank to the right he lost his grip on Neil and he slipped until Kellan caught him with a vice lock at his wrist. While it was all happening, Neil's feet swung far out to the side and back again where they dangled like loose rags in the wind.

Swaying underneath Kellan by one arm, Neil twisted and turned, completely out of control and relying on Kellan's grip to not give out.

Kellan roared as he tugged on Neil, pulling him back against his chest where he held him tighter in his arms. "Dammit, I'm sorry, Neil."

Neil grunted and then gulped. He was honestly fucking

scared.

Not too far behind Neil and Kellan, the Seekers flew in a full speed haphazard formation, weaving over and under each other like wild banshees. From their vocal sacks they continuously pitched high frequency screeches out in front of them because their vision sucked like the blind bats they were genetically created from, which made the high-pitched screams helpful in finding their way through the dark. The echoes speed-blasted toward Kellan, then bounced back just as fast, telling the creatures he was up ahead. With their bat wings flapping, thwack, thwack, thwack, the two Seekers progressed closer.

Without warning, one Seeker, obviously the meaner of the two sped up behind Kellan and grabbed his foot firmly by the ankle, yanking it back hard while releasing a blood curdling scream.

The sudden tug on Kellan's leg startled him and he lost his grip on Neil. His heart sank as he watched Neil fall free, heading straight down. Rage welled up in Kellan and the fight to survive and save his new friend went live.

With his free foot, Kellan side-kicked the Seeker's skull with all his strength. The dead weight of his heel hit hard, and a loud scream emanated from the beasts gullet. The Seeker's hold on Kellan's ankle was lost and it tumbled backward toward the ground, freefalling.

Kellan pulled his wings in tight, back rolled out of the Seeker's reach, and raced with the speed of sound straight down toward Neil. He scrambled for Neil with his hands clawing through space, trying like mad to reach him. Grabbing, Kellan got him by the hand but as quickly as he gripped him he lost hold. Neil slipped from Kellan's grasp, and as he flipped backward, Kellan snagged him by the pant leg, but the downward force pulled at him and Kellan couldn't hang on. Neil slipped away again, looking back at Kellan with watery eyes.

"This isn't happening. I can't lose you now, Neil," Kellan said, biting down hard, clenching his teeth until his jaw ached. He roared to help summon strength and speed to reach Neil. Kellan could see that only seconds remained before Neil crashed into the water. Kellan knew if Neil hit the surface it would be deadly. Was there time? Did Kellan have it in him to rescue the man he could love so easily?

Neil was closing in on the lake below him and just before he hit water, his body jerked when Kellan gripped him by the ankle. Just in time, Kellan heaved Neil in such a way that he arced up, over and then down onto Kellan's chest, at the same instant his wings shifted him over onto his back. The snap of Kellan's wings splashed water as he flew backside down, and then corkscrewed in midflight putting Neil back underneath him. Another rolling twist and a hard downward stroke of his wings shot them both straight upward back toward the stars.

Shocked and on the verge of blacking out, Neil pulled air back into his empty lungs.

"I've got you. It's alright," Kellan said, hugging Neil tight while pushing his head against the pocket between his neck and shoulder. "I'm not letting go this time. I promise."

Neil's heart was beating as fast as Kellan's was. He pulled back and gasped for fresher air.

Kellan looked down and saw the Seekers still after them. "Shit-damn-son-of-a-bitch."

The extra weight of carrying Neil was taking its toll on Kellan's speed and he knew he had to let him go or risk the end result of the battle being much worse. Kellan spiraled higher and flew toward the top of the bridges north tower where he planned to put Neil. When they got there, Kellan set Neil down in the center and hugged him.

"I'll come back for you when the time is right. Just stay put and I be back to get you." Kellan kissed Neil on the lips, held it a few seconds while taking in what he breathed out. Then he let him go, skipped backward in the form of a crucifix, back dropped off the tower, and disappeared from sight.

Neil stood, arms crossed over his chest like he was cold, higher than he'd ever been before, feeling frightened and abandoned. He dropped to his knees and prayed that no harm would come to Kellan.

Chapter 16

Alone, Kellan shot through the sky like a bullet from a gun, drawing the Seekers' attention away from Neil and onto himself. They were after him, gaining speed fast, putting only a few feet between them within seconds.

The Seekers were reckless, designed to be fighters, trained not to give up even if death was the outcome. Their orders were to put an end to Kellan's escape, kill him if they needed to.

Kellan brought himself to a stop midflight, spun to face the Seekers and hovered with slow, steady wing beats in the dark night sky. "Come get me, you fuckers, and leave my new boyfriend alone."

The skilled killers went after Kellan and circled him like a hurricane until they found their place and hung there. While they hovered, the loud thumps from their leathery wings boomed like unsynchronized drumbeats. Their vocal shrieks exploded against Kellan's eardrums, cutting into his senses like a dull rusty blade: metal on metal. The blare crippled his mind and strangled his nerves.

Kellan was shoulder rammed hard to the gut by the Seeker in front of him and it pushed him backward into the batty man at his rear. Kellan's wings folded around the Seeker that tackled him and from there they fell from the sky. As they dropped, inertia pulled at them and they went down faster and faster, like heavy rocks being pulled earthward by gravity.

The Seeker stuck to Kellan like glue, roared in his face with blood-tainted rancid breath that could kill a dragon. All while pounding Kellan's skull with knotted fists.

Anger rose in Kellan like never before. He growled back at the Seeker and then slammed his forehead into the base of its nose with enormous force, pushing it high between its single eyebrow.

Pain showed in the Seeker's dark, ugly eyes as electric shockwaves seared through the stubby bridge of the creature's broken nose. Bluish blood gushed down its grizzly face and pooled in every crevice lining its neck. It howled like a boar being shredded in the woods by wolves.

Without holding back, Kellan popped each of its ears with an open hand, forcing air against the inner drums, rupturing them and making them bleed.

Stunned by the forceful crack to the head, the Seeker pulled back, shrieking louder than it did before.

There was a brief moment where the Seeker weakened; giving Kellan a slim gap in the fight to spread his wings and gain altitude, but when he tried, the weight of the beast still clinging to him yanked them both back down.

Bound together in the clutches of rage, they twisted over and under each other, skim spiraling across the water like a skipping stones. Wings collided, legs tangled, and hands locked around throats as the two winged creatures fought against the splashing water.

Suddenly, another fist to the head by the Seeker pushed Kellan sideways and into a wing propelling spin. He lost his grip and corkscrewed farther away from his impending killer.

On release, the leather-winged Seeker inhaled deeply, dragged fresh air into its starved lungs until the fiery burn of their collapse went away.

A few feet away, Kellan tucked his knees to his chest and

rolled forward, head over heels, turning himself back toward the Seeker who was more eager to kill him than live itself. Kellan's wings flapped fast and furiously, lifting water from the lake that made it rain all around them. Adding a strength-building roar, Kellan shoulder slammed the Seeker's gut the same way it had done to him earlier, and the force pushed its back into the cement base of the bridge's south tower. The impact was so hard that the concrete cracked, spewing bits of cement and chalky dust from behind the ugly monster's back. Pieces seemed to sizzle when they hit water.

Kellan jaw chopped the Seeker with his elbow and the blow knocked its head against the broken wall, turning its eyes backward in its head. At that same moment, the other Seeker sneakily coasted in and latched itself to Kellan's back, trying to choke him from behind.

Swiftly thinking, Kellan threw his head backward, bashing the Seeker's nose, followed quickly by a backhanded fist blow to its jaw. Stunned, the Seeker went slack, fell backward in the water and floated limply with its outstretched wings wavering above the lake's surface.

Seconds later the chopper flew in with its beam of light pinning them all.

Looking over his shoulder and into the light, Kellan unfisted his hands and let the Seeker he was holding onto drop. Wasting no time, he acted on instinct, flew to the body floating in the water, grabbed its feet and lifted. With strained effort, he beat his wings to go higher, dipping a shoulder that started them spinning. He savagely spun the Seeker faster, matching each turn with the blades on the chopper. With a strenuous roar he let go and the Seeker tumbled chaotically through empty space. Suddenly, as if shocked from a dream, the Seeker broke death's grip and took off after Kellan again. It screamed louder still and bared its jagged teeth.

Kellan circled around the rear of the chopper where he stopped and hovered, blade forced air filling his wings.

On the other side of the helicopter in front of him, the Seeker flew at him, bursting with rage.

Kellan broke to the right and dived at the same moment the chopper spun to face them.

The Seeker flew at him hard, moving fast.

As Kellan dropped to fly away, a grated mess was made when the beast connected with the chopper's blades. Body bits and blue blood were slinging everywhere and those pieces were the only evidence that the Seeker ever existed.

The chopper strained and sputtered until it stabilized. From there it raced away and shot to the sky, empty handed. Its lights swept across the water's surface like a paintbrush on canvas before it rose higher and fastened its lights on Neil.

They knew.

"Fuck this shit. I told you to stay away from my fucking boyfriend." Furiously, Kellan stretched one arm in front of him in a Superman pose, banked wide to the left around the back of the south tower and took off at laser speed to rescue Neil.

When Kellan reached the top of the north tower where Neil was, he noticed the chopper was lagging behind, but still climbing. Neil was in the same spot where he'd left him earlier, on his knees and appeared to be praying.

Kellan quickly circled in front of Neil before landing in a tight spot behind him.

Ready to see Kellan, Neil turned around and stood up. A little shaken, but doing okay. He was strong, as usual.

They had to move fast, there was no time to waste.

Kellan's wings back-beat to keep him in place while Neil cautiously shuffled backward into his open arms.

The chopper thumped in front of them, the nose light of the craft directed at their eyes, hopeful of blinding them or scaring them off the edge. It burned hot and bit right through their eyes.

"Come. Hurry. I've got you." Kellan opened his arms and his wings to Neil, inviting him in, ready to fly.

When Neil reached him, Kellan pulled Neil's back tighter against his chest. With his hands pressed to Neil's bare skin, Kellan drew him even closer and back-stepped while he watched the spinning blades of the chopper move closer, daring them to lose their heads. It was like a Wild West standoff, but nobody had a gun.

In what seemed like slow motion, Kellan opened his wings and plummeted backward off the edge of the tower while giving the pilots on board the fuck you finger. They entered into a graceful fall like they landed on clouds, Neil on top of Kellan, tightly locked in his arms. Together again.

Kellan drew one wing closer to his side that spear-spiraled them until they were flying face down, parallel with the horizon. Kellan rose with an angled twist that shot them back up toward the sky again, and as he did, spun Neil around until their bare chests met, held him tight, and looked him in the eyes.

Kellan thought again how beautiful Neil was to him, and almost wept that he could have lost him just then. Kellan squeezed him and went even higher, leaving all the damage behind until the air around them turned thinner and everything below them disappeared from sight.

With the oxygen level getting lower, Neil grew weaker and struggled to breath. He went pale and was close to passing out.

Luckily for Kellan, he was engineered to take on any obstacles that got in his way, and in this case, he could easily withstand low oxygen levels for extended periods of time. He could breathe just about anywhere, that's how they made him. He inhaled deeply, holding it in until the molecular orbital structure changed, placed his mouth over Neil's, and gave him the breath he could not get on his own. The oxygen wasn't the purest, but it was the kiss of life that Neil needed, and it was Kellan's supreme pleasure to be the one who gave it to him.

Chapter 17

With the air as thin as it was where Kellan and Neil were flying, the enemies that were fixated on them may not have the ability to fly safely. Bats and helicopters understandably have their height limitations. Several minutes had passed and there didn't seem to be any sign of the Seeker that Kellan thought was still alive, or of the constantly thwacking helicopter.

Kellan circled the sky a while longer, observing everything around them while passing puffs of air into Neil's lungs that would help him survive in the oxygen deficient air. The way Kellan held Neil against his chest and kissed him over and over again with breaths of life turned what would have been a terrifying experience into a romantic engagement.

The temperature was dropping and the air around them felt more like an icy winter's night than a cool autumn evening. It was crisp where they were and the limited oxygen around them changed quickly to cold microscopic snowflakes.

Before Neil turned to ice and his blood froze, Kellan

dropped a wing that took them lower and lower in a wide-open circle. He could feel the temperature around them rise as they descended and he could see the color returning to Neil's face.

Neil coughed a few times and his eyelids turned less heavy, his beautiful brown eyes sneaking a peak through thin crescent slits.

"There you are, handsome," Kellan said and then blew one last puff of breath into Neil's lungs.

As Neil became more conscious, the memory of what had just happened was coming back. He jerked, both arms instinctively clamped around Kellan's neck and locked, seeking safety.

"It's alright, I've got you." Kellan held him closer, transferring the heat from his body to Neil's.

On a whim Neil kissed Kellan and held it.

Kellan kissed Neil back while slowing his flight to a hawk-like soar. Wings extended to their fullest.

Kellan's ability to see through darkness allowed him to scan the area for any remaining choppers or Seekers before descending to the sandbar where they'd left Dylan. From what he could tell, there didn't appear to be any manic killers hanging around, waiting to attack again.

As they got closer to the sandbar they could see Dylan wasn't on it. There was actually no sign of him *or* the sandbar. The moon that floated straight above brought the tide in higher than it normally does, washing a thin layer of water over top of the bar and possibly taking Dylan with it. They landed, raising a splash of water when their feet hit the nearly submerged sandbar.

Neil fell to his knees when Kellan let him go, tripping twice when he tried to get up. Neil's mind wrestled with gut-wrenching fear that his dog had been taken by the Seekers, or maybe the guys in the chopper. "Oh God, where is he?" Neil sounded hysterical, water splashing everywhere as he spun and scrambled to find Dylan.

"Fuck." Kellan immediately pounded his wings against wind, preparing for take-off. The tips of his feathers tapped the water's surface with light splashes while he ran up behind Neil to scoop him off the bar. "We'll find him, Neil, but we can't stay here."

Neil's dripping feet swayed from left to right, and his shirt almost came off when Kellan grabbed hold of him. He silently begged that Dylan had simply swum home. He's a smart dog, he would do that. He's done it before. Neil's stomach churned as if hell's fire was burning inside him, and he felt like throwing up. He ached inside not knowing if Dylan was alright.

Kellan skimmed the grounds around the house on their way in, looking for any activity that shouldn't be there. He saw no choppers, no Seekers, and he certainly didn't see Dylan wandering around or running up to meet them on their approach. Kellan back flapped his wings, slowing down to a hover at the front side of the house.

Neil's feet lightly touched ground and he anxiously ran for the house calling Dylan, not giving any thought that there could be an intruder waiting for them inside.

Kellan chased Neil, half walking and partly flying, tugging at his arm before he made it inside. "Wait, let me go first." He squeezed past Neil, gracing his cheek with a few feathers as he stepped up to the front entry. The door was left open, possibly unable to shut due to the damage caused by the Seekers' forced entry, and the breeze moving over it caused a repetitive knock against the jam in the few minutes they were standing there. Kellan pushed against the door with his finger and stole a peek inside as he slowly opened it. His wings went darker as a way of camouflaging himself from eyes that might be watching him, turned back toward Neil, and pressed a shushing finger to his lips as a signal to be quiet. Kellan tiptoed across the threshold with Neil holding his wingtips from behind. Both looked like prowlers breaking into their own home.

Whispering, Neil asked, "Do you see him?"

Kellan shook his head, not looking back.

The typical bark or speedy greeting to the door was missing. A bad sign.

Dylan was a bright dog with chromosomes that could create one remarkable animal when combined with the extracted stem cells of man.

A ghastly image entered Kellan's mind and he tried like hell to dismiss it, but he couldn't. It was a horrifying thought, but a theory that could come true if it hadn't already. The laboratory managed to bring his existence to life when they spliced human and avian genes together, so why not mix canine and human? The lab was building smart machines with animalistic instincts and when they came across the perfect specimen, they took it without asking. Human, insect or animal.

"Oh Gawd, they took him," Neil alleged. "Why would they take him?"

"Stay here, I'll be right back." Kellan charged out the door so fast that he took the storm door off its hinges. Within seconds, he was gone.

Neil didn't listen for shit. He ran after Kellan and chased him outside.

Like a hurricane coming across the Atlantic, Kellan raced around all sides of the house looking for Dylan. He hovered high, looking down, scanning everything. Nothing. The dog was gone, and understanding the way the maniacs at the lab worked led him to believe the military had taken him.

When Kellan flew back around to the front of the house, he saw Neil on his knees again, but this time he was crying. Kellan dropped fast and stood above him, one hand on his shoulder, consoling him. He knelt on one knee next to Neil, held him close against his side and tented him with his wings.

"We'll get him back," said Kellan. "I promise."

Neil covered his face with his hands, catching every tear he could that was for Dylan. Some fell to the ground and the rolling tide took them away.

All of a sudden Kellan's senses perked up, his eardrums vibrated from the thump of what sounded to be helicopters. He gripped Neil's arm, pulling him up. "C'mon, we've gotta go."

Neil stumbled as Kellan lifted him. "But Dylan?"

Kellan whispered, "We'll find him. But right now we've gotta go."

Shit, they're back.

Kellan stood and pulled Neil into him, looked up into the sky at the same second two choppers came around the house, one on each side, at sharp angles. He spun in the dirt as the whirlybirds took a wide arc out over the water and then came back and faced them. Kellan push Neil behind his back and raised his wings to shield him, arms out, and ready to fight all over again. He turned his head over his shoulder and hollered, "Get in the house and into the shelter. I'll take these fuckers down and be right in."

Neil back-stepped toward the door, one slow step after the other, keeping an eye on the choppers in the sky the entire time and glancing at Kellan every chance he could get.

Kellan stood still in the sand and waited, his eyes raking the area for an escape.

Things were about to get worse.

As expected, the hovering choppers geared up to attack. The engines revved, pushing the noses forward that aimed beams of light directly down on Kellan. The side doors on each chopper opened and two Seekers plummeted to the ground where they stood in front of Kellan. Clinging to the frame of each open chopper door were a few big men balancing guns across their knees.

Kellan crouched down, sprang from the ground and took flight, staying low at first and then quickly banking off to the left around the house.

As instructed, the Seekers hurried to get Kellan. One flew over the rooftop and the other raced sharply around the side of the house. They worked fast, trapping Kellan with his back to the trees, not leaving him any room to move.

Kellan had nowhere to go but up. Pushing his wings toward the ground, he shot like a rocket straight up. Leaves and bits of earth trailed in his wake.

Infuriated that Kellan slipped by, the Seekers howled, then surged skyward behind Kellan in twisting spins. One caught hold of Kellan's ankle, the other raced above him to block his ascension.

Kellan quickly dropped backward, flipping the Seeker attached to his foot over his head where it slammed into the Seeker above him. Kicking free, Kellan dived sharply downward to get away. Behind him, the Seekers circled around to force Kellan to the front of the house.

The blades of the two choppers banged in the wind, dispersing like dragon flies over the water where they came back around, racing straight into Kellan.

As if he had brakes, Kellan stopped in midflight and hung

there. Down below he saw Neil looking up and when their eyes met, his heart sank.

That was it, he was going back.

A pop from a shotgun sounded and Kellan felt the sting of a sharp dagger penetrate his left thigh. Dizziness seized him as the tranquilizer serum clogged his bloodstream.

As his consciousness faded away, the pain of missing Neil punched him in the gut, and plagued him heavily inside. It spread fast, which forced the ache in his heart to grow larger, pushing it closer to a massive explosion.

Should he scream for help or pray for death?

The sensation of pricking heat spiked his body and he descended the same way his heart was melting, heading down, heavy and slow, mimicking a bad dream.

Two pops from each chopper went off, one right after the other, firing two sling nets through the dark. The nets covered Kellan, tangling in his limbs and taking him down.

When Kellan hit the dirt, the Seekers flew in, tied the nets closed and pinned him to the ground.

Neil reacted as any loved-one would, he didn't care if anything happened to him, or if the Seekers took him too. He needed to get to Kellan, needed to help him. Neil sprinted to the net; belly flopped on the ground, and grabbed hold of Kellan's hand.

Kellan's head slowly went down and he laid it gently against the sand. He placed a finger over his lips to hush Neil, and before he could finish telling Neil everything was going to be okay, his lids went heavy and slowly shut.

"I can't let go," Neil wept. First his dog, and then Kellan.

The Seekers went vertical and dragged Kellan across the dirt like a bag of trash, leaving a trail of disheveled sand and shells behind them. So what if they injured Kellan, they didn't care.

The choppers were still there, but hovering low to the ground this time. The Seekers lifted Kellan to the door where men waiting inside pulled him in.

Neil suspected a trap and sensed he was next to be shot, lassoed and carried away. But unlike Kellan, he'd show up to the party dead. He couldn't let that happen, he had a dog and an angel to rescue.

Neil knew he had seen what nobody was ever supposed to see, which made him extremely disposable. He clawed at the sand and stood up, grabbing a feather of Kellan's which was lying a few inches in front of him as he did, and then made a mad dash for the house. Dirt lifted in his tracks as he hurdled up the steps, slamming the door shut as much as he could in its damaged state as soon as he got inside.

Behind Neil an electronic voice rang out, "Get him."

The doors on the choppers banged shut and when the two machines lifted in unison, they did a three-sixty that aimed both aircraft noses straight at Neil's house.

Another electronic voice called, "On three."

The count of three came and went within seconds, and just like that, an automatic door from the underside of a chopper lowered. From it a missile was summoned and tore through space with a mission of death and destruction. It busted through the front window of the lake house, drawing the front door inward when it dragged the outside air with it.

Before the next second passed, the house blew apart. The rooftop first, followed by the walls that helped it stand. The entire house exploded within a few fast seconds, and the forced winds from the blast sucked the choppers inward and then pushed them back again. Pieces of the house and what was in it were hurled everywhere. Hardly any of it any longer identifiable. Survival outside the blow was slim, and if anything did live through it, they'd be blessed to tell the tale.

Chapter 18

As it was, Kellan was gone, Dylan was gone, and the home Neil lived in - gone. Everything Neil possessed seemed to be disappearing, taken away; leaving him alone.

The house was flattened, and so were most of the trees that circled the property. Whatever explosives the choppers let loose did a fine job making sure any evidence and anyone with knowledge of Kellan's existence disappeared, wiped out as if they had never been there.

One thing was for sure, Neil's house was beyond unlivable. Hanging heavily above the house was a cloud of smoke that suffocated any flames still trying to cling to life. Heat rose from the ashes, and a spark or two attempted to reignite what little was left to burn.

There was too much debris strewn about for the inhabitants of the choppers to tell if Neil was dead or alive. No detectible movement either, except for loose papers the breeze picked up and tossed around the yard, and the slowly rising ash that hid away any sign of life that may have existed beneath the broken home.

A flash of fury left Neil angry while he waited for everything above him to simmer down and settle to the ground. He could hear the crackle of timber and the whistle of the wind through the storm shelter door as he pushed it open to crawl out. On exiting the shelter, he could feel the wind blowing more fiercely than it was earlier, as though the place was irritated by what just happened to it. A huge tree in the yard swayed and violently bent like it was angered too. Small branches broke free from the limbs, and it appeared to Neil that the gigantic maple tree might be wrenched from the ground at any minute. It saddened him to see the wind-whipped tree, knowing after today he might never see it again, at least not rooted to the ground the way it should be. As he stood silently and took in a breath, his lungs filled with ash-plagued air that made him cough, and he knew the moment he turned toward his house it would be in the same wicked shape as the tree. Busted and broken. The blast he heard when he was inside the shelter translated to him as able to cause major damage, and while he was down there, he felt the ground shake as the house came down on top of him.

Knowing what he was going to see when he turned around would be bad, Neil did it anyway. He looked.

Right then he spoke no words, he couldn't. His emotions were snarled between sad and furious, but he was more angry than sad because those maniacs from the laboratory stole Kellan and Dylan from him. Neil's connection to Kellan and Dylan was strong enough to feel they were still alive. Somewhere. And he was sure that somewhere was the Laboratory in Traverse City that Kellan spoke of. It had to be that place. Where else would they have taken them?

Neil could complain all he wanted, break down and cry, but he had a new path to follow. The purpose of it all was unknown to him, but he couldn't turn back now, he had to move on. He was still alive but the Seekers and the MPs probably wrote him off as dead. So there was hope.

Neil sat on the ground, thinking, but not for too long. Vivid memories surfaced of holding Kellan, kissing him, and they congested Neil's mind. He felt him as though he was near, could smell him too. Tears welled in his eyes and right then he knew he needed to find Kellan and Dylan. There was a sense of emptiness, the feeling of a primitive bond that was missing, which instantly made him turn cold.

He shook his head, wiped his face and nose with his sleeve to remove the evidence of emotion. He needed to move quickly, there was still a chance that the choppers and Seekers would come looking for him to make sure there was a time of death on his bloodless soul.

That wouldn't be good.

He scrambled back to the storm shelter, felt around in the dark for anything useful that he could take with him on his hike to the bay. He wasn't sure how he was getting there, his car was buried in the garage under burnt timber, and because it was so late at night, public transportation was not an option.

He stopped and stood quietly for a minute before leaving the storm shelter, glancing at what he was able to see for the last time. A chill stroked his spine when he heard a thump of a chopper blade. It couldn't be, one thump was far less than what a whirling blade sounded like. He dismissed it as being his ruined house shifting above him. Never the less, he needed to get out of there before the room caved in completely or the chopper had truly returned.

He left the storm shelter with a paper bag that held a few select items to get him through to the next day.

He dropped the shelter door into place and everything went black.

Chapter 19

Over at the Laboratory, it took three brawny MPs to carry Kellan to his cell where they tossed him in like old laundry and left him there as punishment for running away. His wing bones bent beneath him, held there by the weight of his own body when he rolled over them across the floor. He lay like a dead man while they shackled his feet for safekeeping.

Kellan was a superior creature, more capable than what was expected, and those in charge needed to keep him under total lock down to be sure he wouldn't be taking off again.

A few hours passed before Kellan's eyes eventually opened, discharge oozed when his upper lids pulled away from the lower ones. He blinked several times to clear away the blurriness, his gaze burned while trying to focus on the unexpected chains around his ankles. They clattered when he moved, turning the military police outside his cell room toward his door.

The last thing Kellan remembered was a sting in his upper thigh followed by a spidery net coming at him while he was hovering in front of Neil's house. From then on, everything else was blank until the moment he woke up. He couldn't remember anything that went on between the two points. It probably didn't matter anyway.

There was no use fighting the restraints they had on him, or trying to escape again. Not right away anyway. Instead he picked himself up off the floor, shuffled to a chair by the window and sat down.

The entire time he stared outside into complete darkness, wondering what Neil was doing; wondered if he was safe, if he was content, but most of all, prayed that he was still alive. Kellan connected with Neil in such a perfect way that he couldn't stop thinking about him. He wanted to hold him, kiss him again, and make love to that man. He wanted to be with him so badly that his heart burned. The feeling was strong, so strong, that he knew deep down he had to get away and find him.

~~~~ O ~~~~

In another part of the same building in which Kellan was kept, Neil was held in a different type of cell, locked behind bars like a criminal. All he had in there with him was a toilet, a tiny sink and a single mattress laid out on the floor. It was worse than a prison cell and more like a cold, sterile cage for a wild animal.

The only good thing about it however, was that he found Dylan, who was lying in the corner of a smaller cage across the way, not socializing. By the dog's actions, it seemed he was missing Neil. It was a familiar sight that Neil hated seeing and avoided as much as possible. His precious boy was gloomy, and a sad dog made Neil an unhappy prisoner. He tried to quietly get Dylan to look his way without drawing too much attention to himself, but failed on every attempt. Their cages were too far apart.

Neil pressed his face between the open bars of his cell and glanced around the open lab in front of him. The whole place reeked of no good, from the cold cell he was put in, to the institutional color painted on the walls. Everywhere he looked, he saw stainless steel laboratory tables and rigid equipment that looked like the same ones found in a veterinary clinic. And given Kellan's form, the setup didn't come as any surprise. Neil
~~~~

wondered why he was put in the vet wing and what plans they had in store for him.

Strange noises that resembled echoes bouncing off the walls in a locker room shower stall were heard around the lab, but from Neil's viewpoint, he couldn't tell where the sounds were coming from. He was almost sure they weren't human because the echoes he heard were similar to chirps, squeaks, whimpers and roars. From that he thought of Kellan, and imagined what he heard could well be mixed breeds, part human, part animal or even part beast.

Was that the plan those maniacs had for him? Were they going to alter him somehow or possibly use him to make a new fucked up creature?

The thought of it did a number on Neil and he lost his ability to breathe for a minute. He let go of the bars, backed up and dropped down on the mattress, freaked out.

What had he stumbled into?

Sensing Neil's fear just then, Dylan lifted his head and spotted him in another cage across the room. Seeing Neil made him go crazy happy, but his tune quickly changed to a whimper when he figured out he wasn't able to bust the gate open and go to him. Dylan sat down with eyes full of sadness.

Recognizing Dylan's cry, Neil returned to the cell bars when he heard him getting restless. Neil waved at him and tried to hush his noise by telling him everything was going to be okay. Neil wasn't too sure about that or if Dylan heard him, but he said it anyway for his own sanity as well as for Dylan's.

As time went on, Dylan and Neil did the best they could to interact with each other from across the room. Facing Neil, Dylan tucked his nose tightly against his caged wall at the same time Neil extended his arm out between the bars as far as he could toward Dylan. They weren't touching, but at least they were closer. Several times throughout the day, they both dozed off in crumpled lumps along the floor of their cages, but snapped out of it every few minutes to make sure the other didn't feel lost and alone. They were too connected to let that happen. Eventually Dylan's eyes turned red and watery, and so did Neil's.

Every few hours, it was feeding time, and the guard on duty would push a tray of food through an open gap along the floor of

Neil's cage that would slip and slide across the floor the same way it would in prison. Spinning and rattling. Neil would eat what he could of the flavorless hospital style mush and then push the tray back through the gap where he would neatly stage it in front of the bars in a way that nobody would stumble into it.

Dylan's dinner was funneled down a chute that gathered kibbles in a dish on the floor at the back of his cage. Thankfully his drinking supply replenished itself all day long with a constant flow of fresh water.

From what Neil could tell, there didn't seem to be any cruelty to the animals in the part of the veterinary facility where he was housed, just lonely hearts that would turn anybody sad.

A few days went by before Neil was allowed to leave his cell to bathe. If one more day passed by without a shower, he'd have reached the point of no return and be mistaken for garbage.

The MP on duty walked with Neil to the shower room the same way they do criminals in prison, closely at his side, gun at the ready.

As they passed through a cleaning and pharmaceutical stock room on their way to the shower chamber, Neil looked around expecting it to be more organized than what it was. Most everything seemed misplaced except the refrigerated section that housed the medication that required temperate control. The hospitals that Neil worked at were never messy and disorganized, and because he was at a government institution, he figured the place would be maintained the way he expected a military hospital would be, in keeping with white glove standards.

When Neil finally reached the bathing facility, there wasn't much room for a person and the tub with the spray nozzle was only waist high. He glanced around and could tell he was in a pet grooming bathhouse, not a bathroom for a standard sized human being. That explained all the animals he'd been sleeping with, as well as the supply room that appeared less sanitary than a medical center was required to be. Neil was in the vet ward for sure. The grooming room was the final puzzle piece that put it all into perspective.

Neil's situation wasn't the worst, but the small tub he was given was perfect for a pecker, tits and ass scrub down. That's all he was getting, and frankly that's all he needed, so he went with it. Trying to think positively: it was better than no bath at all.

During Neil's first bathing experience at the Lab, he was watched the entire time by the police on duty, from beginning to end. He truly felt uncomfortable with the whole eye contact thing going on between them, but after a few days he got used to it, and eventually let the military police get his thrill on for the day like Neil knew the man wanted to.

As soon as bath time was over, Neil was pretty sure the man would take up a private corner and jack himself off, give relief to the hard-on he got from watching Neil soap up, caress and rinse his private parts.

The policeman wasn't bad looking, and in all honesty, he was somewhat Neil's type, but being unwillingly on the giving end of a sex show, made Neil feel violated.

The days went by and toward the end of the week, Neil had slowly befriended the officer on duty to the point that he now gave him more privacy in the shower. Finally, Neil could relax and enjoy his bath without being ogled.

The first time Neil was left alone was on the seventh day of his lockdown, which gave him an opportunity to observe the area more closely and think about a plan of escape. He had a good idea what to do, he just needed a little alone time to search for what he needed to pull it off.

Each day that passed by allowed Neil to keep a catalog in his brain how the refrigeration section in the medicine room was organized. The cooler near the grooming doorway was the tranquilizer and anesthesia box, which was the one he was most interested in. Perfect. The only thing he needed to do was get his hands on a few syringes and possibly a dart pistol to round out his plan.

Neil wasn't the type of person who would be a friendly pretender to somebody and then stab them in the back when they weren't looking, but his situation called for it, and he needed to change his ways about that, just this once. He had to or else.

Even though Neil became cordially conversational with the police on duty, Neil still remained locked up behind bars as tight as when he got there. It was no big deal for the time being because when the time was right to make his move, Neil would know it.

With each day that passed, the MP gave Neil a little more

rope to roam, let him have some extended freedom that allowed him to walk to the bathhouse through the storage room alone. What mischief could Neil get into? He seemed harmless.

Could it get any simpler?

Without even trying, Neil was able to get his hands on the sleeping drug he was in need of. Acepromazine Maleate was the perfect choice, right there on the refrigerator shelf like it was calling out to him. Coincidentally the medication was originally used as an antipsychotic treatment at the hospital when it was a ward for the mentally and criminally insane, but might currently be used to put animals to sleep during surgical procedures and other strange experiments. An injection of fifteen milligrams of the stuff could put down a four hundred pound animal in less than a minute. Neil knew what the drug could do from his extensive medical background as a nurse, which put the idea in his head to use it.

All Neil needed was the tranquilizer pistol, as well as the darts that it used. It made sense that the dispensing pistols would be someplace within the animal housing wing, he couldn't imagine them being stored anywhere else. Whenever Neil had the chance to be alone, he searched a few medical cabinets for the guns and darts.

When he was down to his last option, in a place he never thought to look, he found that all the medication he needed was kept in one drawer at the bottom of the refrigerator. There he found several tranquilizer guns lined up like they were ready for use, or were planned to be used, but never were. It made sense for them to be next to the Acepromazine Maleate. Why wouldn't they be?

In any case, the location of the guns didn't matter. But what did, however was confiscating a pistol or two and getting them past the guard on duty.

Instead, Neil decided to leave the loaded guns where they were for now, and when the moment presented itself to escape, that would be the time to pull them out, point and shoot.

That made more sense. Change of plans.

Chapter 20

In the southern-most wing at the Laboratory, opposite where Neil and Dylan were kept, Kellan was connected to monitors and various contraptions that would tell the doctors if everything was okay with him. They were checking to be sure that there were no injuries or internal damage. It was important to be sure after the fight he had with the Seekers and the tangled net that had been used to confine him.

Honestly, they couldn't permit Kellan to be injured or damaged after all they put into him, and all the years of prepping him for combat. He was a billion dollar project that would be put into action to help ensure everybody's future survival. They were concerned for him.

The clinicians carefully nursed his scratches and bruises back to health before sending him back to his cell where he was able to rest and think about the stupid thing he'd done. They were punishing him for being a bad boy and running away from home.

In the room where Kellan was strapped shirtless to a chair

being examined, his first crush, Seth was also there as part of the medical team.

This time however, Kellan no longer had the affection for Seth that he had before he escaped the facility a few days ago, and Neil was the reason why.

Seth was a good guy, and probably always would be. He never purposely meant to harm Kellan, and would probably never do it intentionally. He was around only as the nurse who took samples of Kellan's blood, shaved his chest, and checked his vitals every now and then. They talked a lot about nothing: it was more like chitchat, played cards, challenged each other with board and computer games, interacted, as well as schooled together. They were like brothers, and as far back as Kellan could remember, Seth was always around. There didn't seem to be a time where Kellan knew Seth to ever be much younger or older than what he was now. The man didn't seem to age. That philosophical bit of evidence got Kellan thinking.

Seth was simply an all-around nice guy, pleasant, carefree, and friendly. Maybe that's why Kellan liked Seth, and confused his kindness with love. Seth always made him feel adored and safe, so in return, Kellan loved him, or thought he did, until he met Neil who really touched his heart and tugged on it, and when that happened, Kellan discovered the difference between love and admiration.

As soon as the medical tests on Kellan were completed, Seth had the honor of taking him back to his room. It was a civilized walk, unlike the one he took earlier when he was manhandled so roughly by the brawny MPs as they dragged him to the lab to be tested. Seth was gentle as usual and treated Kellan as he would his own family. Like a brother.

"Are you doing alright, Kellan?" Seth pushed the cell door open and held it.

"As good as I can be," Kellan answered.

"Why'd you do it?" Seth asked.

"I guess I was tired of feeling trapped. I wanted freedom." Kellan shrugged, and when he did, brushed Seth across the cheek with his wing.

"I wish you could understand, it's not that bad here," Seth said.

"How can you say that? Prison isn't a good place," Kellan said.

"Prison?" Seth leaned in. "Is that what you think of this place?"

"I'm locked up aren't I?" Kellan pointed out.

"You weren't before you left," Seth reminded him.

"I wasn't allowed to go anywhere and haven't been beyond these gates in all the twenty-eight years I've lived here, so that constitutes being locked up if you ask me," Kellan said.

"We've been good to you though, right?" Seth asked.

"Well… Yeah," Kellan answered.

"Okay then," Seth said.

Changing the subject, Kellan asked, "My tests. Did everything look good?"

"Everything was normal. No irregularities or changes in your form. You have a few stress marks on your wings, a few missing feathers, but other than that, you're in excellent condition."

"Really?" Kellan replied.

"Yes, really. You were built to last," Seth said. "You even took down two Seekers and came out of it with hardly a scratch."

"Oh shit, that's right. I forgot about them." Kellan went white. He'd never wanted them to die. He didn't have it in him to hurt anybody and he didn't have a clue where the motivation came from. At the time of the fight as is the case with the male of many species, when danger lurks, instincts to save yourself and those you love go into overdrive.

"It's over and those things have no souls. You didn't kill anybody, Kellan. You were just saving your own skin and it wasn't your fault that the shittin' bat flew into the blades of that chopper. That thing turned off its own lights, not you."

"Those things bleed, Seth. That means there must me some sort of soul in them."

"Listen, those monsters were built, not born like you were. I know what I'm talking about. These… Things… that I never cared for because they can't be trusted, don't give a shit about anything, they don't feel, they don't cry, smile, or even have a name. You can cut off one of their limbs and they won't even scream," Seth said.

"Maybe it's my intellect? I don't know. They have a human form, so to me it's like I hurt a real person," Kellan said.

"Look, they have the body of a human but on the inside they're like a machine built to take orders and obey commands. That's all. So don't dwell on beating the shit out of two monsters that were planning to probably bludgeoning you," Seth said frankly.

Kellan huffed, "The whole thing is fucked up now. I never should have run away from this place. If I hadn't left, none of this would be happening and I wouldn't be a murderer."

"Stop it. You're not a killer and never will be. You just have a conscience and a heart of gold that makes you think you are. If you didn't beat the shit out of them, the military would have. You're far more valuable than those bats. The military never would have let them kill you. The police were there to protect you as well as get you back."

"Wait… what?" Kellan's head tilted. "How do you know that?"

"I've said too much, Kellan." Seth stepped back. "No more questions."

"Alright, enough about the Seekers, but I'm going to ask you one more thing and I need you to honestly give me an answer." Kellan leaned in so close to Seth, he could feel the heat of his peppermint breath.

"Always, what is it?" Seth said.

"There was a man I met outside and I need to know if he's okay?"

Seth looked to the floor. "Can I plead the fifth?"

"No you cannot plead anything," Kellan said.

Seth turned his head to glance over his shoulder, looking for anybody that may be nearby, and for some reason unknown to Kellan, turned his back on him when he spoke. His voice lowered to a whisper. "They brought him here, Kellan. He's in the animal ward with his dog. Locked up."

Kellan thought it was strange that Seth turned his back on him, but smiled anyway when he heard Neil was not dead and he was nearby. Knowing they had Neil locked up in a cage disgusted him, and his smile quickly went crooked and then flattened. "Can you take me to him? I need to see him."

"I can't do that and you know it," Seth said.

"Maybe later?" Kellan pressed.

"I'll find out about him and let you know, that's the best I can do," Seth said.

"Alright, maybe later then," Kellan still pressed.

"That's not what I said." Seth pushed Kellan's shoulder into the room. "I've to get going."

"Wait," Kellan called.

"What is it?" Seth gripped the door handle.

Kellan hesitated a minute before speaking. "I got him into this chaos so I need to make sure he's okay and try to get him out of it. Safely."

"I'll find out what I can for you," Seth said.

"I really like this guy, Seth, so please let me know as early as you can," Kellan pleaded.

"I know you do, and I will," Seth replied. "Shush, someone's coming."

What now?

Kellan shuffled into the cell he was being kept in and turned back toward the door to watch it close. His eyes met Seth's the second the door latched, and he wondered how Seth knew there was something going on between him and Neil.

Seth stood in the hallway looking at Kellan's face through the small glass window in the middle of the door. Kellan's bright eyes were gray with melancholy, and from what Seth could tell, the depression was deep.

And Seth knew why.

They all did.

Chapter 21

"Oh Gawd, Oh Gawd, Oh Gawd." Neil broke out in a sweat and suddenly had a panic attack. It came on like an abrupt thunderstorm on a sunny afternoon. It wasn't supposed to be there and certainly not without warning. There were no signs of it showing up, it just did, and there was no stopping it when it got started.

The cause of the attack, to Neil's knowledge, was a combination of things, mostly the recent events, being locked up as an innocent man, not getting the rest he needed, and what he was planning to do in the next few minutes. All of it added to the anxiety building inside him and he hated every second of it. He needed to get out of there and get out fast, before he exploded from the inside out.

Neil nervously clawed at his thighs while he sat on the edge of the mattress, eyes darting everywhere while he waited for his bath break to be announced. He tried to calm down, but nothing was working. The step he was about to take was a big deal. At least to him it was.

He had his plan laid out in his head, and there was only a short time left before he brought it to fruition. The more he thought about it, the more nauseous he felt, like he was closing in on a jam-packed vomit fest. Ready to blow chunks.

His first mission was to get by the military police outside his door, which was the easy part; he's had that planned for days. If he didn't know any better, he'd think the night time officer was going soft on him, and because of that, Neil was feeling regret for what he was about to do in order to save himself, Dylan, and Kellan. He kept telling himself it was the dart that was going to do it, not him, but the dart. He was going to stick the man with a dart that would drop him into a deep sleep for hours.

"Oh Gawd, Oh Gawd, Oh Gawd," Neil hummed again.

He knew Kellan was in the building someplace, but where, he had no clue. And it didn't help his situation that he didn't know how big the building was, or the layout of it. The whole thing sucked and the chances of a successful breakout were far from being in his favor considering the laboratory was run by the government and laden with MPs. But he had no choice other than to make his great escape happen. He needed to get out before he went even crazier than he thought he already was. If he was, then he was certainly in the right place for it to go down.

Over the next few minutes, Neil just waited. He looked at his wrist as if he had a watch strapped to it and was checking the blasted thing for the time, but was quickly startled when he heard the lock on the door handle click a couple of times. Pulling his gaze from his invisible watch, Neil spun toward the door and watched it open.

Neil's jaw tightened when the man who walked in was not the military police he was expecting.

Damn, release plan meltdown.

"Neil?" the man said as he entered.

"Yes," Neil answered.

"Are you doing okay?" The man repeatedly snapped the clip on his document folder like he had a nervous twitch.

"Fine," Neil spoke shortly.

"Good to hear."

"Are you here to escort me to the bathing room?" Neil

asked.

"No. I'm just here to check on you, make sure you're doing okay."

Neil tilted his head, wondering why this new person showed up today of all days. Was he here to spoil his plan? Did they know?

"Is there anything you need?" the kind man asked.

Neil shook his head.

The man stood in front of Neil, almost too close for comfort because the room was so small, opened up his document folder and turned it toward Neil. Inside was a quick note written on parchment paper that said Kellan was alright and the two of them would be together soon.

Neil's jaw dropped and a slight smile graced his face. "What's going on? How do you know this?" He began to calm down.

"I have to get back up to my floor, but Kellan wanted me to let you know he's okay. I will tell him the same about you."

"Wait." Neil stood up. "Who are you and why are you telling me this?"

"I'm Seth, a longtime friend of Kellan's. I was assigned to take care of him in his later years here, watch him grow up, help him find his way."

"Where is he?" Neil begged.

"He's safe and the tests show he's healthier than a steroid fed fox. That's all I can say."

"What tests? I thought you said he was okay?"

"Just standard tests we always do on him. Other than a few scratches that'll heal overnight, he's solid," Seth assured.

"Will I be able to see him soon?" Neil asked.

Seth tilted his head and smiled without giving an answer. That's it, just smiled, and Neil couldn't read anything from the stunted motion.

Was that a yes or a no?

Getting nothing, Neil coiled downward like a snake and sat on the bed as Seth left him alone in the room. At the same time, the MP outside stepped in and waved for him to follow, presumably giving Neil the okay to take his bath time break.

Chapter 22

This was it.

Turning back once, Neil strolled with a casual whistle into the pet grooming room where he flipped on the sprayer that would help conceal the noise he'd be making while rummaging through the drawers for the gun and drugs he needed to pull off his escape.

While he reached for the single dart gun he had hidden in the drawer beneath the tub, Neil sang a song from the eighties he always liked. It helped stabilize his nerves somewhat as well as made it appear he was actually in the tub taking the bath he was supposed be taking. The last thing he needed was the MP showing up unexpectedly to watch his bath time ritual as he sometimes does.

Crouched against the tub, Neil made sure the gun was loaded, and then peeked around the door frame to see where the MP was located. Ideally, the man would be right where Neil needed him to be, outside in the common area with his back to him, where the perfect shot would be right in the ass. A meaty spot, it will take the shot deep without biting bone or taking out an internal organ.

With nerves rattled more than ever, Neil changed his words from the calming eighties pop lyrics to, "Oh shit, oh shit, oh shit. Fuck me up the ass." He felt like shouting for moral support.

When Neil emerged, gun level with his shoulders, he quietly tip toed through the supply room toward the military policeman standing guard. His hands were shaking due to unsettled nerves, and he hoped it wouldn't fuck up his shot, but he pressed on and aimed the gun at the buns of steel in front of him. "Fuck me," he said again.

Just then, he saw the MP lift his head from the magazine he was reading, but before he turned around, Neil squeezed the trigger. Within seconds, the tranquilizer dart entered the man's ass, the sting of it caught him off guard, and before he knew what stuck him, he went down.

The noise like a toppling building echoed around the room when the man with the grimacing face fell across the tabletop he was standing next to. Sleeping, he lay flat on his stomach with his arms hanging over the edge, one swinging side to side like a dangling rope. No movement from the man other than shallow breathing told Neil he was out cold, hopefully for a while.

Flash-like, Neil ran up to the MP and grabbed the messenger bag hung over his shoulder, dumped everything out of it, and then pulled the magnetic ID card from his belt that would give him access to any door in the building.

Neil pedaled backward to the refrigerator while keeping an eye on the guard the entire time, making sure the man planned on staying frozen where he lay. Any sudden movements out of him and another dart was going in his ass, or better yet up it. Neil grabbed every gun he'd loaded earlier with tranquilizer darts, pulled extra equipment and drugs from the shelves, and stuffed everything in the bag so it was ready to use.

Out of the blue, Dylan barked, reminding Neil not to forget him, which made the monkey across the room bellow like a badass bitch. Neil thought quickly, and threw a banana bunch into the monkey's cage so he'd shut the hell up. Within a split second of letting the bananas go, Neil raced across the room to get

Dylan.

They hugged a few seconds, and then took off.

With Dylan creeping behind, Neil slumped deep in the gloomy recesses of the building, looking for anything that would lead him to Kellan.

Wherever they were located inside the building, it was dark and dank like a basement. Why they kept the place so hot and dark was a mystery to Neil. Hospitals were supposed to be well lit and cold.

Neil pushed past many rooms. Some were empty, but most were filled with random junk that didn't make any sense as to why those particular items were grouped together in them.

Neil expected the place to be filled with more than what he saw, like more people, lab centers, equipment, experiments gone wrong. But from his viewpoint, it was lacking all of those things.

Weird. Where the hell was he?

For assurance, Neil had one hand on the dart gun at all times with intentions of pulling the trigger if anybody popped out of a corner or a crevice. The only thing he hoped for was that he had enough ammo to take down anybody that got in his way.

His mission started on a floor he thought to be underground, but the windowless structure made it impossible for him to be sure. The darkness in the depressed corridors made him think he was *well* below ground. How far down, he didn't know.

"A fucking directory sign would help," Neil talked to himself and to Dylan if he was listening.

Neil remembered Seth mentioning he had to get back up to his floor, which made Neil think the direction they needed to go was up as well.

Neil trekked one foot at a time, quickly but cautiously until he came to a room where a monitor was on and the screen showed movement like there was a camera attached to a helmet or a set of goggles. Somebody had left the room unattended with the monitor running, which Neil found to be very odd. Was it break-time or did everybody retire for the night?

Making no mistake, Neil punched the visual search mode on the computer and watched the monitor scan many areas of the building. The images changed every ten seconds and it made him dizzy. He had to step away for a second before going back to see if he could find anything that would point him to where Kellan might be. His education with computers helped him navigate well enough to find a few things, which meant poking around the system was quick and easy.

He stumbled on a detailed topographical map of the building, and wherever there was a camera positioned, there were pings of red that blinked on and off. He figured them to be the active ones, so he clicked on one to see what it was aimed at. The image popped up into view on another screen next to the one he was working on and it showed yet another empty room, but this time in the corner was a burning lamp that glowed red. To him it meant that there were light sensitive objects, items for research of some kind in that room. Perhaps photographic material that would be damaged if exposed to any light, or other creatures that could only withstand the evening sky or the red synthetic light. He wasn't interested in finding out, so he moved the switch to another light on the map and clicked the mouse.

Dylan stood patiently by his side like the good dog that he was, watching the door they had come through the whole time.

Neil clicked on a different camera and that's when he saw it. The room he was looking for. That quick. He could see Kellan in the small room, and from what Neil could tell, he was doing fine, but sitting sadly in the corner looking out a bleary window. There was no visible sun beyond the glass and to Neil it looked like it was raining outside. He couldn't hear a thunderstorm, which reinforced the idea he was probably underground.

Neil watched the camera reposition a few inches to one side, while still staying focused on Kellan. Somebody else in another area of the building was controlling its angle, because he was sure he didn't touch anything in front of him to make it move. The controller was most likely stationed outside Kellan's door. It was hard to tell.

Neil kept watching the camera move, trying to get an idea where Kellan was, like a room number or a landmark. Something. Anything.

The only thing Neil could do to figure out where Kellan was inside the building was to try to see what was outside Kellan's window when the camera moved past it, look for a tree, or a car, a bush, structural landmarks, something that would help him when he finally reached a window he could look out of.

Neil felt like he was running out of time. He needed to hurry for many reasons, but most of all, he wanted to get Kellan back in his arms. His plan had to work. It was a must.

Finally after a few minutes, the camera moved back to Kellan and crossed in front of the window. Neil leaned in closer to see what was outside. Through the raindrops he could see there was a parking lot down below and the rooftop corner of what looked like a portico or entrance for emergency vehicles. He could also see a large stone fountain that might suggest the front of the building. From what he gathered, it appeared that Kellan was someplace on the third floor, maybe a fourth if one existed.

Back to the graphic layout of the building on the screen to his right, Neil tried to put the puzzle pieces together, place Kellan someplace on the map. He minimized the graph, but there was still nothing to go on. It only showed outlines of rooms and locations of cameras, no labels, room numbers or even which level of the building he was looking at. Useless.

Neil's nerves were rocking and his eyes were blurring. It was time to take this dog and pony show to the next three-ring circus.

He left everything as it was and called on Dylan to follow.

They crept back out into the corridor and followed the yellow line running the length of the floor that would hopefully take them somewhere closer to their goal.

For no reason, Neil ran his hand along the wall as they walked, as Dylan pranced beside him. Up ahead but not very clear was what looked like a glowing exit sign, and alongside it was a yellow placard that displayed a set of stairs with a stick figured man with no feet floating up them. A good sign to see and possibly the only way out.

Getting ready, Neil gripped the tranquilizer gun in his hand for protection against unexpected invaders.

Neil moved slowly, one foot at a time, gun held against his shoulder, ready to drop in to position and fire if anyone popped out of the dark in front of them. He breathed deep and made the corner. In front of him was nothing but a shallow cove with two elevator lifts and a closed door with a set of stairs behind it that headed up. Perfect, they were on the right track.

Thinking they were the smarter choice, Neil decided to take the stairs. A running lift would only bring attention to him that he didn't need.

He ran the access card through the magnetic reader and the latch on the door clicked. Another good sign they were on their way out.

Neil whispered to Dylan to follow and they both took the steps two at a time.

Gun still propped and ready.

They passed two sets of doors on the way up, one that read Floor One and the other was labeled Floor Two. Before he opened up the door that said they were on Floor Three, he pulled in a deep, soothing breath. There were no windows in the door to check for danger on the other side, which meant he had to be ready for whatever was waiting for them when he opened it.

He ran the card, cracked the door open slowly, and spotted someone in the hallway, thankfully with his back to the door.

Shocked as Neil was, the man in black spun around and pointed a pistol at him without even checking to see who was there. Neil backed up and let the door slam shut. On the other side, a foot stopped it and the door flew back open.

Falling back, Neil pumped one off and a dart stuck in the man's meaty thigh just above the knee.

"Fuck me." Neil threw himself against the wall, pushed Dylan to the other side, and watched the military man roll head over heels to the bottom of the stairway where he lay unconscious and drugged.

"Fuck me twice," Neil said again, chest heaving, out of breath.

Neil stuffed another dart in the empty gun chamber, noticeably shaking from rocking nerves. He clicked the shuttle pump a few times to get it ready for another fire, and as he did, he heard movement on the other side of the metal door.

"How the fuck are we supposed to get through that door?" he whispered to Dylan.

The look on Dylan's face purely said, '*Not*'.

A better idea and what Dylan thought exactly, was not to go through it at all. Instead, Neil took the stairs up to the fourth floor, where all the flights going up terminated. "This is it, Dylan. We either go through this one or we don't go in at all."

Neil heard an awkward approach creeping up behind him. He was exhausted, physically and mentally, but he was ready to blast darts and fistfight if necessary. In his hand he carried the loaded tranquilizer gun, and unfortunately the time to fire it had approached again.

Neil turned, leveled the gun and squeezed the trigger.

POP

The dart spun fast and penetrated the left shoulder of the man coming at them. It was another MP who quickly dropped on his ass, and then backslid head first down the bumpy steps. When he finally reached bottom, the man looked dead.

"Fuck me again. Dammit!" Before entering door number four, Neil pressed an ear against it. The steel was warm, on the verge of being hot. His eyes circled in their sockets as he listened and heard nothing.

Neil was still breathing heavy. "Why don't any of these doors have windows, dammit?"

Dylan moved in, sniffed the crack at the base of the door, backed up a few steps, and looked from Neil to the handle as if telling him it was okay to open it up. Dylan was trying to say nobody was there or at least he couldn't pick up a scent.

"Good boy, Dylan." Neil ran the card through the reader and crept slowly through the door with Dylan a half step beside him.

It was quiet, and as Dylan suspected, there was nobody around. The emptiness was eerie, and being alone was a good feeling after the last door bust at Level Three and the recent rear invasion behind door number four.

It seemed as though Dylan and Neil ended up someplace in the middle of the laboratory housing. The corridor went left as well as right.

Neil turned to a window on the left side of the stairwell and looked out. Down below he saw the fountain and the portico at the end of the building that were displayed on the camera in Kellan's room. He was getting closer and the view from the window made it known to go left.

Things were about the get worse. Neil could feel it.

Before moving another inch, he prepared himself by pulling out two of the guns from the messenger bag. He held them with a death grip at his sides, knuckles white with bloodlessness.

Shit, he was nervous.

Every step Neil took, his heart rate skyrocketed, and he swore it reached one-hundred thirty beats per minute within the first five steps. He could hear the boom in his ears at the same time he felt the pulse in his neck. It was crazy. Was he fucked?

They both crept through the spooky hallway, Neil with his back pressed tightly against the wall, while Dylan sidestepped him a couple steps ahead.

The fourth floor was strangely quiet, which left Neil to deliberate if his next move was a wise one. Going against the voice in his head that screamed *go back,* he still sneaked forward like there were pins and needles under his feet.

The closer they got to the end of the corridor, the more they were able to hear quiet noises from inside the rooms up head. Neil wasn't quite sure yet, but it sounded to him like hums of printers, digital processors and cooling fans, all of them overpowering voices within each room.

Neil went to another window, looked out and could tell they were getting closer to Kellan, the fountain and the portico outside was just ahead.

Sensing the distance closing between good and evil, Neil gripped the pistols in both hands, fingered the triggers, and prepped to shoot.

As a measure to protect Dylan, Neil took him to a room close by and told him to stay.

On his way back through the corridor alone, Neil snuck toward the end of the hall where he thought Kellan was being kept. The lights were on so it had to be it.

The closer Neil got to the end, clinical technicians appeared and disappeared, walking from one room to another, muttering nonsense, and thankfully not paying attention to anything but what they were doing.

The only way for Neil to pull off his mission was to blend in, take to the halls wearing a confiscated lab coat, and appear as part of the night crew. There were very few on staff at night so going unnoticed would be less of a chore.

Despite his growing anxiety, Neil slipped into action to rescue the man he was falling in love with. There was no turning back.

Holding his head down, Neil walked by two technicians who walked on by without looking up or acknowledging that he was there.

Perfect.

At a quicker pace, Neil scrambled for the last door on the left where he thought Kellan was, swiped his card, and walked right in. He rolled along the wall and tucked himself under the camera he knew was above his head to the left.

Neil's favorite words came out of Kellan, "Fuck me."

Shushing Kellan, Neil pressed a finger to his lips. He finally exhaled and then smiled at Kellan.

Kellan's eyes automatically rolled toward the camera and then back down on Neil. They happily watered a little when he saw him. "You scared me," he said.

Neil whispered even though the walls were solid. "Stay right there." He raised a hand and then pointed above his head at the security cam.

There was a spark that shot from Kellan's eye that made Neil blink, resembling the flash of an instamatic camera. What the fuck?

Without warning, the door to Kellan's room blew open with a bang and with it came two MPs holding rifles. Big ones that looked like cannons. A screech from the hallway rang out and then the place went silent.

Startled, Kellan froze and Neil slumped to the floor to stay hidden.

Too late, the MPs aimed the guns at Kellan. But before they got shots off, Neil pummeled their asses with darts.

In a snakelike twist, both MP's spun to the floor where they lay with each other in a restful heap, like one was butt fucking the other.

"Holy fuck, Neil," Kellan said. "You killed them."

Neil jumped up. "No, these are just tranqs. They're only sleeping. Let's get out of here. Hurry." He grabbed the semi-automatic weapons from the two slumbering guards, wrapped one over his shoulder and tossed the other one to Kellan.

Kellan pulled his wings in, caught the weapon, jumped over top of the two men on the floor and followed Neil out the door in one quick breath.

Neil blasted the weapons at the ceiling in the hall as a way of clearing a path.

Another terrified scream echoed from a clinician as Kellan and Neil raced by.

A different voice yelled, "Shoot 'em. Don't let 'em get away!"

"Get to the elevator, Neil. I'll hold them off," Kellan ordered.

"No, you're coming with us. Dylan - come!" Neil hollered, slapping a palm against his thigh.

Kellan's bare chest expanded as he stood sturdy, pointing the gun from his extended arm at the men running toward him. Squeezing the trigger, he fired several rounds, but only at the ceiling.

Everybody below the blasts dropped, and as they did, Kellan spun with flapping wings and shot like a bullet down the corridor toward Neil, passing him until he reached the elevator where he stopped and called it to their floor.

Neil and Dylan hit top speed to get to the elevator. In stride, Neil pulled two more loaded pistols from his bag and tapped the safety keys to off.

Behind them, footfalls were closing in and a voice hollered, "Don't let 'em get out. Shoot the fuckers. Shoot them."

Like a warrior, Neil barreled down the corridor with both guns in hand. He dropped to the floor, spin-sliding on his knees while squeezing the triggers on both guns, fired one shot after the other, and watched two more men go down. As he got up to run, he spun backward on one foot while at the same time he pulled another gun out and shot the last man running toward them.

Neil was a super virus, eager to infect anybody that got in his way. He was fucking impressive with a gun, fucking awesome. Like a born sniper. He popped people off like a pro.

Dylan's nails clicked across the slippery floor as he tried to stop. All four feet back pedaling until he crazily banged into Kellan's feet.

Jamming fingers into the elevator call button, Kellan

screeched, "Fuck this thing. It's too slow. Get to the stairs."

Neil's forward momentum finally stopped when he reached Kellan and Dylan. Sparing no time, not even a second to breathe, he swiped the security card that opened the stairwell door. "Go—Go—Go!" He pushed.

Dylan groaned when Kellan picked him up and they took off down the steps at lightning speed.

"Get off at the second floor. Nobody ever uses it and we can figure our way from there," Kellan ordered.

In less than a minute they were on the second floor standing cautiously in the corridor when they heard a noise down the north wing that sounded like clinic technicians coming their way.

Kellan whispered, "This way, quickly."

Neil and Kellan ran past a lab-like room, out of sight from the others. A door in the far wall led into a smaller, less congested room containing a few pieces of furniture. There were mostly computers, printers and processors in there that looked like the heart of a control center.

They looked at the monitors steadily, ignoring Neil's stomach growling. Probably due to nerves, because he certainly wasn't hungry.

The image on the monitor was peculiar and it was exactly the same thing they were both looking at right then, like two facing mirrors reflecting the others image that goes on forever. They both looked into the screen that took them as far as the eye could see.

Without looking away from the screen, Neil reached for Kellan's jaw and turned it toward him. In an instant, the side of Neil's face was clearly posted on the monitor, recognizably coming from Kellan's eye. "Fuck me."

Neil paused as if to give Kellan time to reply, rubbed his hand across his mouth, really feeling twitchy with an onset of a headache.

Kellan whispered, "No, Fuck me." He had no expression, his face crusted with blood because he'd been hit by something during their race through the halls.

Minutes went by before Neil spoke, "An implant. A mother fucking implant. That explains how they always knew where we were. Oh, Gawd, they know everything. Everything we've done."

"And said," Kellan added.

Neil glanced at Kellan and then at the door, "Kellan," he said, with a tone of urgency grinding his voice. "We need to get out of here, but first, should we fix that eye?"

"Shit to hell!" Kellan squawked. "I need to see."

"No, we'll look for the main server and smash it. Blow the fucker to bits." Neil said. "Do you know where it is? Hurry, where is it?"

"It's gotta be in here somewhere," Kellan said.

"Look for the coolest spot. Quick. Those things need to be kept cold," Neil mentioned. He looked across the ceiling for any large air ducts that may be blowing air. That was a start.

Kellan quickly looked out the doorway to make sure they were alone.

"Over here. I think I found it," Neil said. "Watch the screen and tell me if it goes off."

Instead of walking, Kellan flew over and landed in front of the monitor that was looking back at him in a weird way.

Neil lifted a clear protector cap on the server and flipped the switch downward.

Kellan hollered. "It's off. You found it. The son-of-a-bitch is off."

"We need to move fast, because everybody who is viewing a monitor just experienced the same thing we did."

Nemil pulled the semi-automatic rifle from his shoulder and held it against his chest. "Get ready. This is going to shut down the brain when I start firing."

Kellan picked Dylan up and carried him to the hallway so the both of them were away from flying debris and blasting noise. "We're ready," he said.

Neil walked backward as he pulled the trigger. Over a hundred rounds went off, popping motherboards from where they stood to Mars. Electrical sparks flew everywhere with each connecting bullet. The whole place shattered like a bomb went off.

"Neil. Look out." Kellan pushed Dylan down the hallway like a bowling ball and then flew over to Neil and whirled him out of the way and against the wall.

A screech from the south wing came barreling at them like thunder, tackling Kellan to the floor in a knotted ball.

Kellan back rolled, kicking the Seeker off him, sending it spinning like propeller blades across the waxy floor. Its leathery wings smacking against tile, sounding as though they were wet.

Neil wanted to shoot, but couldn't risk hitting Kellan. He pounded on the elevator key to call it to their floor. "Fuck, fuck, fuck. Dylan, come."

Kellan snapped his wings and flew over to Neil where he stood firm, chest out like armored steel, and then pushed Neil toward the elevator door behind his wings.

Screaming, the Seeker rushed for Kellan, but Kellan moved aside and took Neil with him.

Unable to stop in time, the Seeker smashed into the elevator door and tumbled down the shaft, taking broken steel with it and snapping cables along the way.

As quickly as the Seeker disappeared down the shaft, it flew back up and looked right at them, and this time its breath was as hot as fire.

Neil squeezed the triggers, one and then two, expelling a shot of Acepromazine Maleate from each pistol. One sank into the Seeker's thigh, and a second one punctured its chest, sending it back down the shaft like a heavy rock.

Kellan grabbed both Neil and Dylan into his arms and jumped into the elevator shaft where they dropped down onto the rooftop of the lift's car. Next to them lay the crumpled Seeker Neil just took out.

"Stand back." Kellan gripped the steel doors and folded the metal back. He pushed them aside and helped Dylan and Neil boost themselves to the main floor in the lobby.

"Get to the exit. We don't have much time. They'll be after us soon." Kellan pulled himself up and rushed them to the laboratory's front entrance.

The darkness swallowed them up and they disappeared into the night.

Chapter 23

Invigorated by a rush of adrenaline, Kellan generated heat that felt to Neil like the sun was radiating against his skin.

With Dylan in one arm and Neil holding tight to the other, Kellan's speed dragged to a slower burn. That was better for the time being and the tranquility of a slower pace brought them to a calmer place.

They headed north over the bay and then up the coast to Neil's house. It might have been a big risk but they had no other place to go and it probably made some sense to see how badly it had been destroyed.

The run down lighthouse on the island in the middle of Lake Michigan was the only other place they knew of where they could fly to, but if they were being followed by the military police, Kellan preferred to keep their only safe residence to themselves for now.

"Are you sure you want to go to the house?" Kellan asked.

"I do," said Neil. "I've already seen what happened to it, so the shock factor has passed. Just keep your eyes peeled for those flying bat men." In mid-flight Neil wanted to kiss Kellan desperately, but facing the ground made that task too difficult to pull off.

Night had fallen across the foothills south of town, and with the moon hidden someplace behind the clouds, the blackened sky seemed darker.

Unlike Kellan's, Neil's vision was limited, but the lights twinkling on the suspension bridge up ahead of them meant his house was somewhere down below on the right, and from that, he had a good idea where they were. Part of him was happy to be back home, away from that miserable cell, yet his sane side had reservations about seeing his house in a condition he didn't want to see it in.

Compared to any trip by roadway, the flight was quicker, only taking about twenty minutes from the bay in Traverse City to the coast of Mackinac City.

Neil felt Kellan's shoulder drop to one side, and with it went his wing. The slight shift took them in a wide descending circle out over the water and then back again, giving Neil the impression they were closing in on the house.

The wide circle Kellan made grew tighter the closer to the ground they got, feet dangling as Kellan back flapped to set Neil down.

As drained as Neil was feeling, he figured it was close to midnight or a bit later. He'd reached the point of total exhaustion but wasn't sure if it was due to how late it was or from the trauma he just endured brought on by their laboratory escape.

The air was stagnant when they landed, no wind at all, and silent, not a sound. The stillness seemed fitting for what Neil and Kellan were going to encounter next.

With the absence of Neil's house, they were in a dark clearing circled by broken trees. Many had been pushed back from the blast, some were still standing but lying low.

It was unsettling to see all over again. Neil thought he'd be okay with it, flat like that, but he wasn't. He kept trying to tell himself that it's just a house, and that a house could be rebuilt; however the sting of losing a home stayed with him no matter how hard he tried to rid his thoughts of it.

Until a short time ago, Neil's house was standing full of life with an inviting doorway. But looking at the condition it was in struck a nerve with Neil. It was his family home, it had been for years, and now it was gone and all of its memories went with it.

Kellan flipped his wings out of the way before weaving an arm over Neil's shoulder to pull him closer to his side. "You gonna be alright?"

"Yeah, I'll be fine," said Neil. "It's just a little shocking to see it like this again."

"We can go if you'd like. We don't need to be here," Kellan said.

"No, it's okay. I'm good." Neil crossed his arms over his chest and put a hand over Kellan's.

Dylan let out a yip, letting them know he was there to provide doggie type support. As usual, he was a good distraction from an unsettling situation. Dylan had the ability to change Neil's mood even during the worst of times. He was remarkable like that.

Kellan stretched a wing open, moved it down and nudged Dylan on the hind end to corral him closer to them. They huddled together like a tight knit family.

"Okay, enough gloom. Let's say we head out of here," Neil said.

Kellan agreed, but gave Neil full authority to decide when.

"Thank you, Kellan," Neil mentioned.

"For what?" Kellan said.

"For being here and for saving my life back there."

"Remember, you came to get me," Kellan said.

"I wouldn't have made it out of there without your set of wings though." Neil spun in Kellan's arms and grabbed his hands.

"The wings helped, yes. But you were amazing with those firearms. I was impressed with the way you handled the guns." Kellan scanned the sky, above the trees and out across the lake, checking for invaders, just making sure.

Neil grinned. He was no marksman or sniper, so his untrained natural ability to shoot a mean pistol surprised him too. He put his hands over Kellan's shoulders and locked his fingers together behind his head and held them there.

Kellan's wings quivered and stood up. "Why'd you do it?"

"You mean come get you?" Neil asked.

"Yes. What turned you into a superhero for me?" asked Kellan.

Neil smiled. "Because I missed you."

"But you just met me," Kellan said.

"Doesn't matter," Neil said. "I like you so it made me miss you."

"Damn, I was worried about you." Kellan ran his hands along Neil's arms, from his wrists to his shoulders, around his back, and into a hug. He gave Neil a kiss that went deep, taking as much of him as he could. He wanted Neil, he needed him.

Chapter 24

Kellan let go of a wry smile as his wings spread open to funnel the cool night air against his bare skin. His wings wafted wide at his sides to take hold of the breeze that lifted them both off the ground and spun them to the music of an orchestra that only they could hear. The heat between them spiraled and with the kiss that tied their hearts, they drifted away to dreamland.

They were airborne again, but this time they were falling in love. The earth below them spun away while the pleasing wind lifted and held them in an impenetrable place.

From the moment they left the ground, Neil weakened in Kellan's embrace. An urge to connect with the angelic man swept over him, and his raging erection came back without a hitch, pushing forward alongside Kellan's.

Trembling from Neil's intense invasion, Kellan pulled him tighter against the bulk of his chest, and kissed him deep with a dancing tongue. Kellan's heart sped up and the heat within him changed the cool air around them to a warm breeze.

Their lust reached an intense level, and the impulse to trade specific genetic matter from one to the other was rushing both their minds.

All of a sudden Kellan froze as though an ice block had just been swiped down his spine. The strange feeling that they were being watched rolled over him, and he stopped and squinted through the darkness, looking around. The fine hair on the back of his neck stood up and his senses geared up for another battle. He knew trouble was lurking, he felt it closing in on them, and it seemed to be coming fast.

Neil sensed an instant change in Kellan's emotions that let him know there was something wrong. Neil's heart stopped and then jumped into his throat where it stayed a few seconds before dropping back to his chest.

Within seconds of feeling danger closing in, cracking noises snapped through the sound barrier. Trees and foliage broke open as several Seekers abruptly emerged and went after Neil and Kellan. The beasts sliced through thick woody brambles, snapping branches before taking to the sky like a swarm of stinging hornets bursting with anger at whoever disturbed their nest with a bludgeoning stick.

Where did they come from and when did they get there?

The power swelled inside Kellan, flowing up and out of his center to group in his furled wings. He locked Neil in his grip, took to the ground and lifted Dylan in the other arm. The disadvantage Kellan had against the Seekers stung him, but he was made for war, he could take them on.

Screaming, the Seekers surrounded them at every turn, black wings flapping angrily with thuds loud as thunder.

Kellan peered into the darkness and made a snap decision to fly straight up. In midflight, he dipped his shoulder and lurched into a sharp upward circle, forcing his foot into the chest of the Seeker reaching out to grab him, propelling the creature backward out of the way. Kellan screeched as loud as the Seeker and almost breathed fire when he did. His body was hot and the flaming fury within him needed release.

Neil reached for Dylan, bringing him down to let him hang beside the messenger bag around his neck.

To the right, Kellan flew, wings beating hard, up and down.

Behind them, a small flock of Seekers soared, five, maybe six of them. They were moving too fast to count, and the problem lay with their being only one of Kellan, slowed down by the load he carried, and many of them.

Kellan heard the whup, whup, whup of choppers that followed before actually seeing two of them up ahead, guns in position, aimed right for him, and ready to shoot. He quickly identified a swirl of air that chased after a dart speeding his way. He dipped, spiraled downward, out of the dart's path. As it passed overhead, it clipped the bell of his wing at the joint, scattered a few feathers, and dug deep in the skull of a Seeker attacking from behind.

The screeching monster flipped backward, dropped from the sky like lead weight, tumbling and twisting toward earth. With a deadweight splash, it hit Lake Michigan at the north side of the bay. From there it vanished and went under water.

As if brakes had been put on, Kellan stopped and went up at a sharp ninety degrees. Straight up without stopping, spinning like a corkscrew the whole way.

Below Kellan, without their notice, a Seeker grabbed his ankle and tugged. Kellan lurched backward that caused Neil to drop Dylan.

"Dylan!" Neil yelled, struggling to get away and reach for him.

In an instant, Kellan side kicked the Seeker's skull, throwing it into the path of the second dart that was intended for him or Neil. The stinking fucker went down, landing next to its battle buddy already at the bottom of the lake.

Only seconds flashed by after breaking free from the Seeker's grasp when Kellan rolled wings down to press Neil as hard as he could off his chest into the sky, growling as he did. A millisecond after releasing Neil, he flipped back over, drove unbreakable wing beats toward his feet that sent him speeding toward Dylan where he snatched him within an inch of hitting water. Spinning quickly, Kellan shot back up toward Neil, who was coming down, catching him in one arm, and setting them in a wild spiral, Dylan in one arm, Neil in the other.

Kellan sensed the Seekers rapidly approaching from the rear before he saw them. He turned back to check the distance between them, meeting their eyes, that were dark and expressionless. The rest of the Seeker's faces were a festival of gore, their razor-like teeth snapping with every screech.

Kellan hollered, "Do you still have the guns?"

Nervously Neil scratched for the messenger bag, clawing for it as it swished beneath him. "Uh, yeah... yeah. Yes, I do."

"Use them," Kellan yelled.

Shaking, Neil lost his grip on the bag three times. "I can't get it."

Kellan did his best to fly steady. "You can. You have to."

The choppers were zipping around them, pumping out shots in rapid succession.

Kellan swerved several times, dodging darts.

Everything shook, and Neil lost his grip on the bag again.

Kellan dipped below the chopper that spun in front of them, forcing the messenger bag against Neil's chest.

Gripping tight, Neil reached for the gun, pulled it from the bag and aimed.

"Shoot 'em. Shoot 'em. Shoot 'em. Now!" Kellan circled around to face the rancid creatures. "Take the shot."

Just when Kellan spun to face the Seeker, a disturbing squeal pierced their ears as the maddest Seeker in the pod side kicked Kellan's feet to one side, spinning Kellan, and at the same time jolting Neil's aim off kilter.

Neil's throat closed when he lost his grip on the gun, and watched it spiral toward earth. "Dammit. Fuck."

Kellan shot higher to regain control, heaved Neil and Dylan into place, spun around, and took off toward the two Seekers that continued terrorizing them from behind. "This is it. Grab any guns you have left. These fuckers are going down."

"Got two, that's it," hollered Neil. His shaking hands reached inside the bag for the remaining guns. He held one in each hand, tightly. He closed his eyes and begged, only wanting two good shots at them, just one lethal, brain splattering shot each that would put the Seekers out of their misery for good, or at least to sleep. That's all he wanted.

Kellan pushed his wings back one more time, tapping his heels, and they soared at top speed into the breath of the Seekers.

Neil's heart raced and he lifted the pistols to fire. For a split second, he squeezed his eyes shut, and when he opened them, they were face to face with the angered Seekers. As quick as that.

Kellan flipped his wings in a way that slowed their flight.

Inches in front of them, the Seekers roared.

"Now," Kellan spat.

Neil leveled the two pistols, one in each hand, and seconds apart, he squeezed the triggers.

POW, POW. The darts pierced the Seeker's midriffs and they went down like the others.

Before the choppers had a chance to get a lock on Kellan and shoot, he pulled his wings in tightly and they instantly dropped.

The last Seeker tailed them, swinging its clawed fingers at Kellan's feet, screaming a death knell during the harried chase.

Like a fast-moving torpedo, Kellan sped northeast toward the suspension bridge, zigzagging, spinning and back tracking to upset the choppers strategic flight, confuse them and hopefully make them crash.

Kellan plummeted and flew under the bridge where he circled back around the south tower. Chasing him, the Seeker and both choppers tagged his ass, one behind the other.

The Seeker still clawed and screeched, working its last nerve to snag Kellan's feet and take him, Neil and Dylan out of the sky.

At close range, the choppers thumped, hacking at airspace.

Kellan circled the tower a second time, followed by a third, and on the forth revolution, he shot straight up, then zipped way out and back again, and headed straight for the cables on the bridge.

As he planned, the choppers whizzed behind Kellan, not missing a beat and mimicking his movements. They chased him, out, around, and back again.

Kellan powered his wings harder, extended them to full width as he rotated on his side and buzzed between the cables on a downward trajectory.

Behind him, the Seeker and the choppers hunted him.

Violently, engines revved and fought to wind down, but their speed kept them moving forward. Sparks flashed as the two choppers bit and snarled in tune with the other, trying to pull out of a mad hawks fight against momentum in the sky. End over end they cart wheeled into the suspension cables where Kellan wanted them to go, and there they tugged at metal that tossed fiery sparks to the bridge's pavement down below. In a twisted mess, the choppers ripped into cables, tangling them with the dying blades. Screeching metal on metal, they flipped nose over tail down the snapping steel cables where they landed in a diesel-fueled fireball at the base of the bridge, nearly taking out the few cars traveling the road that late at night. The bridge shook from the choppers' impact before they blade-chopped across the pavement to the edge and teetered into the water with an enormous splash and sank.

Chapter 25

Kellan tucked his wing in on one side so they'd spin around in time to see the fiery helicopters go down below the water's surface. The sizzling flames could be heard from where they were and the bridge swayed in front of them.

Broken cables dangled toward the water as if sending down ropes to any survivors.

While watching the choppers sink from a distance, Kellan also spotted the last Seeker crazily flying toward them. It seemed to be injured, but being familiar with its chaotic flight pattern, he had to assume it wasn't. The only Seeker left and it was built like a warrior.

Kellan knew the chase wouldn't be over until the Seeker was extinct. He had to first fight it off and then get Neil and Dylan back to the lighthouse where they would be secluded and somewhat safer than they were.

Beneath Kellan, Neil was gasping. Not because he was exhausted but from the constricting hold Kellan had on him.

"Son-of-a-BITCH!" Kellan snapped.

"What now?" Neil grunted.

"I need to set you two down someplace so I can finish off that last Seeker," said Kellan.

"Oh shit, is that one of them coming now?" Neil sounded panicked.

"It is." Kellan spun around and flew north, running the length of the bridge as his guide.

"There's a huge empty forest northwest of the bridge with nothing but woods and water. I think its Hiawatha National or something like that. You can drop that piece of shit in one of the lakes up there or feed him to the coyotes."

"Shit, here it comes again." Kellan used the wind under his wings to push them forward, racing against time to get to where Neil suggested. "You have any more darts?"

"None left. I used every one of them." Neil squeezed the bag to be sure.

The seeker was gaining speed, coming up on their left at about one-hundred miles per hour. The bastard was fast, but Kellan was faster.

"Hang on," Kellan said, gripping Neil and Dylan tighter still.

"Oh, Gawd." Neil just about had enough.

They chased wind for what seemed like two or three minutes when they finally crossed from water to land. Kellan veered left and shot bullet-like to the forest where not much of anything was. It was pitch black for miles and the place smelled like pine and maple.

Not more than fifty feet behind them, the Seeker was trailing, bobbing bat-like, swerving everywhere.

The Seekers were fast and strong, and could tear up the sky and whoever was in it with mean fists and sharp teeth.

At their rear and flying faster, the Seeker gained speed and flew closer to Kellan, clipping his heel with its clawed hand.

Kellan's instincts heightened and he ripped through the sky like a MiG-29, dived toward an open clearing where he was able to let Dylan and Neil down until he had the Seeker belly up in the lake. As he left them, Kellan looked down, dropped one arm in a sweeping wave that threw a kiss from his lips to the man he was falling in love with. A thumbs-up gesture came next as he winged away.

Neil fell silent while he watched Kellan race away in hot pursuit of the villainous Seeker. There was no stopping Kellan, and Neil knew Kellan would get it.

Rolling in midflight, Kellan's back faced the ground, and his glowering eyes picked the Seeker out within a second of turning over.

In a surprise attack, the Seeker landed on Kellan's chest and went for his throat with a death grip.

With the weight of the beast bearing down on him, Kellan lost control of his flight and they ended up rolling rigid across the ground, head over feet, lifting dirt, twigs and stones into the air like a tornado had touched down. When they finally broke apart, Kellan toppled one way, and the Seeker tumbled the other.

Choking in oxygen, Kellan was past irate. He back flipped into a crouch, wings high, looking mighty. The power within him skyrocketed and he ran full throttle at the Seeker sprawled out on the ground.

Lifting dust while he clawed the ground, the Seeker jumped up screeching, taking to the sky.

Kellan followed it with determination to shut the machine down. Racing the northern wind, Kellan reached a speed above one-hundred knots as he passed a startled sparrow on his left. Without warning, a hungry falcon sped into view, and Kellan rolled quickly to avoid it. "Shit!" he roared.

Squealing, the Seeker dropped and hit the ground running. He then spun messily, expelling black dust as his claws dug deep into the dirt to help him spin. His feet snagged a root that hurled him into another gravel-raising tumble, spewing dirt twenty feet in front of him. His leathery wings thwacked several times as he rolled sideways repeatedly across the ground.

Sloppily, the Seeker stood, rotated from right to left and back again, looked up and then straight at Kellan. His hands fisted so tightly that its knuckles changed color, turning them from black to deep purple. Attempting to elude Kellan's advance, the Seeker brought its wings down with mighty power and jumped straight up.

Kellan mimicked the Seeker's leap with the same flap of his

wings, trailed it until he was able to connect and hold it vise-like at the back of its knees.

Struggling to get away, the Seeker kicked and wiggled.

Losing his grip, Kellan fell back, but quickly reconnected with it face to face.

Attached they flew; wings beating against the others, tips thwacking tips, both trying to pound the other out of the sky at the same time. Pinned together as they sliced above the lake, water glazed their eyes.

The Seeker lost his bearings as it squinted to see beyond the pecking mist.

They fought in midflight, powerful wings pounding the air unmercifully, and at intervals beating tirelessly against each other's, nasty black leather against pure white silk.

Kellan let go of the Seeker and back flapped until he passed its feet. Quickly he took a diving roll, latching on to its back where he gripped its rubbery wings with his arms, and took control.

The Seeker jerked and kicked, trying to free itself.

Kellan held tight, not letting go. He growled deeply as they circled downward to the lake.

They hit the water fast, skimming across the surface like a skipping stone, spinning, tumbling and slicing waves.

Feeling the sudden collision bend their bones, the impact shoved Kellan's body forward as the Seeker was held back beneath him by the tug of the waves.

Kellan catapulted forward where he spun to a rocky stop in the middle of the lake. Water pelted his vision, stabbing like broken shards against his face and eyes. His thoughts foggy, he managed to pull himself free to fly before he sank.

Within moments of scrambling for the sky, the Seeker gripped Kellan's ankle and pulled him back into the lake. Fighting again, they pounded at one another with tightened fists. White waves engulfed them as raging body parts skated across the water's surface, showering them with waves.

Gaining power, Kellan clamped his hands around the Seeker's neck, forced its head below water, giving the seeker a vision that had no future.

Managing its rage, the Seeker shot above water, throwing Kellan's body to the left, where he dropped back down into the

Seeker's ribs, wrenching his shoulder as they spun to the right.

With a shocking left hook Kellan jammed a balled fist into the Seeker's jaw. The Seeker's nerves rattled when the skull crushing pop came at him with horrendous power. Its jaw shattered and teeth crumbled.

Flipping on its side and then toppling over, the Seeker hit water with a mighty smack. It screeched, squeezed its eyes shut, and waited for another jaw-breaking blow from Kellan. Disoriented, the Seeker's eyes blurred. Gasping as it hung on, the Seeker heard crunching bone as it opened its mouth to screech again. Bone fragments and teeth pieces dropped to the water and sank. Locking his elbows, Kellan pushed the Seeker back under water and held him there. He could feel it kick and try to scuffle to the surface.

Fighting back but weakening from lack of oxygen, the Seeker struggled against the weight of the water and the grip Kellan had around his neck. It somehow mustered enough strength to pull itself free to catch one last breath.

During the harried survival match, Kellan found his way to the Seeker's back, and cracked the bell bone of both wings.

While fighting back, the Seeker gurgled with rage and pain as it sank. Kellan went down with it. The beastly Seeker flailed in Kellan's grip as he twisted and kicked under water.

Deprived of air, the Seeker's head lurched above the surface and inhaled deeply. Soggy air filled its starving lungs, blistering its throat on the way in. Every limb went weak and the broken wings lay limp against its back.

Bursting out of the water alongside the Seeker, Kellan slammed his forehead into the bridge of its pug nose. Blue blood poured down its ugly face and swirled across the surface of the lake, turning the white froth around them to a shimmering crisp cerulean.

Piercing pain gouged at the Seeker's eyes as electric shock waves seared through the bridge of his crumpled nose.

Not holding back, Kellan popped the Seeker on each ear with cupped hands, forcing air deep against the drums and they also bled.

With an effort weakened by dizziness, the Seeker lobbed itself backward, pushing a rippling wave away from them. A sullen groan escaped its gullet before it fell silent. Suddenly the flames in its eyes went out. Unconscious from the blows, it floated limply like a deflated raft on top of the simmering waves. Its legs bent at the knees, dangling below the surface, and its head lay bobbing like a feeble balloon floating at sea.

Wanting to kill the crazy bastard but deciding against it, Kellan dived beneath the surface and swam like a fish until he reached the shallow edge where he stood and shook out his wings, leaving the demented Seeker to drown on its own in the middle of the stirred up lake.

Kellan heaved his wet body from the fresh water lake, dragging light cerulean swirls behind him. The Seekers blue blood snaked after him, grabbing at the purity of his being as if trying to take his soul.

On his way out of the lake one step at a time, Kellan looked back and said, "Swim with the fishes, bitch."

Limp and waterlogged, the Seeker lay unconscious on the water's surface, sinking slowly, but looking like it was going down.

Catching his breath with no time to waste, Kellan stripped away his ripped and blood soaked pants, dropped them in his tracks where they hit the ground with a squishy splat. Wearing nothing more than the day he was born, Kellan freely ran with the wind, pushed off the ground with beating wings, and took his flight back to Neil and Dylan.

Chapter 26

It was tense from what Neil was able to see and he laid low with Dylan by his side in the bushes where Kellan left them. They nervously waited for Kellan to finish the fight that recklessly turned their stomachs. There was so much noise and alien-like blood that Neil worried Kellan may not come out of it alive.

There wasn't much that Neil could do other than sit with Dylan in the brush, hugging him for needed support. He was fear stricken beyond what he could grasp.

Even though Neil turned out to be a warrior earlier that evening, to his own surprise, he didn't seem to have the strength to wage another battle with the monsters the way Kellan was able to. The power that angelic man had was above anything Neil had ever come across before. Kellan was amazing.

Every time the wind blew, branches picked at Neil, making him flinch at the thought of it being a Seeker or a security agent lurking in the bushes right there next to him.

He sat quietly and waited for Kellan to return.

~~~~ O ~~~~

Kellan landed in front of Neil, stark naked and pretty much taking Neil's breath away. His hair was a mess and hung down his forehead, a few wet strands dangled in front of his eyes, making them look even bluer than usual.

Neil wasn't expecting Kellan to return without his pants on, but it certainly took his mind off the recent events. His nerves were still rocking on edge from being chased by killer bat men and witnessing the fight between one of them and his angelic boyfriend to be, so with all that he wasn't able to focus on Kellan's natural beauty for more than a few paltry seconds.

"We need to get out of here," Kellan said. "I'm pretty sure they have a trace on that Seeker."

Neil hesitated for a few more seconds before he looked away. "Unh - Yeah - Right. Dylan, come." He stood up, trying to shake the vision of Kellan from his mind. It wasn't easy. The angel was magnificent, with and without clothes.

Kellan reached for Neil. "Hey, you doing okay?"

"I'm fine. You just caught me a bit by surprise is all," Neil explained.

What Kellan meant to ask was if Neil was okay health wise after being chased by villains, but hearing him say he was fine just might be enough. Kellan curled a wing in front of him to shield his swinging dick from the world, hopeful to set Neil's mind at ease so he could concentrate on getting out of the bush.

"Is it dead?" Neil asked.

"I'm not quite sure, but it doesn't seem to be going anywhere anytime soon," Kellan said.

"We should get out of here, yeah?" Neil suggested.

"Exactly. Grab your things," Kellan said. "Can you carry Dylan okay?"

"Yeah, sure. Where are we going?"

"Back to that small lighthouse on that island we found. It seems to be deserted. Nobody'll know we're there," Kellan said.

"Good idea." Neil pulled the strap on the messenger bag as he corralled Dylan around to be lifted. "Do you want my shirt to cover up with?"

"That would be nice. I'd feel less out there with something
~~~~

on." Kellan reached out.

"I'm fine with it." Neil stripped off his shirt and handed it to Kellan, and as he did, both of them looked at each other's form, marveling at the other. Neil's chest was solidly built, and from the first time Kellan saw it bare, took him no time to be enticed by its strength and outstanding beauty. The distraction at that moment was a godsend and brought the both of them back to reality for a split second.

"Thanks, hun." Kellan wrapped the shirt around his waist.

"Don't mention it," Neil said. Smiling at being called Hun.

"Let's fly," Kellan said, then kissed Neil on the cheek.

They were getting ready to take off when Neil mentioned he had a few syringes and bottles of Acepromazine Maleate in his bag.

"What is that?" Kellan asked.

"Oh, sorry. It's a tranquilizer," said Neil. "Do you think that Seeker will stay down or should we stab it a few times with this sleeping drug."

"It looks to be comatose for the time being. I think we better save that stuff for later," Kellan said.

"Oh Gawd, don't tell me that." Neil backed in to Kellan's arms with Dylan wrapped in his. "Let's get the hell out of here."

Kellan's wings hit the down stroke and they took to the sky like night owls, leaving the sinking Seeker and whatever else was trying to grab at their heels behind.

Feeling content, but not yet safe, they flew back to Lighthouse Island where they *would* be. Neil had the pleasure of being underneath Kellan where he wanted to be. Kellan had the pleasure of holding him from behind the way he wanted to.

Chapter 27

Making it back to the island without any further assaults by Seekers or helicopters, Kellan, Neil and Dylan found the ugly run-down house welcomed them with a homey hug. It was quiet and peaceful, just the way they wanted. And most of all, they were completely alone, like they wanted.

They were still a little skittish and kept their ears and one eye open at every turn.

Kellan's eye cam connection, to their knowledge, had been destroyed. At least temporarily, and as long as Kellan didn't look at anything that anyone at TC found familiar, they would be lost to them for the most part. For the time being, they were in the old house to stay.

Even though he was a small sized dog, Dylan stood at the front door like he was a big German Shepherd on guard while Kellan and Neil looked around the house for anything to make their stay a bit more comfortable. Everything was dusty and old, but still usable. The condition of the place and what was in it really didn't matter to either of them anyway, as long as they were together and safe.

Kellan was the first to make it back to what they both presumed to be the main living space of the lighthouse, dragging a mattress he found leaning against the wall in a smaller room that looked as if it was a large closet, or maybe a tiny bedroom. When he let the mattress fall to the floor, a dusty breeze wafted up all around him, blowing his wings and hair back. He coughed and waved the space in front of him with both hands.

The thud made Dylan turn around and bark.

Neil came running down the steps with an arm full of graying sheets and a yellow blanket. He whispered, "What the hell?"

Still coughing and fanning the place, Kellan smirked as he waited for the dust around him to settle. He laughed because the dust storm inside the house struck him as funny.

Neil handed the yellow blanket to Kellan and then snapped the sheet open above the bed, let it parachute down so he could make it while fighting with dust particles as he did.

After dropping a couple of pillows on the mattress, Neil stopped dead fast next to the fireplace and looked at Kellan standing shirtless in the middle of the room. Being that Neil was a little more relaxed, he could absorb the good looks that Kellan had to offer. Bracing himself, Neil pressed one hand firmly against the mantle and gazed upon the glorious sight standing in front of him. The shirt Kellan had tied around his waist was open just enough for Neil to get a glimpse of Kellan's dangling genitalia. Impressive did not justify how magnificent that entire package was. The moonlight coming through the cracked windowpane made every muscle across Kellan's body appear more defined. His open wings took Neil's breath away every time he saw them. That would never end, he was damn sure of it.

"Fuck, me! You are stunningly hot. Damn hot is more like it," Neil squealed. He couldn't help it.

Clearly blushing from head to toe, Kellan stood facing Neil with his wings expanded at his sides, fanning the place in what looked to be him prepping for flight. His broad chest protruded with confidence without him even trying, and his chiseled stomach flexed with every breath he took. He stood like an idol with the flimsy shirt wrapped around his waist, and sprouting out of the knotted arms of the shirt in front was body hair that traveled up the center of his six pack stomach and fused with newly feathered hair that fanned out across his magnificent chest.

Neil stepped up to Kellan to get a closer look at the angel's hairy chest. It seemed to have grown overnight along with the prickly hair that graced his gorgeous face. "You are truly a glorious creature, Kellan. I really like the hair on your chest." He laid both hands against Kellan's chest, gently running his fingers through the short blond hair while he fantasized about the magical man pressed up against his smooth naked body, tantalizing him in a dominant manner.

Neil would so bottom for Kellan, even top the angel if he wanted him to.

Kellan lunged for Neil and kissed him with an open mouth - hard. He tugged at Neil's tee shirt and peeled it over his head, exposing his barrel chest and smooth muscular torso that had been hidden beneath it. Every bulge and every ripple surrendered to Kellan was accentuated by the moonlight coming in from outside.

The freshly grown hair on Kellan's chest teased Neil's silky skin and Kellan's masculine touch conquered Neil. That touch brought about a rock hard erection and a climax that was on the verge of exploding from within him.

"Damn, I want you," Kellan hummed. "But…"

"But what?" Neil gasped.

Kellan kept his lips against Neil's as he spoke, his voice low and muffled, "This will be a first for me. I mean—actually giving myself up to another man."

Neil uttered no words, just labored for air as he went on kissing Kellan, growing harder by the second.

Kellan kissed Neil back, deep and hard, before pushing him away to put minimal distance between them. "Shit, man, you're gonna fucking kill me." He fell back against the blackened fireplace, working hard to catch his breath and keep his cock from blowing semen everywhere. His erection thickly evident through the shirt as it projected high across his hip bone. The shirt was soaked as if he'd already ejaculated.

"Oh shit, you came." Neil tripped backward and gasped

after Kellan let him go, his cock hard as hell and making every effort to break through his jeans.

"Not yet. I'll explain that later." Kellan moved in for another tongue tangling kiss and then backed off, gasping.

"Awesome," Neil muttered, wiping his mouth with the back of his hand and gripping the swelling below his belt buckle.

Kellan peeked at Neil's stocky build while he held back his own cock from busting through the shirt. "Hot damn, you need to get out of those pants, Neil."

"And you need to get out of that shirt," Neil panted, as his chest rose and fell rapidly. He dropped his pants and tumbled backward on the bed.

More dust rose, but neither of them cared.

Kellan opened the blanket and let it float down over Neil. It took on his form as Neil lay beneath it. Next to him, Kellan lay down, only partially under the blanket, with his wings lying flat out across the floor behind him. The warmth of the covers soothed them, made them both feel comforted and secure.

With a forefinger, Kellan traced Neil's lips.

Forearms entwined, Neil stroked Kellan's jaw, finding his bones angular and distinct.

It was quiet.

A long moment passed before Kellan skimmed the back of his hand along Neil's body, caressing him as if he were stroking the full length of a furry animal. Neil lay still, his body indolent beneath the covers.

Kellan kissed Neil's nose, his closed mouth, and then his cheek. He trailed Neil's jawline, breathing in his masculine scent. When he pulled back, Neil's fingers found Kellan's mouth, traced the curve of his lips that he wanted so badly.

Keeping his eyes on Neil, Kellan slid his pursuing fingers across Neil's chest, where he rested them on his rib cage, waiting, fingers being cradled by the muscles in his side. He leaned in and left a trail of soft kisses, like little butterflies, down Neil's jaw. With one hand still on Neil's ribs, Kellan cradled his head in his other palm as his lips traveled slowly, so slowly, across his chin. His mouth opened and their lips touched.

Neil arched his back and rose up to meet Kellan just as Kellan's palm slid up Neil's body and covered his bare chest. Neil traced Kellan's naked back, around his wings, skin like molten silk, his muscles hard and rigid.

Kellan's mouth moved from Neil's lips to his chest where his glossy teeth grazed his nipples, giving him chills that strengthened his erection.

Kellan breathed on Neil's chest, his breath warm until he licked at his left nub, and then slid his lips across his chest to the other. His tongue was hot on the sensitive points, producing a rushed pulse that made his erection throb.

Neil trailed his hands up Kellan's body, from his hips to his shoulders and up his neck until he found the cleft where his skull meets his ear. He wrapped his hands around Kellan's head, holding him in place with needy whimpers. His touch made Kellan's wings expand; they fluttered and fanned the place, bringing cooler air to a very heated moment.

Kellan shifted his body between Neil's legs, balancing on his elbows to hold most of his weight. Kisses traveled over Neil's chest and ribs, traced the trail of hair running down his stomach, and then moved across his abdomen, from one hip to the other. Wing cooled air followed the heat of his wet mouth.

Neil groaned, heated and passionate as the covers slid away.

Kellan moved his mouth across Neil's rippled abdomen, followed the deep V that took him to his pelvis where he stopped and breathed in the scent of the hair that surrounded Neil's cock. His tongue lashed out, circling the sensitive glans that was enlarged and drizzling pre-ejaculate.

Neil's legs opened in invitation, and then Kellan paused, pulling the covers away so he could see all of him. He liked to watch Neil's body move, go tight, putting every hardened muscle on display for him, needy and demanding.

Taking Kellan's shoulders, Neil pulled him close, locking his angelic blue eyes with his own. Neil reached between their bodies and clutched Kellan's erection. Moaning, Neil's tone changed from pleading to desperation.

"Not yet," Kellan said, his tone rough with his own need to connect with Neil. He turned Neil, putting his face to the pillow. Neil tried to rise, but Kellan held him in place with a hand to his back, pressing down and caressing him. He stroked Neil's spine, down to his sides, and then trailed his hands from beneath his arms all the way to his thighs. The hair was soft there and felt good on Kellan's palms. Kellan moved slowly. Neil shivered, wanting Kellan to join with him, wanting him inside. Neil breathed Kellan in, took what he was giving, tasting his scent.

Kellan's tongue gratified the dimples above Neil's buttocks, swirled at his crevice and moved slowly up his spine. Neil quivered when Kellan's heated hands slid between his legs, with a thumb pressed hard against his taint.

Then it happened. The moment Neil was waiting for.

Kellan's internal gland grew full, naturally storing semen that would aid in sexual penetration the way it's done in the wild. Kellan held the head of his cock against Neil's entrance, letting the clear semen flow from the tip like a running faucet, coating the star at the center of his backside with his natural lubricant made within him.

Kellan lifted Neil's hips and pressed the head of his rock hard cock against his entrance that was slick and dripping with Kellan's semen, ready to take him in. Slowly Kellan teased Neil until he couldn't hold back any longer. He entered Neil, one hand holding his hips high, the other stroking Neil's cock, teasing him, but not allowing him to release.

Neil pressed back against him hard, so Kellan would go deep, pushing himself onto Kellan with his hands securely gripping fistfuls of fabric. Guttural groans escaped Neil's throat as Kellan rotated his hips and smoothly rocked into him. Moving easily in and out. Taking his time until every inch of him was buried inside Neil. The hair surrounding Kellan's cock warmly caressed Neil's hard, tight ass.

Neil needed more of Kellan, wanted it all, every thickened inch of him tunneling deep, going for his heart. Neil's body begged with his actions and his expressive sounds. But still Kellan moved his body slowly, very slowly, his perfect rhythm was like a timed oil well, pumping in a leisurely beat.

The heat around them rose as waves of desire elevated and engulfed them.

Kellan's thick erection slid in and out of Neil, touching every part, making him squirm. Neil's vision blurred by lust, but below him he could still see Kellan's hand, as it moved slightly slower over his cock, milking it, making it ooze with his pregenetic essence. He went mindless, about to explode.

When Neil thrashed, arched his back and moaned, Kellan withdrew from his ass, fast, leaving him empty. Neil bit down, gasped and held in the roar of pleasure trying to escape.

In a second, lightening quick motion, Kellan turned Neil again, dropped to the mattress on his back, Neil landing with a forced puff of breath. He pulled his knees tightly against his chest, holding them there and exposing his hairy entrance to Kellan for a second penetration. He couldn't wait. He craved him desperately. Kellan was propped above Neil, his large exquisite wings extended high. It was magnificent, on the brink of being unreal.

Kellan wasted no time. He gripped his cock with a spit soaked hand and plunged hard, slamming into Neil with his entire length, filling him up, digging and fucking him deep. Neil felt the hair above Kellan's cock scrub against his balls. Neil's head fell back, his mouth popped open. He groaned without any control, throaty and breathless.

Their bodies meshed, fitting together like perfect puzzle pieces. Locked as if they were made for each other.

Kellan lifted his body above Neil, braced his hands on either side of his head with locked elbows, his blue eyes staring penetratingly into Neil's face. Kellan's full strokes filled Neil and then retreated, piercing him rapidly with the perfect rhythm that hit the deepest part of Neil with internal blows of desire. Neil spread his legs even further apart, wanting Kellan to go deeper, wanting him closer.

Kellan lowered his body against Neil's, elbows now along both sides of this head, bearing the brunt of his weight, chest to chest, grinding into him with a consistent rhythm that went deeper still. As he rocked his body into Neil, Kellan's mouth found Neil's nipple, grazing it with his teeth, licking until Neil gasped with pleasure.

"Fuck, me," Neil moaned, back arched, his heartbeat banging like thunder.

Neil's body tightened and his knees went deeper into his armpits, opening himself up as wide as humanly possible to Kellan. He took Kellan's ass in his hands, fingers gripping and digging in, drawing him closer while his body naturally pulled and sucked Kellan in.

Passion whirled from the depths of Neil's being, pinging every single one of his nerves with impending orgasmic explosions. Kellan's eyes were heavy with pleasure, but locked on Neil's, watching him. Sparks of pleasure raced from the center of Neil's body and looped in his groin. Every extremity buzzed, and he moaned louder each time Kellan pressed deep.

"Ejaculate into me," Neil threw out a whimpered beg. "Now."

Kellan thrust, ferociously pounding Neil, his cock going in and out the same way a piston pumps inside an engine. The feathers on his wings fluttered and fluffed with air. He was getting ready. It was time.

Electric waves burst inside Neil that crackled and burned like embers in a fire, rolling through him, stroking his skin. Lust and need took over, he thrashed vigorously beneath Kellan, and his volcanic release was seconds away. "Holy Fuck Me-eee," Neil hollered. He couldn't control his outburst.

"Omigawd, you feel amazing," Kellan grunted. His pelvis buzzed, electric sparks shot up his spine, from top to bottom and back again.

Together for the first time, they were going to burst. Neither of them could stop what was about to happen. Suddenly, they surged simultaneously, as though Kellan's sperm was passing through Neil's whole body somehow.

Kellan's muscular chest expanded and his wings snapped wide, every feather filling with air. His erection, snugly tucked inside Neil thickened and went deeper still. He growled, tossed his head back and forcefully rolled his hips into Neil's ass. Thumping, digging deep, pounding, fucking wildly while he dumped several loads of his pure silken genetics up inside Neil's slurping cavity.

In time with Kellan, Neil drew in what he gave. Kellan's eruption flooded inside him, drowning every part of his body with an orgasmic fit. He couldn't hold back his own explosion. His skin went numb at the moment semen gushed from his erection, splattered his chest, his face, and pooled in the wells of his sculpted torso.

The power of cumming together joined their souls, and just then they were united. Right then they were whole.

After Kellan emptied his spunky essence inside Neil's craving body, he collapsed against his sticky chest and kissed him, breathing in Neil's scent that kept him hard. He shook his wings as they came down and blanketed them. His hoarse cries of deliverance echoed Neil's.

They lay quietly afterward, fully spent, heated, and breathing loudly with tortured lungs, as if they were starving for oxygen.

When Kellan could move, he slipped himself out of Neil and settled more tightly against him on his right, his weight moved off to one side so Neil could breathe more easily. They lay there, head to head, while Kellan's hand rested in the semen that had pooled across Neil's chest. He liked it, the way it smelled, felt and tasted. Shifting slightly, his wings stretched off the edge of the bed and across the wooden floor, the same place they were before he and Neil had fucked.

"That was intense," Neil huffed. "I can't believe that was your first time."

"Well, I've had some alone time to perfect my skill. Dreamt about it, how I would do it and how I would give it all up. You just happened to be the one to help me attain my ultimate and long awaited fantasy." Kellan grinned.

"Thank God it was me. That was the greatest fuck I'd ever had," Neil confessed. "I'm glad you saved it for me."

"Actually, right now, I can't imagine anybody else I'd rather give myself to." Kellan looked into Neil's eyes. "Everything about it felt so natural to me, like it was meant to be."

"I felt the same way, Kellan," Neil said.

"I imagine you're feeling quite satisfied, and full." Kellan laid a hand on Neil's six-pack and rubbed it with small circles.

"Well you could say that." Neil grinned. "And it's perfectly fine with me. It feels good to know there's a part of you alive inside of me. Kind of warms my soul."

"Aw, sweet." Kellan pecked Neil's cheek.

"Do you normally expel that much semen or did I make that happen?" Neil laid a hand over Kellan's.

"Actually both. Just so you know, Neil, it's always going to be like that. It's not just a one-time occurrence," Kellan said. "To start me off, I need somebody that will get my sex drive elevated, in this case it was your hot sexy body that did me in, and when that happens, my body makes loads of semen, which eases the penetration of my mate. That's the way it's done in the wild, you know. It's part of my animalistic abilities. My seminal vesicle is about four times the size of the average man's and when I get an erection, it releases clear semen, lots of it, as a lubricant. At least that's what I've been told by the doctors as being the reason so much comes out of me even before I make the flash flood at the end."

"That's incredible," said Neil. "I have to ask this. Do you feel the sensation of an orgasm the entire time you're pumping out semen?"

"A little bit. But not as intense as the big finish when I shot all up inside you," Kellan answered, and he laughed.

"Must be nice," Neil mentioned.

"Yeah, it is. And fun. And messy," said Kellan, grinning. "And now, both of us can enjoy what comes out of me, if you don't mind."

"I don't mind at all. Hell, I can take it," Neil finished.

Chapter 28

Kellan chuckled as he relaxed.

"Why are you laughing?" Neil turned his head to look Kellan in the eyes.

"It's just," Kellan hesitated.

"Just what?" Neil breathed.

"Just… that you were so amazing. You felt so good to me. I liked being inside you." Kellan kissed him on the cheek, taking semen in his mouth when his lips left Neil.

Neil let out the air he was holding. Relieved that Kellan's laughter wasn't because of his squealing while getting fucked in the ass by a big thick dick.

Kellan rose on one elbow while swirling a finger in the spunk splattered across Neil's chest. "That was the first time I've had sex with anybody. I enjoyed it so much and it made me very happy. Gawd, you were amazing."

Right then Neil laughed, though it was more like a contented giggle, thrilled that Kellan thought him amazing in bed.

He'd never heard those words from any guy he'd been intimate with, they never mentioned his performance so honestly and he was pleased to hear it now, especially coming from somebody as spectacular as Kellan. "First time huh?"

"Well, my first time with another human being," Kellan said.

"Wait—What?" Elbows propped behind his back, Neil rose, concerned that other species may have been entwined in Kellan's past copulating exploration. "Please tell me they didn't make you do anything weird in that place?"

Kellan flattened his hand against Neil's chest, pushing him back down on the bed. "Oh, Gawd, no… wait. I meant that I've never hooked up with anybody that took care of my business before."

"Okay, that's better. You scared me for a minute," Neil said. "You have experienced getting off before though, right?"

"You mean by myself?" Kellan asked.

"Mmm-hmmm," Neil answered. "You know - beat the meat, choked the chicken, jacked off, bopped the bologna?"

Kellan was embarrassed at first, but then laughed. "Oh, lawd, I may as well be honest, so yes; I have, many times. Once I figured it out around the age of fifteen or sixteen, I did it about three or four times a day, whenever I was alone. You know, like you said, beat my meat."

Neil laughed. "Beat your meat. I love that you picked up on that one. I'll say it's the most fitting for what I saw and felt earlier. Meat definitely describes that slab you have." He laughed again.

Kellan poked Neil in the rib and then covered his mouth with a semen soaked hand.

Neil licked his lips beneath a constricted laugh, tasting his own spunk as it coated his tongue. "Oh Shit!" he exclaimed.

"What?" Kellan said.

"The eye cam." Neil pointed.

"We smashed it. I don't think they can see us, or you, through my eyes. Oh, that's weird." Kellan rubbed his eye, and then brought his hand down and focused on his palm as if it would reflect back the secret within his eye.

"I was talking about what they saw you do in private for the past ten-plus years. You know, beating your meat."

"Fuck me to shit!" Kellan winced. "Did you have to mention that? Oh, Gawd." He covered his face with his hands. The left one felt sticky and smelled like man spunk. He liked it. And because it was Neil's spunk, he liked it even more.

"It's done and over with, so we might as well move on," Neil said.

Kellan cringed. "Maybe later, Right now I can't. This is embarrassing for me, that Lab knows everything, everything I've done while I thought I was alone in that room. I know they've seen me without any clothes on many times, that didn't bother me; it was part of the everyday life since I was small. But now that I know they've viewed me ejaculating all over the place and shoving stuff up my ass, I'm totally humiliated."

Neil smirked. "If it makes you feel any better, I would love to get my hands on those recordings. I'd jack off to every one of them, and you could watch me, or better yet, join in."

"This isn't a time for funny business, we have to get those discs before anybody else sees them." Kellan ran his fingers through his hair.

"Come here, let's worry about it tomorrow night." Neil tugged on Kellan's shoulder and caressed his wing.

"Oh Gawd, that explains the drawer full of vibrating dildos, pocket pussies, and tight rubbery assholes in my room. I thought they were left for me to figure out who I was, give me something to do during my *private* times, or maybe part of an experiment that never took place. Holy shit, they saw me do it all, and that means they know I'm gay because I never went for the repulsive pussy thingamajig. Dammit, they know." Kellan's eyes glazed over as he rambled on about popping off loads while shoving a vibrating dildo up his ass.

"Listen. They're all doctors in that place, so I'm sure they observed your private time as medical professionals determining if they created what they wanted," Neil explained. "They're all smarter than you think, and are able to keep personal shit separate from business shit."

"Gawd, I hope so. It's surprising that whoever was watching me fuck myself with a vibrating dildo while shooting spunk across the room was able to keep a straight face when they saw me in the daylight. I'm not exactly a quiet cummer, nor a tidy one."

"Yes, I've discovered, and I like you that way." Hearing Kellan talk about jacking off and butt ramming himself with foreign objects was getting Neil hard again. He was imagining every bit of it as well as wanting to see Kellan in action. He couldn't hold back his grin.

Kellan spotted Neil's cock growing and standing up. "Is this making you go chunk on me?" Even though still slightly bothered by his revelation, he still found the joy in grabbing hold of Neil's thickened erection and giving it a few gentle strokes.

Neil took in a deep breath as he watched Kellan's hand move up and down his stiffening cock, and the added amber light coming from the lantern beside them made the stroking session that much hotter. "Fuck that feels great."

With all Kellan's experience over the years of jacking himself off, he was familiar with all the buttons on Neil that would bring him to another full-blown climax. He stroked slowly at first and then sped up when he went for Neil's nipple and sucked on it, tasting spunk as he did.

The intensity of Neil's nub being tongue lapped, and his dick being stroked by Kellan in the same motion made his back arch off the mattress, pushing him to the pure frenzy of their beef beating session.

Kellan kept the strokes going as he moved his mouth over top of Neil's, passing musky semen from tongue to tongue.

It didn't take long for Neil to groan. His hips raised and dropped, followed by the rigid torso that men get when they're closing in on a full-blown cum fest. His stomach went ripped and then he growled, "Fuck-fuck-fuck, me-hee-ee. Here it comes again."

Kellan pulled back off Neil's mouth and turned his face toward the stone-hard cock in his hand. Neil's head fell back, his body froze, and he released a hoarse groan that let Kellan know he was cumming, and if at all like the last one, it was going to be explosive.

All at once Neil's cock expanded and semen spit from its head. It splattered Kellan's face and hair, some getting inside his open mouth, and a few thick ribbons snaked overhead and landed with splats across Neil's chin, neck, and chest.

With a cream painted face and a mouth full of semen, Kellan glowed like he had just been handed the key to heaven. He enjoyed the taste of his own hot liquid, but cherished the scent and zest of Neil's even more. He swallowed most of what made it to his throat, but wanted to share what was on his tongue with Neil, let him taste the sweet honey that came out of him. Not hesitating, Kellan turned back to Neil and kissed him deeply, giving back his creamy spunk that had coated his tongue. They both moaned as they transferred and tasted Neil's cock blown spunk.

Neil gasped, breathing heavily through his nose. "How's that for round two?"

"Damn, Neil, you've got a lot in you." Kellan was happier than hell.

"It's all for you now, nobody else," Neil said, exhaling harshly.

"I can certainly live with that." Kellan gloated about having Neil as his own, and wallowed in what he knew Neil had living inside him that was all his if he wanted it.

Neil's stomach made a noise.

"What the? Are you hungry?" Kellan lifted his head.

"No,"—Neil rolled his head to face Kellan—"that's just a part of you making a home inside of me."

Kellan laid his head back onto the pillow and smiled.

They spent the night awake, organizing, talking about everything that came to mind, and kissing. They made sweet sugary love, swapped semen, kissed some more until they fell asleep around eight in the morning and woke up sometime close to four that same afternoon.

Chapter 29

There wasn't much to do around the lighthouse other than broom the place down, open windows and let in a little fresh air. Kellan and Neil weren't certain how long they planned on sticking around the island, so turning it into a place to call their castle didn't make much sense. For all they knew, they could be chased off the island as quickly as they got there.

As soon as they were finished polishing the inside of the lighthouse they went outside to catch dinner. While Neil and Kellan fished in the lake for something to eat, Dylan played with a stick along the beach, running in and out of the surf.

Many days had passed since the sun's rays touched Kellan's face, so the warmth it gave felt good as it stroked his skin.

They fished using poles they found in an old shed out back and earthworms they dug up from the wet ground beneath the trees. They waded in the surf while casting the line in and out of the breakers, not paying attention to the distance they put between them, but as they spoke, the water somehow carried their voices back and forth at an understandable volume.

"Neil, I have some things to take care of at the lab, and I should probably go alone," said Kellan.

Neil cast his fishing line into the lake again. "What? Are you crazy?"

"I need to do this, or I'll never be free." Kellan cast, too.

"I'm going with you," said Neil.

"No, that wouldn't be good. I can't risk you getting hurt, Neil." Kellan squinted away the sun that reflected brightly off the surface of the water. It sparkled like diamonds, pinging sparks of blinding light.

"Well I can't risk you getting hurt either, or locked up, or whatever." Neil cast his line out farther, strength came from his rising temper.

"They aren't going to hurt me. They want me alive for whatever they have planned," Kellan explained.

"Dammit, Kellan, I can't risk losing you. Not now. Not ever," Neil raised his voice. "For some reason, I've been brought here to take care of you, and vice versa. You're supposed to take care of us. Me and Dylan. That's how it is now. Period."

Kellan jammed the handle of his fishing pole in the muddy drift, buzzed over to Neil with a single wing beat, and hugged him. "Dammit, dammit, dammit." He pecked Neil's cheek three times, pressed their jaws tightly together, and ground his teeth like he was chewing gum. "I wish this wasn't so fucked up."

"We'll fix this. Together," Neil purred.

"If you go with me, you have to promise that you'll be careful and do exactly what I say." Kellan pulled away, gripped Neil at the sides of his neck, traced his thumb pads along his jaw, and looked him straight in the eyes.

"I'll do my best," Neil said.

"No, Neil, I need better than that. You have to promise me." Kellan kissed Neil on the forehead and then hugged him tighter.

"Okay, I promise." Neil's hands grazed Kellan's feathers as he massaged his back.

Kellan palmed the back of Neil's head that tucked his chin into the crook of his neck. He whispered, "I can't lose you either, Neil."

"You won't," said Neil.

"Alright, but I'll still worry."

"I'm a tough guy." Neil smiled, trying to brighten their edgy subject. He was good at comforting people during rough situations. It was the power of a nurse. Solace comes in the form of a smile.

"I got something," Neil hollered. His fishing rod swam away. They dived for it, belly flopping in the water, both of them.

Neil grabbed the handle and tugged. "Whoa, it's a big one."

Kellan got behind Neil and lassoed his waist. Neil reeled the line while Kellan held him in place.

A deep growl came out of Neil when he pulled the pole behind him over his shoulder. It sharply curled toward the fish that was fighting back. "What - the - hell - did I catch?"

They fought the fish, stepping backward as they wrestled with it.

When Neil tugged again, he lost his footing and fell into Kellan's lap. They landed hard, but as quickly as they went down they got back up.

Upon standing, Kellan's wings snapped wide, shaking away the fishy water that clung to them. As he did, they went up, rising, backward into the sky.

Another grimacing growl came out of Neil as he wound the stringy line back into its reel. All at once the line snapped, and it shot them higher into the sky where they could look down on the big fish that was getting away.

"Oh, snap," Neil said. He let the rod go and it dropped to the ground.

"What the hell does that mean?" Kellan asked.

"Shit, Dammit, Fuck," replied Neil. "Another word for frustration."

"Speaking of which." Kellan pointed to his pole.

"Oh, snap," Neil said again.

"I've got this one," Kellan said. He brought his wings in and shot downward, letting Neil run through the shallow surf when he let him go.

Dylan barked because he thought they were playing.

Kellan shot back up and then did a twisted swan dive into the water next to the line hooked fish. Water splashed everywhere, and to Neil, it looked like another underwater Seeker fight. He hoped for Kellan's win, but secretly wished the fish well.

About a minute later, Neil witnessed one of the most beautiful displays he'd ever seen in his life. Kellan blossomed from the depths of the lake, bringing water and a torrential rain with him. The vision was dazzling, like a magnificent fountain that could only be found in a magical place. Spiraling higher, creating a twisting rain shower, Kellan held the fish he had gone in for against his chest.

High above, Kellan looked down at Neil, giving him a thumb-up with one hand while the fish squirmed in the other. He pulled his wings in and dropped straight down, feet first, fast like an arrow. Just seconds from hitting dirt, he back flapped to stop his descent, and as graceful as a floating feather, he touched ground next to Neil.

He shook himself like Dylan does, throwing water droplets up and back down again.

"Now that's how you fish, my love." Kellan pushed the slippery creature toward Neil. "Let's eat."

Chapter 30

"Look what I found." Neil held out a handful of fabric.

"What is it?" Kellan asked.

"A pair of jeans for you to wear," Neil said.

"Where the hell did you find them?" Kellan asked.

"In a closet upstairs." Neil snapped them open and the pant-legs dangled to the floor.

"But they're faded with holes in them." Kellan noticed.

"Who cares. Frayed denim is stylish now and I think they'll look good on you." Neil pushed them toward Kellan.

Skeptical the ragged jeans would fit; Kellan reached for them anyway and put them on.

"You see. A little snug in all the right places, but they fit well." Neil gave Kellan's visible bulge a gentle squeeze with a cupped hand. "And I like the slash marks. They make you look rugged and very sexy."

"What fantasy is this?" Kellan asked.

"It's not a fantasy, it's the truth," Neil confirmed.

Kellan shook his wings and pulled them against his back while staring into space like he had something on his mind.

"What are you thinking about?" Neil cocked his head and snapped his fingers to bring Kellan back from wherever his thoughts took him.

"I was thinking about going back to TC. There's something I still need to do," Kellan firmly stated.

"Tonight?" Neil asked.

"The sooner the better," answered Kellan. "The best time is around one a.m. It's the quietest time around the Lab and the diehard scientists and caregivers are typically the only ones on duty. They're so engrossed in what they're doing that they don't even notice what goes on around them."

"I'm in," Neil immediately said.

It was only a matter of time before they were headed to TC to be chased, shot at and probably locked away for good.

~~~~ O ~~~~

Thirty minutes past midnight arrived too quickly. Standing next to Kellan, Neil was wound tight, his hand clenching Kellan's in what felt like a death grip. He was nervous.

Knowing they were about to walk out the door, Dylan stared at them; his mind seemed to be wondering, *am I going too?*

"Bring your bag," Kellan said to Neil.

"Check," Neil grabbed it.

"You ready?" Kellan asked.

"As ready as I'll ever be," answered Neil.

"Let's do this." Kellan pulled the door open.

"Dylan?" Neil called to him. "You wait. We'll be right back. You stay and wait."

Dylan dropped his ears and sulked, turned his back on them and rotated his head back over his shoulder to watch as the door closed behind his people.

~~~~ O ~~~~

The night air seemed damp to Neil while he and Kellan flew through it. It was cooler than it usually was, and with the lake being warmer than the air, fog rolled off it like a creepy Halloween image. Chills crimped his spine while he looked around for the zombies he expected to emerge from the fog and get them.

That was a ridiculous thought. Zombies don't exist. Only angels do.

Kellan and Neil circled over Traverse Bay a few times before taking their flight to the Laboratory in the village. On the way over town, they could see the streets were abnormally busy. All the bustle was either due to late night travelers who had forgotten what time it was or there was an event going on Neil and Kellan didn't know about.

They made it to the Laboratory grounds flying low, where they then hid in the trees to think their plan through.

Fifty-five minutes past midnight arrived, giving them five more minutes of solace before they followed through with the intended mission to make Kellan disappear.

Tenderly, Kellan leaned in and kissed Neil, gripped his jaw, and breathed him in deeply. He held the kiss while he softly spoke, "Remember the promise, Hun." He hung on to their kiss a moment longer before he moved back slowly, so slowly, looking into Neil's dark eyes the entire time he pulled away.

Neil whispered, "I promise." His chin quivered and his eyes misted over. He gulped, trying not to weep. He didn't want this, didn't want Kellan to hurt anymore, and with all the worry came a bad feeling about everything. Nothing about what was in store for tonight was good. Nothing was good about it. Nothing. He could tell.

Kellan gently cupped the back of Neil's neck, pressing their foreheads together. "We can do this, Neil. You got me, and I definitely got you."

Stalling for time, worried his head might explode at any moment, Neil bit his lip and looked at the front of the building he never wanted to see again. *Hello institute, we're back.*

They slipped out of the trees and onto the walkway beside the main rear entry. Hunched over, they crept across the asphalt to the four-story building, staying quiet the whole trip. They sidestepped with their backs against the wall like prowlers, doing their best to remain inconspicuous and keep away from any shining lights.

It wasn't easy. Those damn lights were everywhere.

Kellan's voice lowered to a whisper, "Do you remember where you picked up those tranquilizer guns?"

"Yeah, the vet clinic on the lowest level," Neil whispered, placing one hand on Kellan's shoulder from behind.

All the main entry points were always locked from the inside, and in most cases; unless something major called the MPs away, each was heavily guarded, giving them no chance of getting in the easy way.

"Come." Kellan tugged on Neil's hand, holding it tight.

They skimmed along the wall until they reached an older part of the building that still had built-in ventilation systems under each window.

"Look, our way in." Kellan pointed, knelt down, and ran his fingers along the edge of the vent plate to see if it was loose. The first one they tried wasn't loose, so they moved on to the next one. Not that one either, so they moved on again. After they made it to the fourth window, they found a vent that was rusty as hell that looked like it was about to fall away from the wall on its own. He traced the frame with his fingers until he found a spot where they easily slipped behind the weakened plate. He tugged, pulling it free. Part of the wall crumbled with it. He then used his foot to kick the air unit on the inside off the wall.

They both winced when it clanked to the floor on the other side.

"I'll go in first to make sure it's clear." Kellan nudged Neil aside, crawled through the opening on his hands and knees, losing a couple feathers along the way. When he got inside, he crept to the door and peeked down the corridor, to the left, then to the right. Clear. Thank God.

He flinched when he turned back around where Neil was standing a few inches behind him. "Holy shit, you scared me." He grabbed Neil's hand.

"Sorry." Neil kept his voice low and breathy.

"We need to go left. There's a set of stairs at the end of the hall that'll take us down to the basement. You have the keycard, right?" Kellan said, keeping his tone low and quiet.

Neil opened the messenger bag and felt around the bottom for the key Kellan just asked about. "Here it is. I forgot it was in there." He put it back in the bag where it landed on top of several bottles containing Acepromazine Maleate. He forgot about those too.

They crept down to the end of the hallway where they came across the stairwell they intended to find. Neil grabbed the key from the bag, swiped it, and through the doorway they went. The well was dark and dank, just like Neil remembered, which told him they were on the right track.

When they reached the next door that would take them to the veterinary level, Kellan pressed a hand and an ear against the door before opening it. Not hearing anything from the other side, he reached for the lever. "It's fine. Key it, Neil," he whispered.

Neil swiped, the door clicked, and they went through it.

At that moment, a white coat walked from one room to the other about three doors down from the stairwell. Kellan pressed Neil backward up against the wall, hoping they would be hidden behind the archways constructed every few feet.

Kellan peeked around the archway with one eye and saw another white coat swish across the hall. He quickly tossed his head back, hopeful he wasn't seen by the man. "Dammit."

"Do you think we're gonna make it?" Neil whispered.

"We'll be okay unless the Seekers pick up our scent. Till then, were all good. These guys are just pill pushers."

Breathily, Neil said, "I'm kinda freakin' out here. Is the coast clear yet?"

"Looks like it," Kellan breathed. "Just stay close to the wall. Any fucked up surprises, I'll take over. You just keep going and get the guns out."

They crept down the hall, slowly, and as soon as they reached the doors where the white coats entered, they took off running for the vet lab, skidding by it at first, then turning back to duck in.

"Shit," Neil yelped.

"It's you." The white coat in the room spun in his seat and looked at Neil.

Neil recognized him from the time he was locked up. In fact, he was one of the guys Neil shot in the ass with a tranquilizer dart.

Kellan jumped between the two of them, opened his wings and built a wall.

Thinking fast, Neil pulled the Acepromazine Maleate filled syringe from the inside pocket of the messenger bag, spun on his knees around one side of Kellan and stabbed the white coat in the meaty part of his calf with it.

"Not aga-ainnn..." Down the white coat went, hitting the floor in front of them.

Continuing the spin, Neil spiraled upward where he stood. He then skittered into the supply room to grab a handful of tranquilizers, half a dozen pistols, and few more syringes. When he turned around, Kellan was there dragging the white coated man with him. He wasn't expecting anybody to be standing there, and because his thoughts were on intruders, he flinched and grabbed at his palpitating heart.

Kellan sat the man in a chair and pushed it to the corner of the room. "Hurry up, we've gotta go."

They heard footsteps just outside the supply room. Neil tugged on Kellan's wing and pulled him into the dreadful bathing room. Bad memories returned, but he fought them off. While they were in there, Neil loaded the guns with darts, getting them ready.

Kellan moved to the back when Neil inched to the doorway to look out. He was horrified by what he saw, couldn't believe it. Another white coat came in, went to the refrigerator with the drugs in it, and pumped his veins with some shit he pulled from the top shelf.

Incredible.

Neil backed up, bumped into Kellan, and held his breath.

Kellan leaned over him and watched the drug buzzard stumble back out the doorway. Kellan couldn't believe what he just witnessed either. That man had been his pill pusher a few times, and for all he knew, could have slipped him the wrong medication while wasted.

They lost time while patiently waiting for the fucking addict-bastard to finish poisoning his bloodstream with that shit.

Not taking any chances that the guy passed out in the chair would wake up soon, Neil stabbed him one more time with about fifteen milligrams of A.M.

That sleepy bitch wasn't getting up until morning.

They squeamishly passed by the cages of weird

experiments, made it safely to the hallway, and then up the stairs, but this time, they didn't stop until they reached the third floor where the storage room they were looking for was located.

Kellan recognized the layout of the third floor when he saw it, remembered the green arrow on the wall marked: This Way to the Ice Room.

The ice room wasn't actually a place where ice was made or kept, it was called that because the place was the main technologic heart of the entire building. All the electronics were kept in that room and to keep the place from blowing up from the heat they generated, the temperature inside was held at a high fifty-two degrees Fahrenheit at all times, which made it feel like an ice room, thus the appropriate name.

As Kellan said earlier, one o'clock in the morning would be the best time to roam the halls in order to remain somewhat invisible. For the most part they did, other than a few encounters here and there that were quickly obliterated by the prick of a hypodermic needle.

Surprises could happen at any turn. They knew that first hand from previous experiences, and were reminded of the fact when they passed under the green arrow pointing south.

There was no telling where the Seeker came from, but suddenly it was there, in the hallway with them, like it appeared out of thin air. A magic trick perhaps, or a newly developed breed that was bred with an invisibility feature. Its large hand gripped Neil's shoulder, digging in with sharp claws, at the same time a leathery wing batted Kellan in the head.

Thank god there was only one beast in the hall, but it was one monster too many.

Shocked by the touch, Neil spun around and ducked while Kellan raised a fist and undercut the Seeker beneath the chin. It did a back flip, landing flat on its back across the floor. As quickly as it went down, the Seeker got back up, reached for Neil again and took off down the corridor, dragging him by the leg in its monstrous grasp.

"Fuck this shit," Kellan growled, and went airborne, clipping his wings against every surface as he flew. Outraged, he turned beastly as he flew along the walls, floor and ceiling during the winged chase to get his boyfriend back, spiraling through the corridor like a child's spinning top.

Without pausing, the Seeker tossed Neil over its shoulder by one leg as if he were only a flimsy towel, his arms dangled at its back between the Seeker's thick leathery wings. Picking up speed, the Seeker moved quicker. The bastard was fast.

Terrified but still lucid, Neil kicked and wiggled for all he was worth. His head lifted and he spotted Kellan flying behind them, outpacing the Seeker but not fast enough. Kellan's face was clear; it showed anger and determination as he strove toward them at top speed.

Neil continued to struggle, beating the beast, punching at the Seeker's back, pounding with all the strength he had in him, and all his efforts seemed to have no effect on the maniac that took him away. That bastard Seeker was tough.

Gaining speed again, Kellan was almost on its tail. He reached out and clipped the Seeker's foot, but fell back when it kicked him in the skull. He clawed at the floor on all fours, then he shot forward with increased beats of his wings.

Neil scrambled for the bag around his neck that wildly dangled toward the Seeker's feet. It bounced and twisted, making it difficult for Neil to grab. Pulling it from around his neck, he reeled it in by the strap. While towing it in, Neil was caught off guard by a rubbery wing that knocked the bag from his grasp. He lifted his head and watched the bag tumble behind him across the floor. Every curse word he knew came to mind, but he was too jostled to spit them out.

Kellan spotted the bag tumbling in front of him, kicked off the wall, grabbed it from the floor, rebounded off the other wall and finished his corkscrew flight down the hall behind the Seeker and Neil.

In its wake, the Seeker emanated the smell of dirty blood. It was metallic and pungent, and it made Kellan's eyes and throat sting.

Anger growing, Kellan burned up oxygen as he gained momentum, out-flying the Seeker by sheer strength of will. He ground his teeth and growled, snagged the Seeker around the ankles successfully breaking its momentum.

The next thing Neil knew, they were going down, as though the Seeker's legs were just hacked off at the knees. They hit the floor with a sickening thud and the Seeker lay there completely still, as if dead. Knocked out. Good deal. Time to make headway. Blue blood trickled from its mouth and pooled on the floor around its cheek.

During the tumble, Neil flipped backward over the monster's shoulder. He cracked his head against the wall so hard, he swore he spotted two crows flying by. His legs were pinned under the Seeker, and he frantically kicked, scrambling to free himself from it. The bastard was heavy, he couldn't escape. He felt powerless. He was trapped.

Kellan quickly stood, picked the Seeker up off Neil like it weighed nothing and threw it into a corner by the door they were trying to get to. "Damn that bitch."

Dragging his legs away from where the beast fell, Neil reached for the bag at Kellan's feet, plucked another tranquilizer-loaded syringe from inside it, and plunged it into the Seekers ass. "That'll teach you to mess with me and my boyfriend."

The Seeker laid still, its chest lifted and fell, breathing shallow, polluting the cleaner air around them with its rancid dragon-breath.

"Damn you're good with that shit," Kellan commented. He reached for Neil's hand and helped him through the entrance marked ICE ROOM. Before he closed and locked the door, he dragged the sleeping beast in with them to keep suspicions at bay as to why a Seeker lay sleeping outside the ice room.

Chapter 31

Kellan looked around the room. "This is it. This is where we need to be."

Neil skittishly walked next to Kellan, watching the Seeker on the floor the whole time to make sure it wasn't going to get up and take them out. He'd never laid eyes on such an ugly beast in his life. He could see that it resembled a bat, and knew that's how they got started with its creation. All the facial features were there, as well as the dark skin and rubbery wings. It was ugly and smelled like shit, too.

Kellan glanced back at the door to be sure nothing and no one else was coming through it, and then while he searched the room for the main server and the drive that operated it, Neil loaded all the guns with tranquilizer darts. He wasn't into killing anybody, so knockout drugs had to do.

"Neil!" Kellan hollered in a breathy whisper. "I found it." He pushed the computer mouse and the screen lit up.

Startled by Kellan's breathy outburst, Neil accidentally

squeezed the trigger and fired off a dart. "Oh, Shit." The pistol just happened to be aimed at the Seeker on the floor and the dart nailed him square in the chest. "Well, that fucker will be out for a week."

"Good fucking shot, Neil." Kellan puffed.

Neil scrambled to his feet and shuffled over next to Kellan, looking back every few steps to make sure the Seeker stayed down. With all the drugs in its body, Neil knew it would, but for some strange reason felt the need to keep an eye on the stinking beast.

The monitor started up in front of them, adding a soft green glow to the room.

"Ho, shit, bright light. Can you lower the blinds, Hun?" Kellan said.

While Neil pulled the shades, Kellan went straight to the computer's explorer and searched for his name. It took a few seconds, but sure enough a folder popped up on the desktop. He clicked on it. They were in luck. It expanded and filled the screen.

Just when Kellan was about to click again, the monitor went black and a password request exploded across the screen. "Dammit!"

He tried a few and failed at every one of them.

'Birdman' didn't work, and neither did 'Angel'.

Neil suggested 'Gorgeous' as well as 'Beautiful', but those didn't get them in either.

Kellan looked around the workstation to spark a clue as to what the password might be. There were the usual family photos of the wife, the children, even the family cat and dog. Grandma and Grandpa were on his desk too, smiling back like they were proud of the work whoever sat there did. Kellan lifted a few trinkets that sat on either side of the keyboard. But for some reason no password came to mind. He looked at the nameplate below the monitor and recognized it as the man who hated him. He wasn't sure why, but the man definitely did. Thinking of reasons, Kellan came up with one and thought to give it a try.

"You got something?" Neil asked.

Kellan rubbed his hands together like a feeding mantis and then typed: f-a-g-g-o-t, followed by a punch to the enter key. The time wheel on the monitor orbited, the screen went blank, and the folder labeled 'Superior Experiment-Kellan' maximized.

They were in.

Did the white coat who occupied that seat hate Kellan that much? Was it his superior abilities or that he was gay? The password clearly indicated the latter.

"That's nice. I always knew this guy hated me, and now I know why," Kellan assumed.

There were so many files in the populated folder. Hundreds, maybe even thousands. How was he going to get them all loaded in such a short time frame? They didn't have all night.

To make sure this was what he was looking for, Kellan clicked on a few subfolders and viewed what was there. A million reports popped up, blood tests, growth charts, speech lessons, schooling, everything was there, each one labeled by age and date, right up to the return of his recent escape. All of it in there. Audio and video recordings too.

"This is incredible. Your entire life is inside that tiny little folder," Neil said in a breathy voice, keeping his tone low.

"Do I dare?" Kellan moved the mouse to the folder marked video. His heart sped up and along with it came heat.

Neil felt Kellan radiate fire.

"Sure, but we better make it quick," Neil whispered. He quickly turned around and pointed the gun at the Seeker. Still out. He spun back around to face the screen.

"Remember, this could get ugly." Kellan double clicked the mouse. Another hundred plus subfolders opened, all labeled by age, date, and this time what the folder contained.

At the moment, Kellan was more curious about one particular folder than any of the others, the one pertaining to his private moments alone in the dark. Or until recently, the moments he thought he was alone in the dark. He looked sideways at Neil before going for the folder he really wanted purged forever. He scrolled through them until he came to the most obvious choice labeled 'Self-Discovery and Masturbation' and opened it. It was good to see they labeled it scientifically, that was a plus.

Inside the SD & M folder were over a thousand feed links that filled the screen. "Oh Gawd," Kellan said in a muffled voice, then pulled Neil closer to him with an open wing.

Neil was also anxious, not from excitement to see what was

about to be displayed, but because he wanted to get the hell out of there and go home.

Kellan clicked on a link that was dated recently, hopeful it would be less awkward for him and for Neil.

The media player immediately opened and when the recording started, the purpose and the date of the recording were first displayed. After that came the video. Everything was clear. Out in the open. Everything. Very clearly.

Kellan skipped through most of it by clicking the progression bar at the bottom of the player, stopping in the middle where he was laid out on his back with his legs held high, sliding a black vibrating dildo in and out of his ass while jacking off.

Kellan gasped and quickly shut it off. "Holy shit. I can't believe they saw me do that. Fuck." His wings opened up and Neil rolled away from the embrace.

"It's alright. Who gives a flying fuck? We've all done it. That's how we got started in our younger years. The idiot that sat at this desk did it too. I'm not sure about the dildo, but I can pretty much say for certain he jacked off when he was alone in the dark." It wasn't a good time for an erection, but Neil was thickening a little from what he saw and heard in that recording.

Kellan closed down all the links and sub-folders until he was back to the main folder on the desktop that held all his personal business. "We need to find an external drive. A big one. Help me look around. There's gotta be one someplace."

Neil was within reach of a laptop, so he grabbed it. "Here, use this. It'll store what you need and it'll give us a computer to use later on."

"Brilliant." Kellan took it from Neil, cleared a spot on the table and started it up. While he did that, Neil unplugged the laptop charger from the wall and then pulled all the cables off another PC that he thought would be useful. He handed Kellan an HDMI cable so he could connect it to the main PC as the external hard drive they needed. Within a minute, the transfer process began.

While the transfer progression bar turned from white to green slowly, Kellan asked Neil to help him turn everything in the room on.

Wondering about the reason for that, Neil asked, "Why?"

Kellan pointed to the ceiling, "Because computers, electrical currents, and water do not get along. We're going to flood he place. When we're done, nothing in here will be useable."

They got through flipping all the switches in less than five minutes and the anxiety of it all was rising in both of them. Neil tapped his fingers on the back of the chair while Kellan pushed the Seeker a few times with his foot.

Checking the hallway, Kellan pressed an eye up to the corner of the small window in the middle of the door. It was still dark out there, but the way things go down around the lab, that didn't mean shit.

"Oh my Gawd, how much longer is this thing going to take?" Neil was getting antsy. His nerves pricked his flesh, like tiny hot needles.

The systems progression bar read eighty percent, which meant it was almost done.

"Quiet, I think I hear somebody in the hallway," Kellan whispered.

Neil reached inside his bag and pulled out a gun. His heart raced, and then jumped into his throat. His nerve endings that were already scratching his skin felt like they lit on fire.

Kellan stood in front of Neil, opened his wings and waited. "Ssshhh!"

They heard the card reader beep, and then a clunk against the door. The manual lock on the door Kellan engaged kept the door from being opened, and the thump they heard was a body banging against it. The beep sounded again, followed by another thump and the clatter of the knob being tried.

"Shit, how much longer?" Neil read the monitor at ninety-two percent. His head was hurting from his heartbeat pushing too much blood up to it.

Kellan watched a set of eyes widen in the square window of the door. He looked back at them and scowled. As he did, the eyes went wider and dropped away. "We need to hurry, Neil. There's going to be company any minute."

Ninety-seven percent.

Horror struck and a chill ran down Neil's back. "C'mon, c'mon, c'mon," he begged, shaking the mouse and then impatiently tapping it against the tabletop.

Kellan ran over to the window leading outside and tried to raise it. The layers of paint sealed the damn thing shut and it wouldn't budge. It was opening one way or another, so he needed a chair or a heavy object to pull it off.

Thwack, thwack, thwack. It was the visitors at the door trying to break in. Many of them if the noise they made was any indication.

Kellan reached for a PC drive and threw it at the window. It was the heaviest thing within reach and he knew it would do the trick. Glass shattered as it punched through and dropped three stories to the ground. "Pack it up, Neil."

Ninety-nine percent.

"Two more seconds. We've almost got it." Neil hurriedly pulled the pistols from his bag and stuffed the laptop in it while it was still running, collecting data. Cords and cables remained connected to the main PC, ready to disconnect the second he saw one-hundred percent of the transfer complete.

They heard a screech outside the door.

"Fuck. Seekers," Kellan muttered. "Hurry, Neil. We gotta go now."

Neil looked back at the window in the door and saw a set of teeth that looked like they were bloody and dripping gunk. He spun back around and finally saw *one hundred percent*. He yanked the cables from the computer and then kicked the tower to the floor with his foot. It broke wide open, but kept on running.

"Get to the window, Neil." Kellan flapped his wings, bounded off the floor and knocked the trigger plates from the sprinkler systems in the ceiling. One by one the water jets let loose and saturated everything in the room below it. Most pleasing to see was the PCs and servers popping, smoldering and shutting down. A couple caught fire and melted.

The door was getting looser as the seekers threw their bodies against it, one right after the other. Boom—Boom – Boom. The deadbolt lock was weakening, the hinges too. The screeches were getting louder the closer they got to taking the door down.

"Shit, the guns." Neil jumped over a table in front of him, slid off the edge and grabbed the guns he had left at the white-coat's desk.

Just then, the metal door twisted inward and hit the floor at Neil's feet, forcing loose debris and water into his face. Neil spat and then took off back for the broken window.

Clumsily pushing through the busted doorway were four Seekers and then some. Every one of them looked so fiercely at Neil that it sent a chill down his spine and almost split him in two. A second later the entire crowd burst in. A couple human voices were heard, the rest, Seeker screeches. It was getting ugly.

Neil didn't falter. He leveled both guns and squeezed the triggers. One, two - bang, boom. And just like that, two Seekers went down.

Overhead, Kellan flew to the window and went through it. "Neil," he called, "jump, I'll catch you."

Neil threw the bag to Kellan before standing with his back to him on the window's ledge. Like a skilled sniper, Neil pulled two more loaded pistols from his pant pockets, leveled them at the clowns in the doorway, ready to shoot. The clinicians hit the floor to avoid being shot, whereas the Seekers stupidly charged him.

Not smart.

Neil pulled back on the triggers and two more shots were fired. The darts sank deeply into the Seeker's massive chests and stuck there. The bit of kick back from the guns pushed Neil backward out the window. He allowed himself to fall into empty space, trusting Kellan would catch him like he told him he would. He held onto those coveted words, 'I've got you covered, hun.'

The last Seeker standing scampered to the window and crashed against it, its wings too big to fit through as they were, and it was too stupid to think of tucking them in. It growled while struggling to get outside. Spiked glass fragments sticking from the frame sliced at its wings as it wildly scrambled through it. Blue blood dripped as it flew.

Outside, Kellan beat his wings so hard they ached. He needed to get Neil to a safe place, and needed to find solace for himself. He held onto Neil tightly, flying as fast as he was able, and followed the lane that took them to the street, headed to the bay.

The Seeker got to them fast. It was closing the gap, screaming and screeching.

"I need to put you down, Neil," Kellan told him. "I'll take care of the Seeker and then come back for you. Wherever you are, I'll find you."

"No, we can do this together." Neil grabbed Kellan's wrists.

"I need you to stay, Neil," Kellan yelled, fighting wind. He descended, heading to the stone monument at the Laboratory's street side entrance.

"Kellan, promise me you'll be careful." Neil loosened his grip.

"I will," Kellan said. He gave the messenger bag back to Neil, strapping it over his shoulder where it had started the adventure.

"Like you said before, Kellan, you have to promise me." Neil's feet touched the ground.

"I promise." Kellan spun Neil to face him.

Neil's face was painted with fear.

Holding Neil by the shoulders, Kellan jerked him forward and kissed him. "Go, run to the bay and get lost in the crowd. They won't come after you if people are around. I'll find you later."

"Please," Neil whispered.

Kellan skipped backward several steps, watching Neil the entire time. "Neil," he hollered. "I'm in love with you." Moving fast, as only a mutant bird could, Kellan threw his back against the wind, spun himself face down and took to the sky in pursuit of the last known Seeker of the night. Like Superman, he was gone.

Kellan went one way, while Neil went the other.

Neil clearly heard Kellan say he was in love with him, and with that admission, Neil was determined to survive. He had to. For Kellan.

Before Neil could absorb what Kellan said, another Seeker came at him from above the trees. Trying to get away, Neil took off running, running fast, taking to the streets, heading north toward the bay like Kellan told him to. When he raced out onto highway thirty-seven, he met up with a steady stream of cars racing like maniacs up and down the street. Vehicles took the corners like they were in an old time cops and robbers movie. One car sped by and clipped him. A second car squealed without stopping. He twirled along the front bumper with one hand on the hood, skipped on one foot along the pavement to the side where he rolled along the fender that dirtied his shirt.

When he spun around, Neil hobbled in front of another car coming at him the other way. His hands went up to shield himself from being struck, and within an inch of his kneecaps, the car's bumper stopped. Hopping backward, he then twisted out of the way, looking to the sky as he did, only to spot the dreadful Seeker coming up at his rear. "Shit!" He then spun the rest of the way around on a single foot and took off running back into traffic down the highway's center division line.

Several more vehicles came at him, one speeding up behind the other.

Neil ran back to where he came from only to discover another train of cars coming that way too. "Shit!" he shrieked.

Where were they all coming from?

Turning back around again, Neil tried to run, but it was too late, the cars speeding in skidded to a stop, one after the other. When they met him, he flipped up onto the hood of the first car and rolled, miraculously making a back flip over his shoulder that brought him to a bull legged stance at the base of the front windshield. Without stopping, he raced up the window to the roof, where he then skidded down the rear window, across the trunk, and jumped onto the hood of the car behind it, leaving dents with every footfall.

The Seeker was at his left above the trees. He aimed, squeezed the trigger, and let the dart fly. Another sniper-perfect shot. The beast dropped from the sky, landing somewhere in the trees.

After witnessing gunfire, the driver of the car hit the gas and sped off. The momentum of the vehicle forced Neil to run up and over it and onto a third car coming up behind it that had not yet stopped.

Neil stumbled forward to the roof, this time tripping up the window that pushed him into a face down soar. Before he belly-flopped and struck metal, he was side swiped from the left by an unseen being that came out of the sky.

Thwap.

The shock of suddenly being pulled into flight, Neil lost his breath and his senses blurred. It happened so quickly, his head spun and there was no time to think of whose arms he was in.

In flight they rolled and flew facing up, straight toward a trailer of a semi-truck that was crossing at the intersection in front of them. Neil saw it, and pulled every limb in tight against his body just seconds before they skimmed low, only a few inches off the pavement, spinning like a chopper blade under the rear of the passing truck. Still spinning, they shot out the other side where they spiraled upward into the sky.

"That was brutal. Holy shit," Neil grunted. "Fuck, me. Fuck, fuck, fuck, me."

"Later," Kellan said.

Chapter 32

Kellan forced a downward beat that shot them straight up away from the commotion that was taking place on the ground in town. A few seconds later they were way high, looking down on what they just left.

Flying steadily, Kellan flapped his wings to take Neil home. A stinging down-stroke, then a tender upward, *ouch,* then down again, *double ouch.* Kellan must have jarred a wing somehow when he was battling the Seeker back at TC, but he tried his best to keep his secret so Neil didn't worry. It was well enough anyway, given that he'd heal in about an hour or so and he'd be good as new. His body healed like that. It was amazing.

While soaring in the dark, they crossed paths with the same falcon they ran into a while back. It looked at them as it did in the past, before it backed away to chase the sparrow it was originally after.

Kellan back flapped to pull out of the two birds' flight path, rolled with a downward dive where they just missed out on hitting water at the north part of the massive bay, somewhat skimming it, and Kellan's wingtips tapped the surface with every down beat, lifting droplets into the empty space all around them.

It was good to fly freely. Kellan knew it and Neil now did too.

Anxiety over the possibility of being followed had them taking the long way home. During their diversion along the coast, they followed the bridge north, looked at the damage they caused earlier, circled around the northern peninsula, and then south to the island where they made it back to the lighthouse sometime around four in the morning.

When they got there, Dylan went crazy, dragging a pillow from the bed that showed Kellan and Neil he was happy they were home.

They were wide awake from the forced adrenaline, so it was pointless to settle in. Instead, Neil took Dylan outside to take care of his long awaited business.

Neil sat on the front steps and gazed up at the stars when Kellan came out the door behind him. Before he realized what he was doing, Neil leaned back against Kellan's legs and stared into the trees. Spooked a little.

The tension from Neil's insides raced up Kellan's legs.

"What's wrong?" Kellan asked, stroking Neil's hair from front to back.

"I hope it's nothing, but I thought I saw something moving in the trees. Those bloody bats have me seeing things," said Neil.

"It's probably just a deer or an animal. I don't think there's anything to worry about. Seekers don't stalk their targets, they just barge in and attack. It's the way they've been bred," said Kellan. "Anyway, Dylan would have picked up their stench by now and he'd be letting us know something was wrong instead of playing on the beach."

"I hope you're right." Neil reached above his head and locked his hands in the front of Kellan's jeans, feeling soft warm hair where his fingers went in. It soothed Neil in a pleasant way. He liked it.

"Why don't we go inside and try to find an electrical panel. There's got to be power to more than just the lighted silo." Kellan grabbed Neil's wrists in a way that made him feel captive.

Neil grunted when he stood, calling Dylan in a voice so low he could hardly hear it himself.

Kellan smirked at the way Neil called out to Dylan so the monsters in the bushes didn't hear.

Once they got inside the lighthouse, with Dylan in tow, they wandered around looking for a power box that housed all the electrical breakers. The lantern Neil carried with him cast behemoth shadows of Kellan on the wall that resembled one big ass monster. The man was freakishly large to begin with and the huge winged shadow that crept up the wall and across the ceiling had Neil freaked out. And after the night he just had, the dark shadow easily contributed to what he feared.

Neil pointed. "Look, over there."

At the rear entry was another room that looked to be some sort of breezeway, and next to the door that led outside in the corner was a big gray metal box that had several metal pipes running to it, most likely housing all the electrical wires that road-mapped throughout the house. Having seen that type of box before, Neil knew it had to be what they were seeking.

Sure enough when he opened up the sticky door, there was what looked like a million breaker switches that were all flipped to off. Something small and heavy dropped to the floor at his feet. He froze and his breath had gotten lodged in his throat. Gingerly, he looked down. It wasn't a rat or a mouse, which was what he thought it was, but a key with a leather strap tied to it. He picked it up and looked at it blankly. It looked old, tarnished, like it fit a large padlock of some kind. "Hmmm. I wonder what lock this opens. We can check it out later. During daylight hours."

"Holy shit," Kellan said, looking into the breaker box. "Wonder why so many?" He placed his hands on Neil's shoulders from behind while Neil held the lantern up so he could read the dingy paper that labeled each switch.

It wasn't easy to read, so Neil took a breath and blew. Dust billowed everywhere and a few roaches scampered away. He moved in closer until he found labels that showed switch twenty-three and thirty-one to be for the kitchen and the living room. That's all they needed, perfect.

With liberal effort, Neil flipped the two switches on, followed by a loud pop that brought the appliances that were dormant for some time back to life. Low hums orbited the rooms where power had been restored.

"Ah, nothing like restoration of electrical power to bring life back to normal," said Neil, backing against Kellan's bare chest.

"Good job, mate. However, we need to lay low for a while, which means no lights," Kellan said, kissing the back of Neil's head and then spinning him around to face him.

"What are you up to?" Neil asked.

"Nothing, I just want to look into your eyes," Kellan said, staring. He gripped Neil by the waistband and pulled him against his chest. "They're beautiful."

Their lips met and before Neil could take a breath, Kellan's tongue found a way to push past his teeth. Neil tasted sweet, like honey and fresh spring fed water.

Kellan's cock sprang into action and leaked spunk through the front of his jeans. Neil's did too, but nothing that saturated anything like Kellan's, just stained them a little to show his true excitement for the man taking control of his mouth and tongue.

Kellan was amazing when it came to having a sexual encounter. Everything about him was self-contained. He needed nothing but another man's tight naked body to fulfill his desires and make the perfect connection. It was simple for him. He was a lucky man.

Kellan walked into Neil, taking him backward across the room until his back was pressed against the windowpane that faced outside toward the pines. With their mouths remaining connected, Kellan held one hand at the back of Neil's head, thumb caressing below his ear where skull meets jaw, while the other gripped the collar on his shirt. Their heads rotated as they chewed on the other's mouth, swapping spit with tangled tongues.

Reaching down Kellan's pants, Neil gripped his cock, already soaked with semen, his zipper just about to break open.

Kellan's body twitched every time Neil stroked his hand over the bulbous head of his cock. Semen steadily seeped from it, adding a slickened coat to the shaft and to the palm of Neil's hand. The sharp fragrance of raw honey wafted between them as it rose from Kellan's cock with every movement.

"I need to fuck you, Neil," Kellan groaned, trying not to burst in Neil's hand. His wings stretched wide, lifting air into every feather.

Neil broke the grasp he had on Kellan's cock, snapped the button open and dropped the zipper on his jeans. Kellan's wet erection sprang free, flicking semen onto Neil's shirt and hand.

Gripping the ribbed collar of Neil's T-shirt with both hands, knocking knuckles against the other, Kellan tugged, tore the fabric, and ripped it open from neck to navel, bringing his thick beautiful chest into view. With a crazed sense of lust, Kellan pressed his wet lips to Neil's chest, taking in one nipple and then moving sideways to the other.

Tormented by extreme pleasure, Neil's head fell back against the window. An uncontrolled moan broke through his gasps when Kellan's hand moved over his cock and squeezed it. With no room to move, his leaking cock burst through his open zipper, banging against Kellan's semen soaked pelvis with a slippery smack.

Kellan's heart raced, heating his body to a temperature that challenged the weather outdoors. His blood flowed hotter, pushing his erection to its ultimate size. He lifted Neil in his arms as if he weighed nothing and carried him outside where the wind felt cool against their heated flesh.

They stopped in the sand at the foot of the stairs and kicked their denims down their legs and over their feet. Bone hard erections stood strong, both reaching for the other to come back for more.

Neil kicked his jeans to the side and lunged for Kellan. Pouncing for the other, they dropped to the ground, cocks battling on the way down.

"Damn, I need my cock inside you, Neil." Kellan crawled on top of Neil and trapped him there, running a finger down his chest and stomach until he reached the hair surrounding his cock. He circled Neil's shaft and tugged on his nuts. His warm touch made them retract quickly and then sag just as fast in his grasp. Looking down, Kellan's gaze doting and utterly peaceful, pining for the crucial connection he just mentioned. He rocked his body forward with his dripping cock eagerly tapping at Neil's entrance, making it slick with his slippery semen.

Anxious to take Kellan's cock, Neil glanced across his torso between them, watched Kellan's abdomen crunch tight as he sensed the enlarged head of Kellan's cock pop just inside his begging ring. The increasing pressure of Kellan's stone hard erection and oozing spunk tunneling inside him took his breath away.

Moving forward, in and out, slowly inching further with every stroke, Kellan leaned down and kissed Neil, taking in his tongue at the same time he burrowed his thick cock even deeper. The orgasmic pings of pleasure brought his wings up, filling them with air and trickling wind.

For a moment, Kellan just rocked against Neil, groaning with each stride to push himself deeper. Beneath him, Neil went rigid.

Neil reached up and gripped Kellan's shoulders, digging into his solid muscle as the thrusts from Kellan turned fierce. "I need this, Kellan. I need you," he pleaded.

While on the ground, Kellan twisted Neil's body face down, grabbed his hips, and pulled him up on all fours. He then dropped to Neil's back and covered him, thrusting forward to give him everything, letting out vibrating roars that Neil felt race up inside him.

Out of instinct, Neil's back arched, ass pushing back onto Kellan's intruding cock. He whimpered every time Kellan's cock went deeper inside him, opening him up to the pleasures of an amazing fuck.

"I need you closer," Kellan said, wrapping an arm around Neil's chest and awkwardly pulling him closer. He twisted Neil's jaw into an over the shoulder kiss, where it forced the space between them away. At the same time they kissed, Kellan withdrew completely and then redelivered several bottomless thrusts.

While being bumped from behind, Neil let go of strangled cries, "That's it. Drive it in. Fuck me good." He shuddered while pushing back into Kellan, meeting ass against hairy pelvis. His cock so hard that it stretched up tight against his six-pack abdomen, smacking against it with every rear-ended strike he received from Kellan.

While they fucked on the beach, the sand below them gave way and Neil tipped forward.

Falling into Neil, but before his hands met dirt, Kellan

stopped his momentum with the beat his wings. They rose, separating from the ground beneath them, spinning upward, kissing, with Kellan's thickened cock still digging deeply into Neil.

Kellan held Neil's hips in his strong warm hands, pulling him backward into his rolling hips that drove his cock in and out of Neil's ass as they flew.

In the sky, Neil clamped onto Kellan's pounding cock, pulling him in, stroking him with what he had.

Every beat of Kellan's wings drove his dick in and out of Neil. On the down-stroke, his cock went in, going up, his dick slid out. Semen seeped from Neil each time Kellan withdrew.

Staying joined, Kellan groaned, "Holy fuck, you feel so good." He pulled Neil back tighter against him while he held and stroked his dick. When he spoke, Kellan's voice sounded deep against Neil's ear. "Stroke yourself. I want you to come for me while I fuck you in the sky."

Doing as he was told, Neil reached down and took himself in his hand, brushing fingers with Kellan's as he let go. He pumped his hard cock, matching every plunge that Kellan gave him.

Kellan never stopped sliding in and out of his boyfriend's tight slippery ass. He grunted with each thrust, punching into all the right places that would make Neil cum.

Neil's body convulsed, "Oh fuck me, Kellan. I'm cumming." Spunk flowed from his cock and over his knuckles, and when Kellan thrust harder from behind, the liquid pearl shot from Neil's dick, five feet out in front of him and then arched downward in the dark as they flew through the sky. Shot after shot spit from Neil's dick, influenced by Kellan's dick rooting inside him.

Still fucking Neil deeply in the ass, Kellan made gorgeous noises as his own pooling semen churned. He pulled Neil into his pelvis at the same time he shoved his cock as far as he could into him. Kellan growled at the moment his cock erupted up inside his boyfriend's flexing chute.

Kellan's cock stayed tightly embedded in Neil who let him shoot what felt like a gallon of semen up his sucking ass. As they flew, Kellan's spunk spit so far into Neil's guts that there was no chance it was ever spilling out. Sweet vocal roars escaped Kellan the entire time he pumped spurt after spurt up inside Neil.

Kellan hugged Neil, kissing his shoulders and neck. "That was fucking unbelievable. You okay up there, Hun?"

"Actually, yeah. That was truly the best and most impressive fuck I've ever had." Neil gasped. He liked being called 'hun.'

They flew through the sky, staying connected. Kellan buried deep, still hard, and Neil held on tight, not letting loose.

Kellan soared, keeping low so that Neil's feet would drag the water's surface. It refreshed him, and brought the heat of the moment below a boiling point.

Back flapping, Kellan brought them down softly to the beach. Kellan kissed the back of Neil's neck, tucked his wings behind his back, and pulled his leaking cock out of Neil's body, regretfully drawing semen with it.

"Before we go inside, I need to take a quick swim," Neil said.

Knowing the reason for the bath, Kellan grinned. "I'll go with you. I could use a rinse myself."

Chapter 33

Still dripping wet, completely naked and leading the way, Kellan greeted Dylan in the doorway first. His dick was deflated, but still hung low and large. He was luckier than Neil when it came to a good sized cock, however Neil was lucky to be the one taking it all in.

Neil followed Kellan into the house, carrying their jeans that had been strewn across the dirt earlier. Dylan tugged on them like it was a game of tug-of-war. He always played like that.

"It's getting light out. Why don't you get some sleep while I take care of some things around here? I've got work to do," said Kellan.

Kellan sat down on the floor next to Neil and flipped back the screen on the laptop computer, stared at it for a few seconds before clicking on a file to explore.

He thought about which file to open first, thinking it would be best to stay away from the file that would cause a great deal of self-induced mortification. He hovered over the folder labeled

'Kellan', backed off and then hovered again. "Dammit!"

CLICK! He went there.

Kellan waited for the password splash screen and then typed in that horrible word the maniac at the laboratory computer desk nicknamed him. He tapped enter. He was in.

Kellan scanned through the files on the computer, looking for anything that would tell him what plans the military had for him. Everything he found was so formal, many codes were listed, and he had no idea what they meant, several sub folders within each main folder that took him further into the background of his life. He clicked on some of them, one at a time, and as much as he tried to stay away from the video folder, he just couldn't keep his mind off it. He wanted to know what was posted in them, yet at the same time he didn't. Kellan thought about it for a few minutes and then caved, going for it with one eye pinched shut.

CLICK! He went there.

If he didn't go there, he wouldn't be able to concentrate on anything else until he satisfied his curiosity. He needed to know what kind of recordings they had filed away on him.

Kellan looked down at Neil before proceeding. He appeared to be sleeping, but he wasn't quite sure. Kellan lifted the laptop from his lap and placed it on the mattress in front of him with the back of the screen facing Neil.

Kellan didn't really care if Neil saw what was in those folders because it probably wasn't anything Neil hadn't done himself. It's just that there was a smidgen of embarrassment that went along with what he understood should be kept private.

He glanced at Neil one more time over the laptop screen, not checking to make sure he was sleeping, but because Kellan thought the man was so damned handsome. That smile, that mouth, and those damn eyes. Even with bed-mussed hair, Neil had that masculine edge he liked so much. Kellan looked at his screen and then back at Neil again. This time watching his chest rise and fall while he breathed, and then he glanced at his chest, moving his gaze down to his sculpted torso. He stopped to watch his abdomen flex, wondering how his genes were making out inside that beautiful man's body. He was sure they were doing well, making a nice home in there, because when he was snuggled inside Neil, it was the best feeling he'd ever felt in his life. Kellan thought about their flight all over again, and getting hard just thinking about slipping back inside Neil where it was tight and cozy.

"Aw, shit." Kellan glanced down at the bulge that formed under the sheet in his lap and saw a wet spot had developed already. He smirked at how easily Neil could give him an erection, simply just by looking at him.

Kellan went back to the video file and clicked on a subfolder that was dated a few months back. A whole list of recordings populated, maybe a hundred or so, all within a single day. His heart raced just thinking about what he was about to see, even though there was no reason for anxiety. He was basically alone, so it shouldn't make a bit of difference what was in the folder. He could always tap delete.

Neil was a nurse with a medical mind that thought on a different level than the average Joe Shmoe, who with all respect wouldn't make a big deal out of it if he saw anything weird.

CLICK! He went there. Well so what?

Kellan tapped on fast forward until he came to the part where he stood in the room completely naked. One hand holding a cream colored dildo, and the other gripping a bottle of oil. He knew what was going to happen next, because he was there when it took place in real life, on screen he was about to have sex with a nine inch vibrator. He remembered it clearly. Kellan was talented and over time learned to take dildos even bigger than the one he had in his hand. He watched the recording in horror, but like most tragic situations when stumbled upon, he couldn't look away even if he tried. "Ohmigawd." His jaw dropped.

Shock and horror caved in on him fast. It wasn't because he watched the dildo disappear up his ass while he lay sprawled out on the bed with his feet in the air, but the fact that somebody was watching him slide it in and out of his hairy anus while he blew semen all over himself and across the bedding he was laying on. He pressed stop and opened a separate video linked to the one he was watching that showed a different view of what he was doing. He recognized the angle to be from his own eye. He could tell because he saw several loads of semen shooting into the camera lens and over the top of his head. He said it again, "Ohmigawd."

He moved on and clicked another. This one was a little

different from the last film he viewed where he sat down on the dildo, riding it like a he was on horseback. Horrified again, he covered his face and wondered what the clinicians must have thought of him and how they could carry on a conversation face to face without taking a nosedive into fits of laughter.

About a half hour went by when Neil suddenly sat up and stretched. His eyes were heavy and he looked exhausted. His voice was raspy and low, "Everything alright?"

Startled, Kellan slammed the laptop closed. "Uhn-yeah, sure!"

Neil glanced across the room and looked out the window. "What time is it? How long have I been asleep?"

"It's about seven in the morning. You've slept about thirty minutes is all. You look exhausted," Kellan rambled.

"Did you find anything on that thing?" Neil's voice cracked.

"Yeah, I did," Kellan answered.

Neil rubbed his eyes. "Is it okay that I see it? Maybe I can help you figure it all out."

Kellan stuttered, "Um - well - you may not want to see what I just saw. Or actually I don't know if I want you to see what I just saw."

"Is it bad?" Neil asked.

"It was horrifying to me, however you might find it erotic." Kellan blushed.

"Oh, shit, that's right." Neil crawled to his knees and planted a hand on the laptop.

Kellan stacked his hand on top of Neil's. "Wait. If I let you see this, promise that you won't laugh or make fun of me."

Neil held up two fingers and pressed them to his temple, "Scouts honor. I promise. But I won't look at them if you don't want me to."

"It's bad. I am so embarrassed," Kellan said.

"There's no reason to be embarrassed over whatever you did in those recordings."

"I'm actually more humiliated that somebody was watching without me knowing about it." Kellan circled the top of Neil's hand with his palm.

"If it will make you feel any better, I probably did everything that you did in those videos," Neil confessed.

"But nobody saw your naked ass getting reamed." Kellan dropped his head and brought a wing to his lap and fingered the feathers.

"That I know of," Neil said.

Kellan cleared his throat and flipped the laptop open. "Let's just do it. Might as well get it over with and out in the open. You're gonna see it anyway, be it on video or live in person."

Neil really wanted to see the recorded version, but didn't want Kellan to notice his eagerness. "S'up to you. I can wait for you to show me live."

"It's alright, you can see both, starting with the video." Kellan swiped a finger across the mouse pad, triggering the laptop to wake up.

Neil sat on the floor next to Kellan and waited for him to select one of the recordings. He felt Kellan's wing nervously tap the back of his head, and he pushed it away. Not in a mean way, but gently. His own nerves tingled and he fidgeted, rubbing the back of his thumbnail up and down the deep crevice at the center of his bare chest.

The screen flashed once, followed by the media player opening up. Kellan looked sideways at Neil, watching his actions. He noticed Neil's eyes went wide a few times when he saw how well he could take a dildo up his ass. Neil was honestly turned on by how much semen the man produced and let loose around the room. It was like he was watering flowers with a garden hose.

Neil never had the pleasure of seeing Kellan actually spew any of his semen yet, because every time they were together, all of the spunk ended up inside him. Seeing the recording helped him understand why he felt so full after sex with Kellan, it was a full blast cum dump. He laid a hand on his stomach and rubbed it, wondering how all that lively sperm was doing inside him.

"Have you seen enough?" Kellan asked.

"Yes. Wow. Actually that was pretty hot," Neil admitted. "I'm hard as a rock, and normally after watching something like that, I'd be jacking off to satisfy my self-indulged fantasy."

Kellan let out a grunt as he leaned forward to shut down the player. "Let's see what else we have, shall we?" He spoke dryly.

"You're probably right," Neil said. "I'm thirsty. You want water?"

"Sure, I could use one." Kellan went through data files on the computer, clicking on several of them before he came across one marked 'Creation of Kellan'. "Ohmigawd. This could be freaky."

Returning to the living room, Neil said, "What did you find?"

"My birth," said Kellan.

Chapter 34

"Get ready for this." Kellan tapped the screen.

"Are you sure you want to see more of what they have on you?" Neil said.

"Right now, I'm ready for anything." Kellan zoomed in on the file, expanded the document so he could read it more easily. "Ho, fuck me. Look here."

"Holy crap! They purposely made you gay?" Neil swallowed his water. "That's fucking awesome, for me anyway."

"Thank God I am," Kellan said. "I can't imagine not being gay. How the hell would I survive otherwise? Eww, lady bits, I can't even think about it."

"It would be strange if you weren't," Neil stated. "And I'd be super bummed."

"By all the gene splicing and graphs here, I see how they were able to make me a male, but how the hell did they make sure I was going to be gay?"

"Those people are more brilliant than most people think,

like they are working at being God. I know a little bit about this because I studied some of it in school. Let me get a closer look."

Neil picked through the photos and literature on splicing and gene manipulation that made Kellan the man he turned out to be. What they did to create him was close to miraculous. Neil saw that the lab had genetically altered the XY gene that produces a male, and that Xq28 region of the X chromosome was totally manipulated. There were also notes listed that chromosome eight had markers of alterations as well.

"I've heard of this before, but never continued with it in school because it wasn't the direction I planned to go in," Neil said. "The Xq28 is a touchy area to be messing with, I know. Duplication can cause major defects in a child, like cell building and certain brain activity can be obstructed if the region even mistakenly duplicates it on its own. That extra chromosome in a cell makes that happen."

Kellan watched Neil as he translated the elements displayed on the graphs into what they created him to be. The man was amazing in so many ways, Kellan could tell.

Neil flipped a few pages across the screen. "I see where they fused the homogametic chromosome from a bird with your XY chromosome. My guess is that the all-male genes from the two species made you a birdman and the alteration of the Xq28 region decided your sexual orientation. They knew what they were doing, even though it was dangerous. My other guess is that there were probably many trials and errors that ended up becoming far from what you turned out to be, and they were most likely destroyed inhumanly. Oh Gawd, I can't even think about that."

"How do you know all this?" Kellan asked.

"I studied some of it in college. It was part of the requirement if I wanted to become a scientific engineer of medicine. I opted to take up nursing instead, figured it was enough headache to deal with. I come with a boatload of money, so I didn't need the greatest paying career to survive. My grandparents still own half the wine country in Northwestern Michigan, even after selling most of it off to make a cushy bank account for me. I'm the only one in the family, so I got it all."

"That explains why you don't have to work," Kellan said.

"I work because I enjoy helping people, and what better

way of doing that than being a nurse? It suits my need as a giver," Neil confessed. "I will be your nurse if you'll let me."

"Shit yeah. I think I've found my perfect mate," Kellan reeled.

"That, you have." Neil quickly pecked Kellan on the cheek right after he clicked on another folder that brought up several documents outlining the process of his creation.

"Hey, wait a minute. What was that? Go back." Kellan finger poked at a spot on the screen.

Neil clicked on the document and they looked over it together, scrolling through it slowly to catch as much of it as they could. It mentioned the steps taken that made Kellan into who he was, from splicing his genes, to implanting the embryo into the test tube. The process was actually quite amazing and the fact that they could grow a human being in a glass chamber was extraordinary.

Who would have thought that was even possible, much less could actually be taking place?

From the length of the file Neil opened up, it seemed as though every minute of Kellan's conception and gestation was recorded. Mixed in with descriptions, were links that took them to video profiles that showed the growth progress as well. As a fetus, Kellan moved around, well mostly twitched, as well as grew quite quickly inside the scientific beaker where he lived for only five months before being born. The incubation period for the bird-baby was quicker than the average human being. Everything about his development was accelerated. Even his growth spurts could actually be seen with the naked eye.

Kellan sat stunned when he saw himself as a blob of fleshy tissue floating in a gel-filled tube. He was amazed by many things, but that? That was surely an incredible miracle to see, and to see it as himself was staggeringly unbelievable.

While fast-forwarding through the progression of Kellan's growth, Neil's heart slammed in his chest and almost stopped. He put a hand over his mouth to keep from crying. It was remarkable, overwhelmingly beautiful. He couldn't help himself, he just had to kiss Kellan, the love of his life.

While paging through, Neil learned it was documented that the lab purposely made Kellan gay, and it mentioned they did it to keep him from trying to procreate through the usual heterosexual method. They couldn't risk that happening. It was a procedure that needed to be monitored and done medically. They were geniuses and they had documents that prove people are actually born gay, and these scientists figured out why and how it happens.

"Why didn't they just neuter me?" Kellan said.

Thinking wisely, Neil answered, "My guess would be, if you turned out the way they wanted, they could go after your spermatozoids to make more of you. God knows you have plenty of it, I'm witness to that."

Kellan laughed. "Spermatozoids? That's funny. Never really heard anybody actually say spermatozoid like that before."

"What? It's the proper name. Remember, I come with a medical background. You're gonna have to get used to the words I use," Neil said.

"I can live with it, as long as you can live with my feathers all up in your grill," Kellan said.

"Those wings are my favorite part of you, well, almost my favorite," Neil established.

Kellan grinned.

Neil clicked on another recording that was labeled 'Four Months from Conception', in which the camera was mainly focused on Kellan the whole time. Behind Kellan's test tube, which was staged in the middle of the room, was a wall of glass, behind which was another lab or what appeared to be a holding room of sorts.

Neil swallowed hard and tried to get a grip. Tentatively, he glanced down at the gleaming surface of the screen and saw what he wasn't prepared for. He felt like he was on the verge of a panic attack. He squinted and leaned in closer.

Sure enough in the background were other glass pillars similar to Kellan's lined up along the walls, and in them were tiny mutant like creatures. Dozens of them.

Just like Kellan, only disgustingly deformed and none of them moving. Dead? Possibly. Maybe being stored for later observation and research.

They could actually be gene members of Kellan's. His brothers.

Neil laid a hand on Kellan's shoulder and squeezed it.

Could they be Seekers, or the beginning of Seekers?

Neil closed down the video feed, because he didn't want to see any more.

They flipped through documents instead and clicked on the Seekers folder. Mostly hoping to find out what it takes to bring them down, but during their search, they came across documented facts that were totally despicable and honest to God inhumane. There were snapshots and videos of broken bodies, black and purple, as in death. It showed Seekers being tortured to the brink of bursting, to find out their tolerance for pain. As time went by, in the document, the Seekers became more and more resilient to pain. They took away their nerves and their emotions. Those science freaks were brilliant for figuring that out.

How could they?

"That place is sickening," Neil blurted. A chill chewed at him that deepened by the time he got to the end of the page. "I don't care if those Seekers are disgusting and pitiful, they don't deserve to be treated like that."

Chapter 35

Time flew by as Kellan and Neil went through files and the recorded videos of what went on inside the Laboratory. Neither one could believe half of what they saw. Kellan mostly, because he was right there under the roof the entire time, and missed it all.

"Do you think we'll be safe here for a while?" Neil asked.

"For a while, I presume," Kellan mused. "I figure if they knew where we were, they'd be here by now."

"I pray you're right," said Neil.

Kellan looked out the window, and saw that it was extremely dark. That made it the perfect time to step outside to have a look around. "Stay here. I'll check it out for you." He kissed Neil on the top of the head as he stood up, taking Neil's hand with him, which he let go of at the full extension of his arm.

Neil turned to watch him go. Dylan noisily plunked down next to him, right where Kellan had just been.

"Looks good out there," Kellan said, letting the door behind him creak shut.

"Do you think it's dark enough out there to sneak into town and grab a few things we might need to survive out here in the wild?" Neil asked.

"Sure. I can fly low," Kellan said. "Where to?"

"There's a tiny town northwest of here in the U.P. along the lake called Manistique. There are a couple places up there where I could go in and grab a few things while you hide out in the forest nearby. It should work perfectly." Neil dug around in his pocket for his wallet, checking for the bankcard that's always there and loaded with funds. This time he'd have a good reason to panic as if it wasn't.

Everything Neil owned was on him, all else was brought to the ground and burnt up.

At that thought, Neil wondered what the hell he was going to do about his house. How would it be explained to the insurance provider, or had the military already covered up what they've done? Should he just walk away and call it even? There was too much for him to think about pertaining to his pile of rubble on the beach, and it made his head hurt.

Kellan noticed that Neil was deep in thought, and he ran a flattened palm up and down in front of his eyes to snap him out of his trance. "You in there?"

"Unh, yeah. Let's go." Neil blinked a few times, breaking connection with his thoughts.

Dylan was left once again at the lighthouse while Kellan and Neil took off on a food, snack, butt-wipe, and soap run.

Outside, Kellan spun Neil into his arms, and unfurled his wings, pushing them down against wind sending them aloft.

Kellan swooped low, flew northward above water, holding Neil in his arms beneath him. Up ahead they could see lights, the lights of the small city they were looking for. Buildings to the right, trees to the left.

Kellan pulled in a wing and banked left, landing quietly in the trees where Neil had pointed out a good spot for him to wait earlier.

Neil gave Kellan a peck on the cheek, told him to stay in the shadows before heading off down the street to the small tourist town where thankfully most of the small shops were still open.

Neil went inside the quaint market he had in mind, grabbed

a hand basket and quickly picked out items that would last if stored in a storm shelter for more than just a few days.

When he stepped up to the register, the cashier behind the counter stared at him as if Neil was a criminal. The man never looked away the entire time he ran each item across the pricing scanner. The time that Neil stood there was awkward, and the man's glaring made him feel uncomfortable, the toothless grin adding to the backwoods creepiness.

The last item passed over the scanner, and Neil was finally able to swipe his bankcard through the credit card reader. While Neil waited for the approval, he clamped his hands to his torn shirt to hold it shut.

Finishing his spree, Neil pushed backward through the door, watching the guy at every turn. Flattery maybe, but it still gave Neil the creeps.

As Neil made his way down the street back toward Kellan, he could see the trees in the far distance where he left him waiting. On the way, he spotted a man wearing a large hat, one he must have purchased as a souvenir because it said *'I heart Mackinac Island'* on it, and in his hand, carried a huge pretzel that was already half eaten. Neil was hungry, so it drew his attention, and he willed the guy to hand it to him. He tried to manipulate fate, but the man veered off the sidewalk, pulling the pretzel to him and held the hat from being taken away by the wind. He seemed weird too.

Neil didn't trust anybody. Not the man in the store, or the guy tearing into that mustard covered pretzel. Everybody was suspicious, and as far as he was concerned, they were all maniacs like everybody was at TC, and for all he know any one of them could change into a bat-flapping creature on the spot. It sounded silly, but after what he had witnessed recently, anything was possible.

Neil felt totally spooked, like something bad was going to happen, and even though it didn't, there was still that intense pressure that something was building up inside him. For safety reasons, Neil looked back at the store once more to make sure he wasn't being followed, and kept a close watch on the police car that slowly cruised the street alongside him. Paranoid? Perhaps, but nervous for sure. Thank God the marked car veered off down another street and left Neil to wander the streets alone. He didn't need that added to what he'd already been through.

"Holy shit, that was intense," Neil told Kellan who was climbing carefully down from the tree. Neil's head was still swimming from the brief encounter with the two patrons he'd crossed paths with and the police car that seemed to have been watching every move he made. But when he reached Kellan, everything seemed to simmer down and the feeling of being strip-searched by naked eyes ceased. It must have been the presence of an angel.

They were soon airborne again, flying high, heading back to the island house to settle in.

Chapter 36

Wanting privacy with his angelic boyfriend, Neil closed up all the window blinds to keep any peepers who might be looking through them out. Being alone on a secluded island in the middle of a lake made closing every window seem foolish, but Neil did it anyway. While he was dropping the last blind into place, a tiny hummingbird stared at him through the window, like it wanted in, or was just saying hello. Neil swore he saw the little bugger nod at him before it zipped away. Crazier shit has been happening, so if the buggy bird was greeting him through the windowpane, he wouldn't hesitate to believe it was doing just that.

The darkened room was lit only by the gas lantern on the fireplace hearth. It was tranquil and transported them to a place other than the world they belonged to. It made for the perfect escape and helped them both forget about everything happening in their lives.

Neil turned on the laptop and popped in a music disc he

picked up at the store earlier that evening. A cheap one, not worth much more than the plastic it was recorded on. The disc wasn't loaded with any popular hits, just mellow piano music lightly orchestrated with background woodwinds. When it played, it set the mood for a quiet evening, filling the room with romance. It was nice to be together secretly, possibly explore love again, and pass genetic matter from one body to the other without it seeing the light of day. The music enveloped them, and by the third song, Neil recognized it to be an instrumental tune that was once played across the radio by Air Supply. A popular love ballad he'd always liked.

"You like this sentimental stuff, don't you?" Kellan said.

"I do, when I need to relax and take my mind off things." Neil pulled out the two plastic wine glasses he picked up at the market. They were small and super cheap, but would do.

"Classy," Kellan said, reaching for the plastic goblet.

"Don't make fun. This is the best I could do on such short notice. Wait'll you see the wine I found. It has no cork." Neil reached for the bottle of Shiraz and twisted the cap off like it was a soda bottle.

"This is perfect, Neil," Kellan said, winking at his boyfriend.

"Oh crap, you can drink wine can't you?" Neil stopped. "I never gave that a thought."

"Sure," Kellan answered. "It takes me a little longer than most to feel the buzz, but I eventually get there."

Neither one of them wanted to talk about their night at the lab. It needed to be forgotten. Hopefully go away forever.

"Neil, I have to ask you a question," Kellan finally said.

Sipping the wine, Neil stared off into space, making it look as though he was dreamily focused on the lantern light in front of him, seeming oblivious to what Kellan just said. He cuddled deeper against Kellan's chest, feeling his heartbeat pound against his back, and getting drifts of his breath across the top of his head. It cooled him off in a strange way.

"That day on the beach when you first saw me, what ran through your mind?" Kellan wondered.

Neil looked up at Kellan, seeing only his chin, and then dropped his head back down again to peer back into the light of the burning lantern. "Well – first I thought I was seeing things, maybe dreaming, or possibly dead. I remember thinking to myself that what I was looking at wasn't possible. Nothing so beautiful could be from this earth. I almost ran away because I was terrified, mostly by the notion that I had died and the only way to revive myself was to split. I even though that perhaps I'd gone mad, all fucked in the head somehow. Honestly, Kellan, you scared me a bit. But the longer I stood there in front of you, the more I realized you were real, and possibly just as frightened, or feeling as disjointed in this world as I was. Deep down I wanted to reach out and touch you, help you if I could. There was certain evidence in your eyes that expressed you needed some help. Call it a nurse's intuition. I sense these things."

Kellan kissed the top of Neil's head. "Truthfully, I was a bit alarmed myself. I had no clue what you would do to me, and that dog of yours who was staring at me like I was a chicken bone didn't help."

"There were no injuries that I could see at a glance, so I decided to keep my distance and let you get yourself grounded. I knew by your actions that you were only being cautious, and one thing I've learned as a nurse is that you can't rush anybody into trusting you. The best thing to do is turn your back and let them walk into your space when they are good and ready." Neil snuggled deeper into Kellan, sipped more wine, and set the goblet down on the floor.

"Your logic on so many things astounds me, Neil. You come across to me as being wiser than your years. You are twenty-eight aren't you?" Kellan rubbed his hand across the bulk of Neil's chest, pushing his shirt further open from where he tore it open earlier so he could easily see more of it. He caressed it, running his fingers up and down the deep crevice that separated each hard muscle. The man was built like a steel ship, and Kellan loved every bit of Neil's body, inside and out.

"Yes, twenty-eight. Same as you." Neil ran his hand up and down Kellan's meaty thigh and palmed the bulge that was already growing beneath his jeans. It was like a beast, a wild one that was antsy to break free. The man's gorgeous cock was impressive as hell, and as it grew behind the zipper, Neil's hand moved with it. He unbuttoned Kellan's pants and shoved his hand down into his hairy crotch. It was warm and cozy, as well a little damp from his seminal vesicles squeezing out the fluids it usually does when his cock sensed a need for penetration. Neil treasured that feature about Kellan, and couldn't wait to put it to good use again. Neil's own cock was growing at the same time his rear entrance twitched for Kellan's cock to bulldoze its way in.

Kellan's eyes grew heavy at Neil's amazing touch. "Fuck that feels good, Neil. How did I live without you all these years?"

Neil couldn't get enough of Kellan when he spoke his name, especially when he said it during encounters that involved sex and stroking him to a full-fledged erection. The mention of his name in a breathy manner made Neil feel he was doing everything just right.

Kellan heaved a giant breath and then let it go, his big chest collapsed. "Another question for you. Are you a top or bottom?"

"You're asking me this now, just as I am thinking about taking a seat on your thick dick for another ride of my life?" Neil's concentration broke quickly and he loosened his grip on Kellan's magnificent cock.

"I guess that somewhat answers my question. A bottom then?" Kellan chuckled.

"I find it most satisfying when I spread my legs for you," Neil confessed. "However, I wouldn't mind giving you the big one if you're willing."

"You know I can take all of you without a doubt. You've seen my films," Kellan said.

"I did, and they were incredible to see. So does that make you a bottom? Should I be bulldozing into you, or should we carry on as we've been?" Neil's hand was soaked with semen that was already being ejected from Kellan's stone-stiff erection.

"I go both ways, Neil. But right now, I need to be tucked up inside you." Kellan's cock was slick with semen and the hair that surrounded it was as wet as if he just had a bath. His body was remarkable.

Neil, stood up, licked most of the spunk off of his hand, truly enjoying the taste of Kellan, and then removed his shirt and pants. He towered above Kellan completely naked, looking beautiful and hard. "Give me your hand," he said.

"Where are we going?" Kellan reached for Neil.

"Outside, for a swim," Neil answered.

"Right now?" Kellan screeched.

"Yes, now," said Neil.

"But I thought you were going to sit on my cock and ride it?" Kellan howled.

"I will, I promise. But let's swim first. I smell like hot iron, so I'd like to refresh all your favorite parts." Neil tugged on Kellan's hand, making him stand.

"Alright, but don't let me down. I'm rock hard with quite a load ready to inject into you, and the way I'm feeling, it's not going to wait much longer." Kellan was leaking.

"I won't. I promise. Now, take off your pants," Neil demanded.

"Yes sir." Kellan didn't hesitate.

"Just letting you know, I'm a bossy bottom," Neil said. "Can you handle that?"

"I can." Kellan kicked off his jeans. "I can be one too, you know."

"Well then, with an answer like that, I take it you can be an enthusiastic bottom." Neil grinned.

"Sometimes I can, as you've witnessed on screen." Kellan pulled Neil to him, their cocks battled as he kissed him savagely on the mouth, tasting his own spunk on Neil, a bit of it laced his chin. He eased up a little, pending Neil's response.

Neil kissed back, smashing his words against Kellan's lips. "Good, because as you know and witnessed firsthand, I prefer being under you. But, let it be known, I can top like a rebel."

"Son-of-a-bitch, you're fucking me up, Neil. We better get to the water for a fast cool down before my cock blows ribbons and makes a mess of your beautiful chest." Kellan's wings fluffed up as if they were about to start molting, but he was only releasing cum building chills.

Neil laughed, loving what he could do to Kellan the amazing wonder-bird. "Let's go then. We swim first, then we fuck."

"Son-of-a-bitch!" Kellan oozed.

Chapter 37

Neil sprinted to the lake with nothing on at the same time Kellan unfairly beat him there by flying. They dived in the surf and let the frothy fists take them under. The effervescent fizz scrubbed the dirt away, appeasing them with a spirit lifting rinse.

Kellan swam into the waves, diving under and over them like a skilled salmon heading upstream to spawn. His wings naturally mingled with the water the same way they do with the wind in the sky. The birdman could pelican dive and swim under water like a fish.

Captivated by another feature of Kellan's that he found remarkable, Neil stood by and watched him before wading through the water back to the beach.

Behind Neil, Kellan silently swooped in like an owl, smoothly grabbed hold of him and took him toward the clouds.

Kellan's erection came back hard and strong, skimmed up and down Neil's backside before neatly sliding inside him. The anticipated assault forced Neil's back to arch as he pushed back against Kellan's glossy cock, taking in every inch of the man while he carried him across the sky. Every beat of Kellan's wings helped his erection tunnel deeper, going in on the downbeat, sliding out on the upbeat flap.

They were moving fast, way fast, and through it all, Neil's body sucked on Kellan, pulling him in further.

"I want to see you, Kellan. See your face," Neil rumbled.

Eager to gratify, Kellan spun Neil on his ten-inch dick until they were looking into each other's handsome faces. Kellan lifted Neil's legs up and rested them in the crook of his arms, hooking them at the bend of each knee. His erect cock snuggly buried in Neil's begging ass and their lips locked in a kiss.

Neil's spine bowed and his abdomen crunched tight, putting the nob of his cock only inches from their chins. Their kiss continued while Kellan deeply fucked him, turning their heated bonding into a lustful fuck in the clouds.

Kellan's hand moved between them and was perfectly placed on Neil's erection, stroking it in time with every butt thumping thrust up his rose tight hole. Kellan shuddered as the need to burst crept up on him.

Feeling Kellan's emotion, Neil worked his mouth a few more seconds before pulling away, but kept their foreheads pressed together with a strong hold at the sides of Kellan's skull at his neck, "Don't cum yet, Kellan. Let's make this last." Neil stopped moving, pinning himself tightly into Kellan's lap, holding back every internal stroke on Kellan's cock.

"No. Not yet, hun. Let's make it feel good. Anything you want." Grimacing, Kellan pushed his hips forward and held them there. He released the hold he had on Neil's cock that oozed a little, but that was it. Ropes of clear semen stretched from the head of Neil's cock to the hair on Kellan's chest, shimmering by what little light there was in the room. Terminating his rhythm, Kellan slowly pulled halfway out of Neil.

Staying connected as they flew, Kellan felt Neil's silken channel convulse around his cock, eagerly trying to suck him back in.

With winged power, Kellan brought them down to the ground in front of the lighthouse where Neil's legs dropped, and Kellan's erection slipped free.

They walked lip-locked up the steps, Neil backward and Kellan pushing into him. Their hard cocks battled between them, wetting their abdomens with slippery semen.

Excitement built as they kissed, their tongues as wet as their cocks.

Pinned against the fireplace, Neil didn't move much, he couldn't, just let Kellan thrust against him with his leaking cock, while burying his tongue further into his mouth.

Before they fell to the mattress at their feet, Kellan lowered Neil to the softness of the feathery bed. His fingers tingled as they ran along Neil's sides and then stopped under his arms where it was tender and warm.

Neil squirmed while Kellan's hand moved over his silky flesh, from one sensitive spot to the other, making his entire body tingle and aware his orgasm was growing. He whimpered as the angelic man explored all the spots that made him lose his mind. From his tender lips, along his jaw line, to the dip below his ear, down his neck and chest, and onto the appendage that stood thick and firm between his legs. Neil bit his lip and trembled when Kellan gripped him. Thrusting into his hand, Neil's cock slid through Kellan's forefinger and thumb. Neil went rigid, but still Kellan held him, caressed him, and watched in amazement as his boyfriend went to his orgasmic place in front of him. *Beautiful* was all Kellan thought.

Changing positions, Kellan knelt on the mattress above Neil with the head of his thickened rod bobbing at Neil's mouth, tapping his chin like it was begging to be let in.

Neil tongued Kellan's mushroomed cap, slurping on the tons of semen spilling from it. He opened wide when Kellan popped the head of his cock past his lips. It was what Neil wanted, and he wanted it bad.

Carefully, Kellan moved his erection in and out of Neil's mouth, sliding delicately over his tongue. Slick semen oozed from Kellan, forcing Neil to swallow.

Before he overloaded Neil's throat with hot seed-filled spunk, Kellan pulled out and knee walked along Neil's side until he was kneeling between his legs.

Neil licked his lips and grinned.

With one hand behind Neil's neck, Kellan lifted him for a

kiss, tasting the essence that seeped from his own cock and found refuge inside Neil's mouth. It was spicy and somewhat sweet. He liked it.

Kellan released the lock he had on Neil's mouth. "You ready for my dick again, Neil? You know you can take it." Kellan raised Neil's legs so he could see the entrance he needed to fill.

Neil nodded, his hole was already semen soaked and pushing outward, it clenched, and then gaped open as though it was impatiently begging for Kellan's big-dicked intrusion. He couldn't wait. He needed to feel Kellan inside him again.

Kellan's hard-on pressed against the ditch of Neil's sweltering ass, slathered it with oozing semen, then backed away to watch Neil's wet flexing knot beg for more. He teased Neil with the crown of his cock, probing and circling his blossom before sinking into him with one long push. Neil's twitching ass-lips sucked Kellan in as the length and girth of his hard hot rod burrowed home.

Neil's eyes rolled behind his lids and his mouth blew open as Kellan slipped in.

"Omigawd, you're tight," Kellan blurted, moving his hips slowly, keeping his connection smooth and effortless so Neil could get used to his size.

"You feel so fucking good," Neil said. His legs went wide, matching Kellan's wingspan.

"You like my dick inside you, don't you?" Kellan leaned forward; pressing his lips against Neil's to kiss him.

Neil mumbled during their kiss. "Fuck yes. Stay as long as you can."

Kellan pinned Neil's hands to the pillow above his head as he fucked him, and he watched his own cock move in and out of the man he was in love with, stirring slowly at first, followed by hard thrusts of lust that took him as deep as possible inside Neil.

Neil's mouth sprung open at every plunge, moaning sheer bliss as Kellan's dick drove closer to his heart.

"Damn, your ass is nice," Kellan wailed. He rolled Neil onto his side while staying connected to him, twisting his nipples as he drilled him from behind.

It didn't seem possible, but each time Kellan rammed him from the back, Neil felt Kellan go deeper. "Keep fucking me,

Kellan," he growled. "Please don't stop."

Kellan reached round and gripped Neil's erection, jacking it from the front while he fucked him in the ass from the behind.

"Let's cum together, Neil. Shoot with me," Kellan begged.

Neil whimpered, "Fuck, yeah. I want that."

Kellan fisted Neil's cock as he would his own, and he synchronized every pump with each thrust of his dick into Neil's flexing channel.

For the first time, Kellan whispered, "I love you, Neil." He pushed hard against Neil's bottom, feeling his own fiery spunk boiling for the explosive release. "Oh fuck. I'm about to burst inside you. Cum with me, Neil. Let's do this together."

Neil awkwardly twisted his body so that his lips met Kellan's. "I'm in love with you too, Kellan. Stay inside me. I want all you have."

Their breathing was labored. Neither one could hold out any longer. They needed to cum.

Within seconds of hearing those three words from Kellan, Neil's cock spurt pearly ribbons across the printed bed sheets, shooting ten times, maybe twelve. He was full of spunk, and with Kellan pounding at his backside, helped him push out every bit of what he had inside him.

With every stroke of Neil's cock, Kellan thrust into him, pumping one spine-popping load after another, deep inside his boyfriend's ass. The love of his life.

Kellan held Neil close as he filled him with his sizzling spunk, alternating one powerful spurt after another with Neil.

As Neil's spurts slowed, the last of it oozed over Kellan's fingers, like white lava running down the mountainside and into the ravines below it.

Kellan turned Neil back around to face him, spinning his man on his bursting cock. They kissed deeply and long, breathing in each other's masculine scent. Neil's semen permeated the room that preserved Kellan's rock hard cock up inside him.

"Gawd, I love you, Neil. So much." Kellan hugged and kissed him, rolling his hips several more times, sliding his erection in and out with slow venturing jabs, pumping the last of his essence as far as he could into Neil so it stayed.

Chapter 38

It was five in the morning when Neil woke from a dream, a dream that left him rock hard and drizzling cum that stretched from the crown of his cock to a small puddle spreading thinly across his abdomen. He held on to the dream, running it through his mind before it faded away. It was a good dream, involving Kellan, and what took place when he was alone on a sleepless night. He stretched, with the intention of bringing it all to life.

He gripped himself and stroked a few times, being mindful that Kellan was the cause of his raging erection. He rolled over to feel his angel, but when he reached out a hand, found he was lying alone in bed and that startled him.

What alarmed him most was that he couldn't see Kellan and Dylan anywhere. Listening, he heard no sign of them in the lighthouse. He felt his heartbeat race as he thought the worst.

Did the maniacs from the laboratory find them and take them away again?

Neil kicked the covers from his feet and took off for the

door, totally naked with a hand held tightly to his quickly weakening hard-on, pressing it firmly in place along his hipbone.

What Neil saw next was the characterization of peace.

It started with the sun making an appearance along the horizon on the other side of the bridge. It was the typical sunrise he saw crowning the fine line where the water met the sky almost every day, and as it rose, it cast a brilliant orange glow across the clouds in the sky.

Then he spotted them. Out walking the beach, Neil saw Kellan first, and running in circles around him was Dylan, acting crazy. There was something harmonious about Kellan on the beach that Neil didn't want to interrupt, so he shook away his already fading nerves while he stood watching, wanting to join them. Instead went back inside where he laid faceup on the bed, with an arm propped under his head so he could watch the door.

Minutes later, Kellan shuffled softly across the floor, one sandy foot sidestepping the other, leaving wet footprints behind him, Dylan trotting at his side. He quietly knelt on the bedside, trying his hardest not to shake the mattress and wake Neil. His wings splayed high above his head, slowly turning from gray to white. He looked down on Neil, taking in every muscle on display, every solid hump and every deep indention. His focus went between Neil's legs where he first gazed at his low hanging testicles that secretly kept his entrance hidden, and then followed the thick shaft up across Neil's hairy pelvis and stomach. There he noticed a raindrop of semen seeping from the bulbous crown that joined the glistening pool already in the crevice of his abdomen. "Gawd, you're beautiful, Neil," he quietly hummed.

Hearing a whisper, Neil arched his back with a grizzly stretch, moved his arm back behind his head, and groaned, "Is everything alright?" His erection immediately thickened, twitching up the center of his abdomen.

"Yes, my love, everything is good," Kellan softly spoke, looking down on Neil before he leaned in to kiss him. His fingers traced Neil's jaw line, moved to the underside of his exposed arm that was pinned behind his head, and then gently traced the back of his nails downward across the bulk of his chest. The touch was gentle, his hand warm.

Neil trembled and let out a subtle moan, one that begged

Kellan to act further on his stimulating advances.

Kellan breathed in Neil's ear, "I see your dream was a good one." Kellan moved his mouth to Neil's chest, kissing softly, drawing in one spirited nipple at a time, circling his tongue around each stiffening nub as he nibbled. The sensation produced the desired arch in Neil's back, forcing his muscular chest to press harder against Kellan's lips, also making his erection twitch and grow even firmer than before.

"It was, and you were in it," Neil gasped between bouts of pleasure.

Kellan grinned, pressed his mouth to Neil's while he grabbed hold of Neil's leaking cock.

Neil lay back on the rutty mattress with Kellan comfortably on top of him, the way he liked it, and seemed to feel most natural to both of them. They kissed at the same time Neil opened his legs for Kellan's massive intrusion, wanting it again.

Kellan lifted himself up and aimed his semen-saturated cock at the begging entrance between Neil's legs, brushing the ceiling with his wing tips as he rose. Kellan was stunning to Neil, and looked supremely masculine as he sat propped on his knees in front of him using a stroking hand to coat his lengthening erection with his spilling semen.

Neil shuddered when Kellan's wet hand transferred the slippery spunk against his pulsing entrance. His eyes rolled back as Kellan pushed the semen up inside him, providing the needed preparation for penetration that will mark him as his all over again.

Kellan seemed eager, didn't ask if Neil was ready for him, he just pointed and pushed his cock in until every thick inch was deeply fixed inside Neil. The soft hair at the base of his cock pressed tightly against Neil's ass.

"Fuck, me!" squealed Neil, his legs opened wider as his angel tunneled in.

Kellan was gentle when he needed to be, but at that moment he wanted to feel himself inside Neil so badly that his will to remain controlled was taken over by desire.

"Fuck me, Kellan," Neil droned, this time issuing it as an order.

Minding Neil and giving him what he wanted, Kellan rolled

his hips hard into Neil's ass, several times, forcing his cock even deeper, taking it to the limit. After digging into Neil a few more times with his probing erection, still oozing semen, Kellan dropped down and passionately kissed him until he noticed a tear greet the corner of Neil's eye. He moved in and kissed it away. His beautiful wings came down and covered them like a warm cozy blanket.

Every time Neil was with Kellan, the feeling surpassed incredible. Every time Kellan moved inside him, it felt amazing. Neil was in love with Kellan, and his uncontrollable tear made it known. At that moment, he knew Kellan was meant to be, destined to be with him, and to be his companion and mate.

Kellan groaned with desire for Neil as he felt his boyfriend's body take him in. Neil craved him, surrendered to Kellan in such a perfect way that it actually pulled Kellan's cock deeper inside of him. Taking hold, not letting go.

Deeply connected, they rocked together perfectly, one gave while the other received.

Crunching his abdomen, Kellan pushed his enlarged erection forward, guiding himself deeper into Neil again, opening him up until Neil felt the angel tap his heart.

Neil emptied his lungs as Kellan's thickened cock inched farther in.

Kellan gazed down at Neil, held still for a few seconds before sliding his drizzling erection in and out of him with slow lasting strokes. The fiery sensation curled Neil's toes each time he felt Kellan grind against him. They delicately kissed, and from it spiked amazing sparks, bringing them both to the edge of their explosive orgasms.

Kellan's hand ran from Neil's hip up his side to his expansive chest, where he lightly caressed him, sending chills through Neil from bottom to top.

Rolling his hips into Neil, Kellan forced himself further. "I love you so much, Neil."

While kissing Kellan, Neil clasped the side of his neck with one hand, and clamped Kellan's wrist against his chest with the other, holding it there. He took every bit of Kellan that he could, everything he had, sucked his tongue, took his cock, his essence, pulling it all in to the fullest depths of his being. The punishing pleasure made him moan. Neil couldn't hold back. "I love you too, Kellan."

Their tongues made contact as the kiss turned intense.

Kellan's rhythm seized Neil with extreme pleasure, pushing him to the brink of frenzy. Neil's entire body went tight, he groaned, and sprayed streams of hot ejaculate between their massive chests.

When Neil's release laced their chests, the rising scent smothered Kellan and an extraordinary buzz to gush inside Neil dominated him. He possessed Neil, kissed him with rising desire. Kellan hummed in his ear as he lay tightly on top of Neil. "You're amazing, Neil." He gasped—wings spread wide. "Take my sperm, Neil." He huffed. "Oh Gawd, take it, Neil." His face changed to a pleasured knot, and his wings flapped as if he were planning to fly. He rumbled, fell rigid against Neil, and kissed him while his convulsing body transferred everything he had inside his lover.

Neil felt the warmth of Kellan flow inside his body at the same time Kellan's chin went to his neck to breathe.

Kellan huffed, "Oh Gawd, your grip feels so incredible. I am truly in love with you, Neil."

Neil hugged Kellan tightly, his soft tone graced his ear, "I'm in love with you too, Kellan."

Kellan lifted his head, held the sides of Neil's with his hands and looked down on him as the last bit of his matter pumped from him inside Neil. A kiss was surrendered to Neil's lips and then Kellan grinned.

Their mouths stayed connected and they both inhaled each other's breath until the final orgasmic convulsion settled.

"Someday we will need to trade places." Kellan's voice was deep and sexy, but changed to a grunt when he grabbed Neil by the shoulders and flipped him into his lap to have a seat.

"If it pleases you." Neil locked his arms around Kellan's neck, looked down and kissed him again. He couldn't get enough of the man who just fucked him senseless, and still remained hard as a sex stallion up inside him.

"I'd be more than pleased." Kellan kissed back, circling his hips to piston his cock in and out of Neil.

"You still at it, huh?" Neil squeezed tighter, pulling Kellan in. "I can't believe this is happening."

"What's that? You and me, fucking?" Kellan threw his weight into Neil, putting him on his back again. When he did, his cock burrowed to its furthest point.

"Yes, you and me. Falling in love. But what really gets me is I have an angel on top of me with his dick and cum filling my ass," Neil mumbled. "Who'd ever thought that would happen to me? Never entered my mind."

Kellan pushed his hips forward again, giving Neil more. He had the energy still in him, so why the hell not?

Neil's head spun and his eyes rolled back in his head just like before. "Holy shit. You're still full of it?"

"Nah. I'm done." Kellan laughed while he pulled out of the man he loved.

Chapter 39

Many weeks back, the most amazing thing Neil had ever experienced in his life met up with him on his front doorstep. He had always needed to believe in something, wanted to, but figured fantasies or dreams didn't come true, so why bother?

The day Kellan appeared, his life changed forever. He knew that. The first night Kellan kissed him, he was sure there was no going back, and the first time Kellan slipped a part of his body inside him, he was even more certain there was no going back.

After a morning of lustful man on man fucking, Kellan and Neil sat together on the bed, facing each other, holding hands.

"Do you think it's safe if we stay here?" Neil asked.

"For a while," Kellan said. "The mess we made at the lab should definitely make it difficult for them to find us, and I'm hoping they no longer have a lock on my ass with any tracking device."

Neil shifted, adjusting his heavy scrotum that had lodged itself underneath him the way it always does when he wasn't wearing anything to support it.

Though Kellan tried not to be obvious, he watched Neil lift everything he had up in front of him.

"Did you ever think about leaving it all behind? Going far away?" Neil asked.

"Of course I have. Almost every day," Kellan replied.

"One good thing is that we can go anywhere. Anywhere we want." Neil scooted closer to Kellan until their knees knocked.

"But where do we go? What about your job?" Kellan said.

The questions seemed completely legitimate. "I don't need a job. Don't forget about my grandparents' vineyards and what they left me." Neil reminded Kellan. "We can go wherever we want to go."

"But that's all yours, not mine," Kellan said.

"Don't be ridiculous. I don't need all of that for myself, and it would make me happy as hell to share it with you," Neil said. "Move in with me. It's where you belong."

"I'd like that, and I promise to earn my stay," Kellan said, kissing Neil on the lips.

"You already have. Trust me." Neil winked, and patted his stomach.

"Maybe we should get out of this place, move farther away from the lab, go somewhere like China or an island in the Pacific?" Kellan suggested.

"You've heard about keeping your enemies close, right?" Neil said.

"I have."

"I truly believe those maniacs at the lab think we're long gone, which makes me believe they are less apt to hunt for us in a place next door to them." Neil's gaze went to the window when he saw a hummingbird hovering there, and as quickly as it zipped away, reconnected with Kellan's eyes.

Feeling a presence, Kellan looked over his shoulder, wondering what Neil just looked at. Nothing was there, but he still questioned his reason for doing it.

Bringing Kellan back to the conversation, Neil squeezed his hands and said, "This place is secluded in the middle of nowhere and I don't think they'll be able to figure out we're here."

"If you're right about that, then I have no problem sticking around this place." Kellan glanced around the room, looking in every corner like he was searching for spiders.

"We have Dylan who can spot an intruder a mile away, and from what I've seen from you, your senses are rather animalistic too. I'd say our odds of staying several steps ahead of them rank pretty good." Neil shifted, getting ready to stand.

"Why don't we figure all that out later. What're we going to do for breakfast?" Kellan spun, cart wheeling his legs over Neil and onto the floor.

Neil ducked to avoid getting struck in the head by Kellan's feet. "Let's clean this place up first. I'm a little too full right now to be eating anything." —Neil smirked—"Thanks to you."

"The plan is afoot." Kellan stood up after pecking Neil sweetly on the cheek.

Even though it was daybreak, the dingy lighthouse felt haunted inside. There was too much gray and pale blue scattered around for it to appear bright and cheery. It desperately needed more than a broom to make it homey.

They opened all the windows to let the breeze in, perhaps blow away most of the musky smell that took the place over. Wall paint would do it some good, but that was something to deal with later and only if they planned on staying.

Neil held the laptop against his chest before tossing it aside on the sofa, contemplating if he should put it down or open it up. A lot of shit was going through his head that he wanted answers to, and the only way to get them was to go through all the files they loaded into the drive. As well as coming across stimulating facts about Kellan, Neil secretly wanted to see him put his dildos into action and watch the talented man blow loads of semen around the room. Neil couldn't get enough of that. It was awesome how much came out of him, and Neil was getting hard just thinking about it. He desired one of Kellan's cum baths real bad.

Getting back to what really mattered, Neil cleared the images from his mind. The question seemed trite at the time, but Neil asked Kellan anyway, asked if it was okay to plug in the laptop and research additional history on him. Neil was intrigued by it all and wanted to know more about his boyfriend and how he got there.

Before Kellan had a chance to answer, Dylan barked. They froze, turning wide-eyed toward the door. All of them.

"Fuck." Kellan dropped the dust rag.

Neil slammed the laptop shut.

It seemed to be nothing but repetition of bad shit for Kellan and Neil.

What the fuck?

Epilogue

A thunderous crack bitch-slapped them while they stood there, and the boom seemed to spread spontaneously around the room, burning nerve-rocking holes in everything. Amazingly, Kellan didn't move a muscle. Neil and Dylan on the other hand just about jumped through the ceiling and out the rooftop.

Not much came after that, so they continued where they left off before the big bang.

The laptop sat on the edge of the crooked sofa just begging to be opened up again, and before any more time passed by, Neil flipped the screen back up and waited for it to start up.

When it did, they poked around at the main folder where all of Kellan's life was stored, and with that came many areas that neither of them had explored before.

Neil clicked on everything, from the irresistible recordings of Kellan during his alone time, and the documents about his growth spurts that eventually turned into his jack-off spurts.

Neil liked that part the best.

Every time Neil tried to watch him ejaculate on screen, Kellan folded the laptop shut. The continuous shutdown was becoming annoying to Neil so he stopped clicking on folders that showed Kellan beating his meat.

Neil moved on to more historical events, in written form, no pictures, still shots or moving, that showed Kellan doing anything that should remain private. That's when he saw it, came across the unexpected.

"Holy shit," Neil muttered.

Neil was trying desperately to give up bad words, but this time it came right out of him and startled Kellan even though the crack of thunder hadn't even made him budge.

The folder they opened seemed to be another part of Kellan's life that needed to be looked into. Perhaps it was a small part of him that they couldn't just leave at the lab or keep hidden in a folder on a stolen laptop.

The details in that folder made them speculate that it was linked to Kellan somehow. The roadmap of information they viewed practically showed that. Neil was pretty sure of it, Kellan not so much.

They both looked away from the screen for a few minutes, neither one touching any part of it. It was too much for them to take in, if what they saw and thought it meant was true.

Within a few minutes, the screen went into battery saver hibernation mode, which they decided to leave as is for a few more minutes so they could ponder a few things that just caught them off guard.

Neither of them could wait any longer to find out more, so Kellan tapped the mouse pad to get the power started.

As soon as the screen refreshed itself, they noticed an envelope flying across the monitor like it was still in screensaver mode. Unknown to them, the laptop had a smart-mail service on it and the fly-by notification told them a message had been sent to the address on the laptop. Neil looked at Kellan who nodded that it was okay to click on it.

'Don't move. Stay wherever you are,' the e-mail said, and then it disappeared. Fizzled away. Poof. It was like Snap-chat, but with words, unable to see it again once it was gone.

Somebody linked to the laptop was either sending them a stay-safe message or was planning an attack. The idea of being pounced on was what they thought most likely, but why would the attacker warn them before showing up with pistols, knives or worse, Seekers?

What really sucked was that they didn't know who it came from or even if it was directed to them. They figured it had to be someone at the Laboratory. Where else would the message have come from? The computer did originally belong to someone at TC.

Kellan quickly slammed the laptop shut and told Neil that it could very well be a way to locate them, like they just sent a tracking bug.

Neil went white.

THE
END

ABOUT THE AUTHOR

Gregory Jonathan Scott was born and raised in Grand Rapids, Michigan where he met and shared a life with Scott that began just out of high school. Meeting by chance in Grand Rapids before relocating to South Florida where they live now with their lovable Shetland sheepdog and a sweet stray cat that showed up one day and decided to make their house a home.

As a child, Gregory was always told he had a creative imagination and the artistic ability to turn a blank canvas into an eye-catching work of art. Shortly after high school graduation, and together with his true love Scott, discovered the thrill of pottery and ceramic art. Here is where the two of them opened a business for ceramists that quickly exploded before their eyes as the number one location for any hobbyist, storefront and scholastic industry looking for supplies related to ceramics and pottery. During this time, Gregory was approached by art magazines to write short articles and educational columns pertaining to the ceramic artistry. Captivating readers by his writing style grew fast, which ignited his desire to express himself further. From there, it began. Finding a love for writing, alongside his artistic hand, gave him inspiration to design and write this M/M romance Novel.

Gregory and Scott are still together and are currently enjoying home life in South Florida.

OTHER WORKS BY
Gregory Jonathan Scott

HEARTBREAK BEAT
THE PLANTATION AFFAIR

www.ingramcontent.com/pod-product-compliance
Lightning Source LLC
Chambersburg PA
CBHW031314170626
46807CB00001B/419